her adult life in the UK, first in Lond...
Previously Fiona has worked in academia, NGO's, public affairs and as an emerging markets analyst. She continues to keep a foot in both continents and is currently spending the majority of her time back in South Africa.

'Melrose portrays [the city] beautifully, full of grace, colour and even fear' *Independent's i* **paper**

'Melrose can undoubtedly write . . . what emerges is her original depiction of modern *Johannesburg* – a beautiful, violent, unforgiving place that is a social reality and a state of mind' *Daily Mail*

'Woolf produced blooms that are impossible to emulate. *Johannesburg* provides evidence of a novelist who can grow inimitable flowers herself' *Spectator*

'To say Fiona Melrose's new book *Johannesburg* is ambitious is an understatement. But she pulls off a stream-of-consciousness success, following a single day in the South African capital through the eyes of everyone from an expat artist to a homeless hunchback. Kudos' *Sunday Telegraph's Stella* **magazine**

'Melrose beautifully describes the South African city's streets and the longing in the hearts of the characters who travel them . . . A mesmerising homage to Virginia Woolf's *Mrs Dalloway*' *Express*

'Moving . . . The reader gets a real picture of this fascinating country and its people' *Hello* **magazine**

'An insightful portrait of a city and country grappling with demons past and p...

Also by Fiona Melrose
Midwinter

Johannesburg

Fiona Melrose

corsair

CORSAIR

First published in Great Britain in 2017 by Corsair
This paperback edition published in 2018

1 3 5 7 9 10 8 6 4 2

A CIP catalogue record for this book
is available from the British Library.

ISBN: 978-1-4721-5286-2

Printed and bound in Great Britain by Clays Ltd, Elcograf S.p.A.

Papers used by Corsair are from well-managed forests
and other responsible sources.

MIX
Paper from
responsible sources
FSC® C104740

Corsair
An imprint of
Little, Brown Book Group
Carmelite House
50 Victoria Embankment
London EC4Y 0DZ

An Hachette UK Company
www.hachette.co.uk

www.littlebrown.co.uk

To Fiona Swaffield Melrose

Fear no more, says the heart, committing its burden to some sea, which sighs collectively for all sorrows, and renews, begins, collects, lets fall.

Mrs Dalloway, Virginia Woolf

6 December 2013,
Johannesburg, South Africa

Early morning

It had been a bad night for nervous dogs. Thunder, and rain, terrible and hot, had drenched the city.

September's flattened cardboard boxes were wet through. From under his plastic sheet he already knew this. The corrugated boxes no longer had the sort of spring he associated with a dry night and a good sleep.

He had been awake for a while but had only just begun to register that he was back in the world. September felt as if his mind had begun to dispatch messages back to his body from a further, more mountainous geography, messages waylaid.

Some days he could leave his garden, walk to his island and set about asking for loose change from morning motorists. A hand would emerge from a car window to deposit a fat five-rand coin into his enamel cup. He would shuffle all along the waiting traffic (blinking, blinking to turn) and only much further down the line would he begin to register the sound (plunk) as the coin hit the bottom of the cup. What had happened in-between he could not say. Such was the nature of his mind these long, hot days.

And today would be no different. And all the days that followed. One, and another and then another.

He began to rustle himself to life. For he had work to do. Justice would not wait.

———

There had been hail. Flowers and leaves had been stripped from full summer stems. It was a storm that announced itself with belly-fat kettle drums and flashes of lightning long before it even came onstage, raging and spitting. Even between wake and sleep Gin had felt the atmosphere refashion itself. So, when the storm had finally rolled away, there was a sense that something in the small world of uniformly laid out streets, swimming pools and flowering trees had been disturbed. Something had tilted by a degree or two on its axis.

But, Gin also knew, as she arched her body (it had crimped as she had slept so long, so deep) that being home and waking surrounded by this jolt of summer was a brazen-lit reprieve after the lacerating early months of a New York winter. So, here she was, to celebrate her mother's eightieth birthday.

Even as she thought it, she felt her stomach flip a little and a matronly little devil-voice told her that it would all fail, her party, her preparations. And she would be judged by everyone who sat there and, of course, by her mother.

She unfolded herself from the covers. Her anchors had sunk deep, deep into the bed. The bedclothes were the very same ones from so many years before, though thinner now, gauzy almost, like a mosquito net.

Gin knew that the day would be thick and cumbersome and it would be too hot for picking what was left of the flowers.

4

*

Mercy had risen early, woken by the rain that had made all the gutters around her bedroom gurgle. She had drifted in and out of sleep until she had finally surrendered to wakefulness and had risen to run her bath. She sang hymns, mostly in her head, and thought about how she could find herself a new phone for a reasonable price. She opened and shut the large rolling kitchen drawers that held pots and pans and below them, in another drawer, larger platters and servers. As she bashed her way around the kitchen she kept one ear on the radio just outside the back door, listening for news on Tata Mandela. It was said that the family had gathered at the Residence the night before.

Gin had asked Mercy to get all the old platters out and wash them. Gin was home for five days only and before this day was done, there would be a party for Mrs Brandt, for her eightieth birthday.

Some of the platters had thin cracks no wider than an ant's foot. Mercy ran her fingers across the fault lines. She liked how they felt and liked too the confidence she had that they would not break. The older things had a strength to them that the newer stuff did not. The same was true of women and girls. Mercy's own daughters worried her. So here, so there and always more money and more things and no work.

She thought too about what had been said. About what Jacobeth and Anna from next door had told her about Tata Mandela, that there was bad news from the Residence down the road. All the family was gathered. The women, Ma Winnie, Ma Graça were there together, Jacobeth had said, and word was it did not look good for Tata. And perhaps he had already passed but no one was saying.

Nkosi, God bless him.

It is sometimes like that with these families Anna had said. But this illness had been going on for some months and maybe today was just his time, his day, in the way that it eventually just is, no matter who you might be.

―――――

From her bed it seemed to Gin that the house, her mother's house, was suddenly silent but for the hum of a lawn mower. Surely it was too early for a lawn mower? The gardener, whose name Gin could not remember as she lay between wake and sleep, liked to sing as he worked. Sometimes in a strange falsetto. Was he called Brilliant or Talent? She could imagine him as he crossed back and forth in front of the French windows that were left open to the verandah and the garden beyond.

It was a Friday. All over the city suburbs, verges and lawns were being shorn into precise shapes, given a cruel crew cut, which nonetheless smelled of childhood and tennis balls and space to stretch and run. And even in her half-waking place, Gin fell back towards those cut grass lawns at their old home, Eden House, not far from where she lay. Up the road, then down, then across the motorway and then towards the zoo. Eden House, where it would take a full afternoon just to cut the front terraces, which fell in tiers. Gin had thought in childhood that these sweeps of grass were tears, and how sad and beautiful it was that a lawn would shed tears as it fell away from the house in a kind of verdant longing. But fall it did, towards the swimming pool and tennis court, which lay around the boundary. And beyond it, in those days anyway, veld, so dry she felt her skin begin to prickle just thinking about it.

Eden House was long gone, sold by her mother just months after Gin's father died (too large, too unsafe for a woman on her own) and then sold again within a month or so to developers who had torn it down, every brick, every roof tile and wooden beam and window frame. They had decimated the roses, the oaks and the willows that once had trailed their skirts over her bare legs as she lay hidden beneath them, pulling the heads from her dolls.

The trees were all cut and felled in four afternoons. And in their place were eight cluster-houses, each an exact replica of the other in the style that had become known as Johannesburg Tuscan. This denoted sienna walls and a terracotta roof, and some fully grown olive trees and cypresses – trees that a hyena-like digger had clawed out of their birth place – brought to the city on the backs of huge trucks and dumped into holes.

Turf would be rolled out to cover the scars and in less than a month what resembled an established garden would grow over the rubble and the rubbish and whatever else the developers wanted to bury. Fountains and lights would be switched on as if it were a theatre set and a king and his queen could walk through the door to play at their new and lovely lives.

And under them, the carcasses of the lives that came before, tennis balls and bones the dogs left behind, secreted in the cannas and the lilies. Somewhere too, was the necklace Gin had lost while tree climbing and never ever found again, in the compost heap that year after year produced pumpkins and granadillas, both so wild and ripe and abundant that they lasted the entire summer.

For this was Johannesburg, commerce was the new colonizer and all else that had come before was diminished and expunged.

––––––

Mercy thought about Gin coming home to have a party for her mother. That was nice. It was a good thing. But if she loved her really, she would come back to live with her, look after her.

7

That was what Mercy had done for her mother and she knew her daughters would look after her in her old age. It was how it was done. White people built old age homes without a blink of shame. The planted their parents in there and paid someone else to look after them.

Mrs Brandt was difficult though, strict, critical. And didn't Mercy know it? Mercy there are still stains in the tablecloths, Mercy why are you late, Mercy this and that, Mercy, Mercy, Mercy on and on and on until she could hardly bear to hear the sound of her own name, spoken as it was, as an insult or a curse.

Mrs Brandt was old. No worse than Mercy's own mother had been. But harder, less kind, and very white, all through her. Still, Mrs Brandt was better than Jacobeth's madam from next door, who just shouted from the time the sun came up. They owned a bakery, Jacobeth's ones – a whole chain of bakeries that supplied all the delis and hotels across the city. They were up with the birds. They woke up angry and went to bed the same. Some days you could hear them shouting over the wall – especially her. One time, she even shouted at her husband for bringing her flowers on her birthday. But Jacobeth reported to Mercy, as they sat, backs to the boundary wall, legs stretched out along the grass on the pavement, that later that same day, the angry bakers went out for dinner and came back holding hands. Later still, they swam together under the stars in their swimming pool that was tucked under the old jacaranda tree.

Mercy went out to the radio. Hymns were playing. The news would be later. Once she had done with the platters, which were too big for her to hold all at once, she being short, she would feed the dog and then see what Jacobeth knew about Tata Mandela. It was not yet seven o'clock.

My name is September. You will know me by my hump. It is a sacred hilltop that rises out of my shoulders. Others who beg on these corners make them for themselves, paper ones, card ones, using supermarket plastics so that people will give them more when they tap on the nice clean car windows. Mine is real. It is an authentic hump. I cut a round circle in the fabric of my shirt so that it rises up like a majestic peak of the Drakensberg. People must know that mine is authentic.

Every day I make my pilgrimage to the Diamond, the home of the mine bosses, the killers of men. I take my protest to their door. If you do not find me there, then my place is on an island. The island is between Eleventh Avenue and the motorway on-ramp. From here I can feel the whole city washing under me like a great tide as the people roar this way in the morning and that way as the sun sets and makes the roads run with its orange blood. I like it here on Eleventh. This is the corner of kings. Kings from Lesotho, Swaziland and those from farther away have come here to see Tata – he has received them now for years. I see them all. Caravans of cars wash along these roads carrying those who come to ingratiate themselves with our own, more golden king. They come to visit the father of our nation. He receives them and so do I. I shout out my greetings as they pass my island for he is our king no matter our tribe. But now, the king is dead. Long live the king.

––––––

Gin showered slowly and deliberately. She craved the cold water. There was such luxury in that shower, all the little bottles of balsams lined up. Bottles from hotels that previous guests had stayed in and she would never see. Gin loved hotels, hotel bars, hotel towels fresh every day, and trays that arrived with breakfasts she would never have the energy to make for herself and would never eat even if she did. She could imagine all of that bounty, there in those little bottles, and she could feel herself waken.

She let the soap fall along her back, milky tides, and she ran her hands across her hips, feeling the reassuring peaks of bone as they protruded through her skin. A clean line, a geographic boundary; here I am, and there begins the world. She despised unclean lines, a shifting veil between this and that, blended margins, undefined borderlands. For this reason she could never work in charcoal. Her studio was airy, cold even, and filled with neatly stacked boxes, all labelled, dated, accounted for. Not one of them contained charcoal. It was all ink, metal even, plaster, bone, something three dimensional and quantifiable.

She dressed. Her jeans and shirt still wearing the fold-mark of their journey across the Atlantic. Her boots were a comfort as were the amulets, old gold, that she wore around her neck and wrists, worn every day in different combinations since, when? She left her hair wet, forming long burnt serpents, dripping venom along her back and arms.

The party.

She went downstairs to establish how rounded the day had become. And to wish her mother happy birthday. She could hear the lawnmower, Juno chasing it, barking with joy.

———

Duduzile had already washed the dishes and swept the verandah before her people woke up. They stayed in bed well past sun rise and then found they were late for everything. She disapproved of this habit as it meant that from the time they woke until the time they left, with at least one child crying, there was chaos. Something was always lost. Someone had always lost this or that. And it created a chaos she was responsible for fixing. Find the car keys, feed the cat, find the child's swimming goggles.

It was December, and the school holidays had begun, which was worse. All day, she had the children at home while their parents worked. At least on this day, someone else's mother was fetching them and they would be gone until after six when they would return already fed. With the children gone, she would be able to take September food.

Her days were preoccupied with planning how and when she would see him, on his island, in his garden, outside the Diamond. His every movement registered on her wristwatch, the kitchen clock, the arc of the sun. So that each heartbeat was both his and hers and his life rested like a bundle of jagged rocks on her back.

I am my brother's keeper.

————

Gin found that her mother was dressing. The household routine seemed to have been transported across from Eden House along with Aunt Virginia's writing desk and Granny's painting of the veld that hung over the fire place, just as it had before. It was more a suggestion of the veld, a heat haze of colour. No more than an intimation of land. The longer you looked at the image, the further you felt you had wandered into the tall grass and knew the harder it would be to get back. The terror of being lost. Gin turned away.

These stories of being lost and never found again were repeated throughout her childhood. The threats and then the proof as yet another person was lost for lack of vigilance. As if being forever lost were always a breath away, an inevitable outcome if one so much as let one's eye drift, undisciplined, across a night's sky. Oh, he had walked in circles for hours, they said of the tourist who had died while they were on a bush trip one drought-addled summer. Damned idiot, her father had said, deserved what he got. That was more or less his attitude to everything.

I don't miss him one bit.

Even as she said it she felt awkward in her venom – just being here, back among these old paintings and sofas and writing desks, brought it out again. As if her childhood was kept inside her bureau and just turning the key, as she had the night before to find a pen, had released that bitterness once more.

Her mother's door was shut.

————

Peter had been up for a few hours already. Even before he had left his apartment, his eyes hardly left the television screen. Anxious-looking news reporters standing outside the Mandela Residence. The foreign press would soon descend and begin their rigmarole suggesting the entire country would collapse the moment Mandela breathed his last. The streets will run with blood. The people are not capable of controlling themselves in the absence of their moral compass. No matter the moral compass had not been seen for months, years even.

Peter considered his holiday plans. A visit to see his parents, now sedately retired at Hermanus on the Cape coast. The regularity of the dread this produced became, through repetition, its own kind of comfort.

His father, an attorney by trade, played golf, his mother, bridge. His father attended Rotary Club meetings, she her book club. For the days between Christmas and New Year, his brother, David, would arrive with his family from Cape Town. They were good-looking, casual racists. His wife was blonde and angelic, their daughters, unfathomable.

Each passing year, his family parodied themselves with increasing accuracy. Every evening, cocktails were served from five o'clock until last man standing. As if pre-scheduled, about midway through (as his father called for more olives and lemon slices) jokes and jibes about Peter being single would be rolled out. Typically, the exchange would reach a point where his mother, unable to betray her primal anxiety, would interject, saying, 'That's enough, now.' And then, 'These days lots of young men are bachelors well into their forties.' His father would make some comment about playing the field and sowing oats. They would all laugh. And, of course, so would he.

Each year he would return to work, pledging never to endure the pantomime again. But every year he booked his tickets and arrived two days before Christmas, mostly because he did not know where else to go.

Peter took the elevator down, nodded at the concierge, strapping on his training-watch as he went and attaching his phone to a strap on his arm. Concierge was rather too grand a word for the slovenly, rotund man who rarely had the energy to return the mordant greeting, let alone reach for the security buzzer to let Peter out onto the busy street.

He ran the same route every day. He liked to record how many kilometres he had covered in a day, a week, a month. He walked to the corner outside his building. Wide streets, sun, sixteen-seater taxis spilling their passengers out onto the pavement outside office blocks, or further up the road near shopping malls.

He set his watch and started running, warming up slowly but finding his rhythm, moving invisibly along, detached from himself as momentum took over. Suddenly, to his left, a crash. Metal, perhaps a bin truck, and birds, ibises, all screaming and flapping across the sky, their screech enough to make him shut his eyes against the din. The noise, the alarm of it was inside of him. He held his hands over his ears to make it stop. When he opened his eyes again the sun-glare had gone, a cloud perhaps, and still more traffic as a taxi blared and hooted trying to attract customers. He bumped into someone, turned to see the woman walking past, and realized he did not know where he was. He could not name the road, could not recognize the trees.

I am lost. I am lost.

He was holding his breath. He released his lungs. Breathing in and out until he no longer had to remind himself to do it. He was suddenly so tethered to the air around his body, so vulnerable to its loss.

I am breathing in, I am breathing out.

September opened the carrier bag in which he kept his toiletries. His sister Duduzile provided them. His facecloth and sponge were getting ragged but no matter, he kept them clean. His body ached, his back of course but his shoulders too. The flesh where his placard rested every day was tender and torn.

He scraped himself up off his bedding and stretched, letting his lungs take in the fullness of themselves. Despite the rain of the previous night, September was pleased it was summer and that Christmas would soon be over and a new year would beckon, then Easter. The familiar passing of time was important. Without these markers, it was so very easy to get lost in the vast wash of days and weeks and years.

He did not like Christmas as much as he used to. When he and Dudu were children, Christmas could never come often enough. They knew that each year they would receive a new pair of school shoes, black, with laces. Dudu liked to wear hers before school began in January, to soften them up and make the long walks across field and veld easier from the first day. But September would keep his safe in their box under his bed, untouched until the first morning of term, when he would be up and dressed, the solid, unbending leather shoes on his feet, before the rest of the household stirred. After two days he would be unable to walk without bandages all over his toes and heels and ankles but he never minded and never listened to his mother's protest.

These days, Christmas never meant new shoes or bags of sweets. Rather it was reduced to what Dudu gave him: clothes, money, things involved in the business of being alive. And every year she would beg him to go home and live in the clean air and the mountains among the people who knew them. Every year he promised that before Christmas he would be home. And he would have kept his promise, only there was the matter of justice. The matter of the bullet that had shaved the side off his face and the men in the Diamond who would not say they had given the order that it be done.

Today I will sing out my song.

———

Neve Brandt was in disconsolate temper. She sat in her dressing gown in her chair next to the window. From there she could see the birds swooping and flopping onto the bird feeders she kept stocked with seed and fruit.

With her door closed she knew she would be left alone. Mercy and Gin would assume she was dressing. She was not dressing and had no intention of doing so in the next hour. Her tea was finished and though she would have liked a second cup, she decided to stay hidden, or trapped in her own bedroom as she preferred to think of it. A hostage. She heard the phone ring. Probably someone hoping to wish her well on her birthday. They could wait. She had no interest in feigning delight and gratitude, for she felt neither. Why was living to eighty more impressive than living to fifty? The process was the same. One day after the other. In that order, and with no alternative.

———

With a cup of tea, dark, strong and sweet, Gin leaned back in her desk chair in the study. She had shouted a birthday greeting to her mother through the closed door of her bedroom. There was no response. Neve was clearly not ready to receive anyone, despite it being her birthday. The study was small and claustrophobic after the sweep of the rest of the house. Gin felt muffled around her head, half-submerged as she began to scroll through the news.

Her phone rang. She quickly turned off the sound.

She hardly ever picked up, she assumed that if someone really wanted her they could send a message, which was by far the more polite way of intruding on someone's day. And it was just past seven. She glanced at the number. Peter Strauss. Just like him. How did he even know she was home? She turned back to the computer screen to read the news. Updates about Mandela had accumulated through the night. The family had gathered, the nation was holding its breath. Prayers and vigils. 'Unconfirmed sources' said he had already passed away. Already it was some sort of ridiculous bandwagon with rugby players and celebrities talking about how important he was to their lives. Gin felt something, a tightness around her throat, a sort of discomfort but she could not name it. The phone began to vibrate again.

———

Mercy watched Gin for a while before she announced herself at the door. Ginny was reading on her computer about Tata Mandela.

She is so thin this one. Hard too, like her mother, but a good person. And she lives on her own over there, in America. No family, no man, no children. And she is forty. About forty. She looks younger though. She doesn't dress like a woman. She needs to dress better. Instead she looks more like a girl. She should come back home where she could be fatter, find a nice man.

Mercy knew it was difficult though. To be a woman on your own was like that. There was no one to help, no comfort, and she knew it. Her husband, Petrus, was dead, shot by the white police in the eighties. No reason. No reason was needed.

This was years ago, when her girls were babies, one still in nappies. And what was there to do? Nothing. She took Petrus home to bury him, mourn those ten days. She allowed herself to weep whilst still in the embrace of the other women: her sisters who slept in her bed with her and on the floor nearby, her cousins who kept vigil in the kitchen, these women who held her. And then it was her mother who had said:

'It is enough. Go back to work and provide for your children.'

Now, see how those children are? One a midwife, the other in teacher training college. This was what a woman's work could do. But Ginny was too thin for babies and she did not like them.

Mercy padded into the study. She was barefoot. She was small on top, bony even and then widened out as she went down.

People, men, used to tell her she had beautiful eyes. But, in the end, she was a woman who worried about things, about life, her daughters.

Mercy always stood with her feet planted wide apart. She knew she tended to over-explain things, which she felt annoyed Gin and Mrs Brandt, but she needed the information to be clear because misunderstandings were what led to trouble, and she could not afford any.

'Ginny. The list. I have written the things we need. For the party tonight.'

'Hey Mercy. Thanks. That's good. Have you seen all of this?' Gin waved at the screen.

Mercy nodded. 'Maybe it is today. Maybe it has already happened.'

'Maybe.'

'It's nice you are here, Ginny. You must come and stay here again. You must come and be with us.'

'Thanks.'

————

Outside the Diamond, Lungisane looked at his watch. Nearly eight o'clock. He was only two hours into his shift. His uniform was uncomfortable. He readjusted the shoulder strap of his gun, which had bunched up his shirt sleeve. It would be a hot, damp day. On the far side of the plaza in front of the building (fountains, flowers, benches) he saw two of his colleagues greet one another. They then separated to patrol the cars and service entrances every hour through the day. He would simply be required to stand in front of the sheet-glass doors and could circle the plaza occasionally to defer the tedium. He had not yet had breakfast.

*

Gin looked down at the list, written in Mercy's clean, neat hand and felt the familiar anxiety over lists and chores and household things she never seemed to know enough about. And now for reasons, complicated reasons around fear and guilt and so much more, she was giving a party, an eightieth birthday dinner. And in order that it be fitting to the occasion and also so that she did not incur the criticism of her mother, it had to be perfect.

The fuzziness that had accompanied her waking was now dissipated. The focus of anxiety had returned. The flowers, the table, the food, the guests whom she had already instructed to dress properly, in case one of them, a cousin too fond of beer and rugby, arrived in a way that was just too casual for the occasion. And all of this fell to her, to Gin who had an oven she never used and had by all accounts failed to be a girl.

She'd had to surprise her mother with the party. She had expected that a few close family members might come over for tea. Instead, a dinner would be held in her honour and, as expected, she had refused the idea even before she had heard what it involved.

'No. I won't be here.'

'You have to. You are turning eighty.'

'Well, I don't want a dinner. What on earth will we feed all of them?'

'There's no *we*. I am taking care of everything.'

'You, my darling, cannot cook. I will have to do it all with Mercy. Oh dear God.'

'Mum. No. I know what I'm doing. I'm taking care of everything.'

'I've heard that before.'

Gin could feel herself beginning to bruise, in that acrid yellow and black way.

'You're turning eighty and I'm having a party for you. Only people you love, no one else.'

'How many people do I love?' Her mother was becoming impatient, which meant cruelty would follow.

'Twenty.' It was closer to forty.

'Oh dear God. A disaster already. I'm not coming and that's final.'

———

Mercy's phone beeped in her apron pocket. She extracted it with one hand as she opened a cupboard with the other looking for clothes pegs.

———

Gin continued to sit at the desk. Her body was aching and wound hard, in a way that reminds you that you are, in the end, still a physical entity, were born with limitations and pain. All that tension of the flight from New York, the allotted spaces, the identical everything and the passengers, in her part of the plane anyway, the tail end, all dressed as if no one was watching. She hated it, the tattiness of it, the lack of imagination, of poetry. She hated sleeping next to someone she did not know, she could never trust them. As if the fact that someone had paid for a seat made it safer and more acceptable. If a man took up his place next to her she would arrange to move. What was more she knew he would spill over into her space and she hated it.

The plane itself never bothered her, the creaking ball of metal and wires. She craved the flight, in the air again, it was a relief to be so utterly powerless: finally, there was nothing she could do. No one who could reach her and no matter what happened, she was not responsible. She never chose the seats near the emergency exits, she could not be charged with the pressure of others' lives, they needed to do that for themselves. The air stewards, so perfectly made up and beautiful in their hats with a small, draped veil down the one side, brought hot towels and neat little dinners. Later, when she had sneaked back to the galley to ask for some water on account of her rasping throat, they had suggested hot tea with lemon instead, and they were right. As the heat hit her parched throat, it was exactly what she had needed. She felt understood and cared for. And she was under no pressure whatsoever to care for herself.

She had gone back to her seat, never bothering to strap on the seat belt and closed her eyes, holding the cup until it was empty. Turbulence over the Sahara. There always was. She knew this from a pilot she saw for a while. He had also told her that, over Africa, there is no radar. Any change in the flight path risked collision with another plane. You had to ride out the turbulence. You had to hold your course, he'd said.

You just have to hold your course.

She remembered repeating it in her head. The pilot himself had become tedious fairly quickly. All she remembered, clearly and very precisely, was what he taught her about turbulence.

And what if the plane had suddenly plunged towards the earth with an engine on fire? But for the noise of the other passengers screaming and trying to cling on to life when it was already too late, Gin felt sure she would have been completely calm. There was simply nothing to be done. She reverted so very easily to death as simply another option in the business of living. Having that option was sometimes the only way she could survive the gales that blew hard against the window panes, the precarious light, the near permanent jeopardy of living. To live with an option, even the option of death, stopped her feeling trapped. It freed her from fear and that freedom, to choose another way, gave her the courage to continue when, at times, those skinless days, there was really no reason.

———

Mercy glanced at her phone. 'Tata Madiba has passed,' wrote Jacobeth. 'It was his day. *Nkosi.*'

Nkosi, God bless him, thought Mercy and crossed herself. God rest his soul. Everyone will have their day. And today was his.

'Ginny, Tata has passed. Today was his day.'

Gin said nothing. Mercy was surprised, shocked even to see that her eyes filled and then overflowed. But she was not surprised when Gin turned quickly away and said in a child's voice: 'I'll tell Mum. She must be up by now.'

———

September had finally sat long enough in the sun to forget the damp of the night and the rain that had lashed through the dark and drenched his legs. He reminded himself to try and find a better piece of plastic, or at least another one that he could add to his own. He would wander past the building site on his way to his street corner.

His days held a familiar course. This routine of his own making was of great comfort. He would rise, beg for money on his traffic island during the morning rush hour. Then, if Dudu had brought him nothing that day, he would take his earnings to buy half a loaf of bread and some *maas*, which was rich and thick enough to be both food and drink. After eating, he would proceed with his placard to his usual position outside the Diamond to resume his daily protest. Then, back to his island, by now bathed in the blood of the setting sun, in time for the evening rush hour. This rhythm, these goals and their fulfilment, gave his life their substance. And that was what mattered to him. A life worth living, something that was done and something achieved.

———

Mercy had looked at the message again. She wondered whether or not she should have told Ginny about Madiba passing. But she had to tell someone. This was something important. Something you would remember until you were old. It was not yet announced, no one from the Presidency had said anything nor anyone from the family. It was only Jacobeth who had said. And perhaps she should not have. There were ways of doing things with that family. It was how it had to be.

———

'Mandela is dead.'

'I can't hear you.'

Gin opened the door a crack; she knew never to enter until her mother was ready. She registered the slight clink as a cup was replaced on a saucer.

'Mandela. He's dead.'

'Oh God, now there'll be a rumpus.'

'Right. Happy birthday.'

There was no reply. She shut the door again.

Back in the study, Gin had a pencil out and was writing herself lists for the party: flowers, napkins, cutlery, place names. She knew her mother was dressing as slowly as possible in some sort of protest. She tried to remember what flowers she had seen in the garden when she had arrived.

I will pick them myself.

The computer beeped, a message from a girl she knew from back home. Gin was not in the mood for other people's success. She rarely was. It was only her own success or lack of it that mattered. She thought, as she often did, that if she wanted to announce to the world her terminal joy at being alive, she would have children and announce it through them.

No matter what Gin wrote in her messages, the friend would revert to her own special kind of brilliance; her life, her husband, her children, her lovers. In that moment, Gin resolved to drop the woman from her life – something she did often and with incredible precision. If someone became too demanding, too intimate, too inconvenient, she would cut them loose. She had briefly been friends with a man who was consistently an hour late, for coffee, for dinner, for anything and affected a false intimacy at every turn. They had met at a dinner of a mutual friend. After a few of these inconvenient meetings, Gin went to Seattle for a week to set up her exhibition space and when she returned she simply deleted and blocked the man's numbers. She had, over the months, already sacrificed over seven hours, a full working day in her studio, waiting for the man to turn up at various venues across the city. A full day.

———

Neve Brandt sat straight and strong at her vanity. What a day it was already. She pushed her hair back from her temples. Dark hair, still, with bolts of gunmetal and ash streaked through it, cut straight and sharp along her jawline. She tucked her hair behind each ear with a fore-finger, before she ran the thick, white, paste-like cream across one cheek first and then the other. Like a Xhosa woman, she thought. Shame about Mandela. The father of the nation. He was ninety-five. And look at me. Eighty years old. I don't look it. Seventy perhaps.

She absent-mindedly sniffed the little gold pot that held the moisturiser. Roses. Gin had brought it from New York for her. She rubbed it in and added another stripe to her forehead. The cool confectionery of it was satisfying. The day would be hot. This will probably be the last happy moment of the day, here alone, thought Neve as she turned her head left and then right to admire her reflection. She put another dollop of cream on her neck, just to feel it roll out across her skin. A party. What could be worse? It was the most miserable possible outcome for any birthday.

———

Gin looked under the desk at Juno, who was dutifully shivering in an agony of neediness and longing. Gin dragged the round of fur up and onto her lap and sunk her face into the secret, lovely place behind Juno's ears. She breathed in all the warm dustiness and said ' 'I love you Jube-Jube. I could eat you up,' and squeezed her arms around the solid little barrel of ribs until it wriggled and twisted and then leapt to the floor and danced around yapping before disappearing through the door towards Mercy in the kitchen. Whichever dogs had conspired to produce Juno were indistinguishable in her constitution. Silky, ginger and white, a sail for a tail, half-cocked ears, a long narrow nose ending in a neat, black sponge. A body too long for her legs. She was Everydog. Gin decided that she would get one when she was back home. A small rescue type – Juno, but smaller – who could hang out in the studio and get covered in paint and glue. She felt herself fill at the prospect. She wouldn't tell her mother. She would just do it. She always considered it and always had a reason not to do it; none of the reasons were good and most of them were her mother's.

The desk chair was her father's. She had buried him in three hours. The funeral had taken less than three days to organize after she had landed back in the city. She had had to pay for the funeral notice for the newspapers in the same place you went to buy tickets for the theatre or the cinema. This still surprised her. She hadn't known what to write so she simply copied another one she saw and changed the names. It was done.

Before her phone rang again she decided to assemble herself and her lists and head out to buy the food for the party, despite it still being so early. She would see her mother properly on her return.

———

After pulling himself together, giving himself a talking to and then, inexplicably, stupidly calling Gin, Peter decided to run in the direction of the Residence. His thoughts fidgeted with each foot-fall. He moved largely unseeing. By the time he looked around, he saw immediately that there had been a change. There were media trucks, buzzing their power and lights, a small woman reporter he recognized from one of the major networks standing on an upturned plastic beer crate, facing into the lights, looking earnest. He had seen her reporting in Egypt and Libya. The Arab Spring.

Stupidly, he felt he would like to call Gin again to tell her, Mandela's gone.

Of course she had not picked up the first time. Who in their right mind would answer a call at that time of the morning? And, he suspected, knew, that she would not pick up any call from him.

She had been back in the city less than a full day, according to his estimations, and already he was lost. And even as he turned his back on the Residence, he knew he would run the route back past her mother's house.

———

Richard plopped himself into his office chair. Deep and leather-smelling despite its age. It had been his own father's chair and it had moved everywhere with him. Richard was already three years older than his father had been when he had died. Sixty-four.

It was too early to be at work but he planned to sign a few things and then be on his way well before noon. Already there was a file on his desk from Peter Strauss with a note, dated the previous day and an instruction to read through the points and make any recommendations. Richard knew that Peter would have been working on it long after the building had emptied. Bloody Verloren just would not go away. Richard ran his tongue across his teeth and tapped his fingers across his stomach. The buttons around the middle strained a little. He would lose some of that walking on the beach in a couple of weeks' time. A lovely, sickle-shaped, dream of a beach. Just the thought of it, the promise of a gush of ocean breeze that would lift his hair from his head, made him rearrange his toes in his shoes. He remembered how the sand felt when it salted to his feet. The terrible bite of the cold sea as it hit his waist and then off, the loss of gravity, the float and pull of the tide, the brush of seaweed as he would roll, seal-like onto his back and bob awhile, entirely a-drift. A castaway. Seagulls, sky, perhaps the call of children as they ran back from the water's edge as heavier waves barrelled in. That was all. And that was everything.

He wanted the newspapers. Mandela on all of them he supposed. As it should be. A good fellow. Disciplined, early riser. Tricky in the early days though. Richard's coffee arrived.

Black, no sugar. Marie brought it along with more files and the papers. She had been his secretary for nearly thirty years. Funny woman, a bit rough when she arrived, as a young girl. Afrikaans of course, terrible accent, fresh off the farm you'd have thought, but organized, a hard worker. Her hair had been the same for all those thirty years, a strange sort of bleached yellow. Cut short. Still, he appreciated her and she had been a great support.

'There you are. Bright and early. Got the papers?'

'Here it is.'

'God, what's wrong with you?'

'Mister Mandela has passed.'

'I know. There's no need to cry though is there?'

'Shame. Shame, there is. What a beautiful man.' And off she went dabbing her nose with a tissue. Oh God, it would be like this all day and every other day for weeks. He could feel it. He hoped someone had issued a press release from the firm, or would do shortly.

Richard ordered the items on his desk. He liked things in order. Rational and neat. None of this weeping and carrying on. There was a note to call Mogomotsi. Something about shareholders. There was a fellow. He would not be weeping. That was why he could be trusted to run things as he did.

Richard opened the newspaper. The front page bore a full sized image of Mandela: A Nation Mourns.

What a beautiful man.

Richard put down the paper and pulled out the entertainment section, as he did every day, first thing. He peeled back the corner of the second from last page just a little, just enough. Furtive. He read to himself.

Scorpio: With Mars in your career house
for the first time since March, get ready for
an intense, busy day. Try to stay focused if
things reach a peak. Tempers may flare.

Richard opened his diary. December. Friday. He noted it was
Neve Brandt's eightieth birthday party that evening. A dear friend.
Eighty. She had been at school with his older cousins. That would
be pleasant enough. He would try to leave early, walk in the park
perhaps. It was December and he was meant to be on leave already.

He wondered if a gift was expected. She was turning eighty,
after all. He would ask Marie. The thing about no longer having
a wife, a good woman about, was that he never knew what was
expected of him in these situations. He missed Anne, still. She
had been dead three years now. She would have been looking
forward to the beach too, as she had even that last time when she
was too weak to walk and he had carried her along the dunes and
then laid her down on a blanket. (She had laughed as he had
nearly toppled over trying to do it.) He had made sure that they
were close enough to the shore that she could feel the iodine spray
coming off the waves.

Before, they would have walked the length of the sickle,
holding hands. He would break away only to get a closer look at a
shell or something else that caught his eye; a jellyfish, a mollusc
and sometimes whales, just off the rocks. He always rushed into
the sea when he saw them. The same with dolphins, great pods
surfing and roaring through the green curve of water. In he would
go, up past his knees as if just those few strides into the ocean
would allow him to see them better. He knew it was nonsense but
he wanted to be as close as he could. He would stand there being

29

buffeted by the waves and the vicious back-rush and he would crane his neck, stupidly, naively calling to Anne again and again,

'Can you see them? It's a whale isn't it? Does she have a calf?'

And afterwards as they continued their walk, and again later in their bed before turning off the light, he would still be thinking about the whale and her calf. And as he fell asleep to the distant sound of the shoreline it was as if he fell into the great darkening waves and allowed himself to get pulled out beyond the reach of land and rescue.

———

Mercy was drinking her morning coffee in the sun under the washing lines.

'Is Mum up yet?' It was Gin.

'No.'

'I haven't properly wished her happy birthday yet.'

'She doesn't like to talk before she is dressed.'

'I know. I just struggle to believe it takes her over an hour to dress.'

Mercy hesitated, then shrugged.

'OK. See you later. I'm going to do the shopping.'

'Yes.'

Mercy looked at her hands and beyond them, her feet. Her shoes were too large, but she liked them, they were good for walking. They used to be red though they were now closer to fish pink. They were cast-offs from the other job she went to on her days off. She liked both the families she worked for, though this one, Mrs Brandt, could be demanding. She put it down to older women.

Mrs Brandt was like Mercy's own mother; impatient, tired. With both of them, Mercy had learned to scan their faces and judge how the weather had settled in them before opening her mouth. And it was a good thing that she liked dogs as both households let the dogs do as they pleased.

Mercy thought she would like to go to the Residence later. To pay her respects. But there was the party. Mrs Brandt was not happy about it. Mercy felt bad for Ginny. She was only trying to do a good thing. She had heard Mrs Brandt say unkind things to Gin the previous night when she had told her people would be coming. She had also seen that Gin had come to the kitchen and stood while the kettle boiled and that tears had fallen. And then Gin had made tea, one cup for her, one for Mrs Brandt, and she had walked back out to the verandah as if no tears had ever been shed.

There would be cleaning to do after the party but then, Sunday. The day of rest, as it was meant to be. Mercy would go to church early and then spend the rest of the day sitting in the sun with the radio on while her laundry dried around her. If it was not raining, and in this city it seemed to rain every afternoon at four o'clock, she would go out onto the pavements, a few houses further down, and sit with her friends to talk. The three would sit in a row in the dappled sun, legs out in front of them so that their shoes aligned neatly. The only one who would sit facing them was Josephine, who would talk endlessly about her children and home and how she had received this message and that photograph. Josephine never did what anyone else did. Perhaps because she drank. She boasted that during the week, when her employers were at work, she would spend the afternoon with a bottle of wine. She would cook their dinner and retreat to her room to watch television before they were home (they were both lawyers) and they would never know. Mercy found this unlikely and if true, unlikeable in Josephine and put this lack of moral fibre down to her being Zimbabwean. Those *Kalangas* were all the same. None of the other women behaved like that. They were all locals.

———

Gin fetched her bag and went to stand outside her mother's door. Juno was there too, wagging and wanting Gin to open it so that she could go in and make a nuisance of herself.

'Hang on Juno. Mum?' She could hear the wardrobe door closing. 'Mum?'

'I'm getting dressed, Virginia.'

'I know, can I come in though?'

'Quickly.'

Gin pushed the door open. Juno shot through the narrow gap.

'Happy birthday Mum.' Gin put her arms around her mother, who shrank away. Gin kissed her cheek. It smelled of roses. Juno was winding through their legs, her tail thumping with joy.

'I'm trying to forget it. As you well know.'

'Too bad.'

Why do I love you so much?

Gin felt so very far away from her mother. Further than she ever felt at the other side of an ocean, multiple time zones apart. It were as if physical proximity raised in her mother the possibility of a true intimacy, one that demanded involvement and consequence. This was something she was unable to offer and so, in order to preserve her scant reserves, on Gin's arrival, a barricade was hastily erected.

Gin understood this. She too had a finite amount of time and emotional attachment she could offer. Once that level was breached, too much taken, too much leached off and apprehended by emotional subterfuge, her world became increasingly perilous. Her work suffered, quickly becoming impossible. So she understood this in Neve. What she did not understand was that there seemed to be no special compensation or separate store of affection held as a dedicated treasure to be lavished on her alone by virtue of her biological proximity.

'Is that the face cream? Is it any good?'

'Yes. It's nice. Maybe I'll get you to send me some more when it's finished.' Brittle, clean.

'Mum, you can't be angry all day. And it's only this evening so at least enjoy the day.'

'I've got a lot to do Virginia. Thanks to you.'

'Well, at least you will have nice rosy skin while you do it. Won't she Juno?'

'Are you going out now? And what is going on with your hair these days? Honestly. It's very dark and all the way down your back. At your age. It doesn't suit you. You aren't pale enough to carry off that colour and you have a very strong face, Virginia, you need to soften it. What happened to those nice lighter streaks you had? And those ends. Did you just stick them in an ink pot? Why don't you get it all cut off this morning? Dye it a pretty colour. I can make an appointment for you?'

Gin, sitting on the edge of her mother's bed with Juno, felt she was suddenly the subject of too much attention. Not at all the kind she had wanted.

'No thanks. You go to your appointments and I will go to mine. Bea is coming later with some tables from her studio. Mercy can let her in if I'm not back.'

'Is she coming tonight?'

'Of course.'

33

'Such a nice girl, Bea. Why isn't she married either?'

'Just lucky I guess.' Gin kissed Neve again and turned to leave.

She hated that she always defaulted to jest and frippery to fend off the barbs Neve slung her way. It made her burn all through. But what could she say? You lacerate me every time you speak. That she wanted more than anything for her to say she was happy, to say she was so pleased Gin had come? Even if it was not true. To at least be kind.

———

The cars were beginning to dwindle. September began to think about his meal and stood leaning against the traffic light to count the morning's takings. Even those who passed a hand through an open window did not bother to look at him, castaway on this island; as if a vagabond were not made from the same star stuff as the rest. The grace of stars was never once bestowed on him, even in jest or anecdote. If he wished to be made whole again, he would have to claim it for himself. Stand outside the doors of the Diamond and sing out his demand that he too be filled with its light.

September had known for months that the king had already passed, in the way that he often did. It was official now though, announced, and all the little boards on the poles along the street were covered with the news. And images too, of Tata's face as if by repeating it on and on along the roads, it were possible to keep him there, keep him safe under the nation's gaze.

September would go back to his bedding, rest, eat and get himself ready for his vigil outside the Diamond. Even as he thought it he raised his hand to the side of his face, where his skull lifted a little and then fell away. For even though this was an important day for the nation, there was no reason to rest now.

And then, September's brain suddenly released a flare, so sharp and hot that he had to turn from the light. It were as if just passing his hand across the flesh had again awakened the pain. He cried out, again and again, just to make the flare burn out. But it would not. So he kept repeating to himself the only thing that made it bearable:

I am made of light, I am made of light.

Mid-morning

Gin fiddled with the keys to the car. It was her mother's. Long and low and black, it was still accessorized with its original chrome fittings. The engine hummed and throbbed until it settled into its idling speed. She pressed the remote-control console on the key-ring and the big gate rolled back on its runners, rumbling like a Highveld thunderstorm. It could not rain later, or the party would be ruined.

Gin just about registered the thrill, the fear of leaving the house, the checking of the mirrors and looking every which way for cars and pedestrians and groups of men lolling on topiaried verges who might have a look of hunger and fearlessness about them. A man approached along the road and Gin felt the old tug of fear and hated herself for it. But that man, of course, passed with a piece of cardboard and hidden behind it some flowers, heading towards the Residence and she smiled at him, her guilty white smile. She looked the length of the street. At the far end she could just about see barricades, television trucks and a police van. A huddle of women dressed in the familiar yellow, black and green of the Party.

Should I go? Should I be there?

The city was beautiful, electric even. The sky was bleached out over the high-rises that flashed and glowed as the sun continued with its flight for the day. It was a blinding beauty.

Like Granny.

A blinding beauty whose parties in the middle of nowhere attracted guests who would travel a full day, wearing dust coats over their linen, to attend. Granny, who always knew how to laugh at men so that instead of feeling slighted, they left her side floating on a plump pillow of flattery.

Gin steered the car up the hill that would take her to the shops. Towers of glass and everywhere more being built – banks, law firms, mining houses, the great and the good of a bygone era still standing despite a crusty patina of blood and guilt. She felt the weight of the car drag behind her before the automatic gear changed, and gravity dropped away.

———

The day was going to be a write-off. Richard had already had three people in his office with nothing else to talk about but Mandela. At least that would take the pressure off having to come out with a statement on Verloren – the media would be busy elsewhere, until January at least.

He was unsettled. He decided he would find Peter and go to the little coffee shop under the trees in the square. Peter Strauss was not necessarily his preferred company but he was a fellow who always had the look of a caged animal about him and as such, a little outing away from his desk might be agreeable to him. Peter *was* a caged animal. Not a lion, more the temper of a confused antelope. Poor chap. He was surprisingly good at his job, given his obvious disdain for the entire sector and all those who worked in it. He needed to find a nice girl. Then he would have someone other than himself to work *for*. Probably still in love with Neve Brandt's daughter. (She'd sent him a message to invite him to Neve's party.) Now there was an odd one. Very attractive. Not swayed by flattery or frippery. Artist, which might account for a lot of it. Hard as nails. Compelling though, in the way that things you absolutely cannot fathom always are.

'Peter?'

'Oh, Richard, I couldn't find you earlier.'

'You look like a man who has seen a ghost.'

'Well, hectic day.'

'And likely to intensify I'd have thought. Shall we go outside for coffee?'

Peter looked disorientated by the invitation. So much so that Richard felt he should add, 'I wanted to get your thoughts on any complications we might encounter if and when an inquiry is held. Patrick Mogomotsi is already half way through one of his action plans. I've just seen him. He wants to convene a shareholders meeting. He may be right.'

'Of course.'

Richard and Peter made their way across the Diamond's foyer, a cavernous cathedral-white void. The chasm was perfectly complimented by a vast suspended sculpture above the central staircase (a suggestion of a mine shaft wheel here, a whisper of a shovel head there, all hinting at the company's pioneering past).

They passed through the security barriers, barely acknowledging the guard who opened the door for them on their way out. Both blinked as they faced the full force of the open sky. In front of them, the plaza. In the middle of it a large sweep of fountains and water features. These designed to cool the area which, by virtue of being bordered by buildings and the Diamond in particular, seemed to pulse a few degrees higher than anywhere else. All around the outside of the foundations, trees and flower beds, benches, umbrellas.

'Oh, that fellow is back again.' Richard used his chin to gesture towards September on the far side of the fountains. He had just arrived and was arranging himself and his placard.

'He's here every day.'

'Should we worry?' By which for some moment he had felt he meant 'Should we care?' But he had managed to correct himself.

'No. He's harmless. I knew him before.'

'Before what?'

Peter took a breath. 'Before he was shot. On the Verloren koppie.'

'Do you mean before someone in our building gave an order to shoot?'

'We do not have access to any apparatus of the state, remember?' Peter had lowered his voice.

'Of course not.'

———

Gin turned up the steep hill that lead from the houses whose entrances were overburdened with topiaries and security hardware. Along those streets, the recyclers rode self-fashioned wagons, long, wide planks of woods with wheels stolen from shopping trollies and fitted with handles from the same. All day they scavenged through bins to fill their loads, then dragged them up the hills. They strained like beasts of burden, their great rolling bundles of refuse behind them. But then, release! How they rode their chariots downhill, standing proud at the rear, one hand steering, a cigarette or joint in the other, a foot to brake.

Gin overtook a wagon and felt the pull of guilt in her stomach. She slowed at the next traffic light and stopped, shaking her head at three men offering pamphlets for cheap 'leather look' furniture, sex clinics and a new shoe warehouse, and then the beggar too with his blind friend who shuffled along next to him, guilt bait. A mother with a baby. Another child.

So she rolled down the window and dropped some coins from her jacket pocket into the tin cup for the blind man's friend. And they clattered like gun fire as they fell.

––––––

Dudu had things to do. Her salary needed to be put in the bank, some transferred to her sister who was buying school supplies for the children back home in Lesotho, she needed air-time for her phone. And she was late, rushing out because she had done something to the new vacuum cleaner – a bit had come out of a cylinder and she did not know how to get it back in. It had to be fixed and working or there would be hell to pay from her madam. And she had to see to September. There was always September.

He was older than her by three years. There had been another child between them who died. Their mother spoke of this child often as if she was somehow still there, still part of them. Though September was older he was, in the end, always the younger too.

She had begun to look after her brother almost as soon as she could remember it. He would leave his bread at home and be hungry at school so that he would cry and attract the attention of the bigger, rougher boys who would chase him with sticks. And she, though slim and wiry, would pick up stones and throw them at those boys. And they would say, she fights like a boy. Once or twice those same boys tried to tease her for having a Zulu name when she should have had a Sesotho one. She gave them a terrifying speech about her father being a Zulu and if they did not leave her and September be, then her father, Shaka's own son, would find them and beat them until they cried.

Later when she grew up and filled out in the ways that women do (though she was still small and still wiry) the boys would say how beautiful she was. But then another would say, remember, she fights like a man.

Dudu, still thinking about the extra piece of the vacuum cleaner, walked as quickly as she could. She kept her head down, her eyes averted, tucking the long loose strands of her braids under her doek. That way she would not attract the attention of the recycling men as they shot past on their carts. They had a wildness to them and used language that insulted her, her body. To be a woman, walking from here to there was no easy thing. She always looked at women in cars and thought how safe they seemed, so dignified. Women who drove cars did not drop their heads. They looked straight ahead.

She crossed the street that lead to up to the Diamond. Out of habit she looked the length of the street in the hope of seeing September. Instead she saw the woman whose face seemed to melt from her skull, begging at the lights. Whenever she saw her, Dudu would raise her hand in greeting, as if raising a prayer. But Dudu also knew that God had long ago abandoned the woman with the melting face.

*

Gin could feel a rage building. It needed no origin. The heat of the car was part of it, the fans so old that they seemed to blow hot engine air right through her. This was a rage that she associated with Johannesburg. She only felt it here. This city with half-naked women on billboards, adverts for strip clubs, metres high and dripping with flesh, its obsession with marriage, its child-friendly restaurants, its noise, edge, vulgarity; all of it combined to make her feel unwelcome.

Johannesburg was the practised master of the endless hustle. It was built on gold. The wheelers, the dealers, the pioneer, frontier town it was always going to be. The drivers, the pedestrians, the constant tap tap tapping on your car window from hawkers and beggars and chancers feigning hunger and destitution and misery, exposed by the headphones and sneakers they wore and by strapping lumps of paper to their backs because a hump means money, and a limp or bent-back sloping shuffle even more. It never changed. The assault of demands.

She edged forward in the jam to show her disinterest in whoever was at her window. She hated everything about driving.

Across the intersection there were two identically dressed clown-like men, rainbow wigs, cropped trousers, painted faces, twirling sticks high over their heads as they did some sort of soft-shoed tap dance, synchronized. That was new. Dance for your supper. It raised a sticky shame in Gin. A near visceral discomfort. Their routine ended and they each made their way through the long lines of cars, holding out cups to carbon-copy white boys on their way to jobs in foreign banks and mining houses. None of them gave any money.

The lights were doing nothing to change and when they did, all the cars which had sneaked through the amber light on one side blocked the path of those going in the opposite direction. They, in turn, returned the favour. Taxi drivers leaned on their hooters as they mounted the pavement with two wheels and shot across an intersection against the red light. The raging white boys hooted and shook their fists and yelled out of windows, which they then quickly closed. Then, one taxi driver cruised over to them and rolled down his window, leaning out to make sure they felt him before he cruised away with the menace of a shark in deep water. She saw two of the white boys throw a glance down to check they had remembered to lock themselves in.

Gin hated them all.

Another tap at her window, the unmistakable clunk of an enamel cup on the glass. She gestured at the tapper to move on but as her eyes scanned up the round body to the face under a hat, she felt her stomach lurch. She shook her head and looked down again in one motion.

Gin tried to look in the wing mirror as the form shuffled along. As the woman turned to tap on the next car window her face was exposed from under the hat she wore. The entire left-hand side of her face was sliding down her skull and neck in huge folds of flesh as if, as a child, she had been held too close to a fire and had begun to melt. She had great pastry-like waves, three or maybe four that dragged her right eye down towards her jaw.

Gin felt a terrible sickness rising. She had to get away from the woman. The woman moved to the third car; it wasn't far enough.

Get me away from her.

Gin's skin was fired and pulsing.

Get me away from her.

She pushed into the traffic, somewhere in the middle of the intersection where she should not have been. There was nowhere to go, whichever way the lights changed now. She couldn't breathe.

What am I doing here? I could leave, get a flight. I should not be here.

Her phone started ringing again. She threw it from the side pocket in her door to the footwell on the passenger side.

Eventually, a bus overtook her on the left to jump a light, allowing her to rush along next to it and use it as a buffer against the oncoming traffic as it blocked off at least two lanes.

Gin's pulse was pummelling her head, her breath was short and hard to the point of pain. There was nothing to see but the melting woman. It wasn't a burn, the skin was smooth and healthy except that it was all wrong, bulbous and thick and falling down and the one eye had fallen down with it.

What am I doing here?

———

Peter had been at work for hours. The meeting with Richard, though brief, had unsettled him. If things went badly for them over Verloren, he would take the fall. He looked at his watch. Then at his tie.

He had been forced, the previous week, to take part in an end-of-year assessment which, among other things, suggested that his personal brand was undefined within the broader structure of the team. After he pointed out that he lead the entire team, he had been helpfully corrected. A position is not a brand, and his lacked definition. He had then, predictably, bought a vulgar tie, bound to define his personal brand. The tie had for the past three days sat in its see-through plastic box on top of his chest of drawers, mocking him relentlessly, as he continued to revert to his usual choices.

He had sent Gin a text over an hour before. No reply. Yet again had tried calling. Nothing but a curt message to leave a number. Virginia Brandt. Even hearing her instruction raised something in him. Not quite a thrill, not quite anger. Something close to fear. Perhaps she was asleep. Or her mother had given him the wrong dates. Perhaps she had not yet landed. He swung his chair around to look out of the window, which reached from floor to ceiling.

From the outside, the building was simply lengths of mirror that wrapped the irregular, facetted frame of the structure. On brighter days (and every day in Johannesburg seemed over-lit, over-exposed) in among the surrounding towers of concrete and black glass, the Diamond could appear from certain angles to be made from shards of sky.

It wasn't meant to be called the Diamond. It was one of those things that caught on in the media. They had thought to control it but in the end, what did it matter? People were talking about it. That was something. They were a landmark, and the cases brought against the company from residents and motorists claiming that at certain times of the day they were blinded by the glare, had all been dealt with. Not so much settled as ignored.

Peter had already instructed their communications girls to send the press release that had been written over a year before.

> With regret and deep sadness we receive the news
> that Mister Mandela has passed. This is a time of
> great sadness for the nation and the Mandela family.
> Anglo Dutch Mines has had a long and positive
> relationship with the former president.

Important to highlight the company's anti-apartheid credentials, of course. It was important that everyone knew where they stood, where he stood.

I am lost.

The last time he had felt this way, or at least an approximation of it, and with far greater severity, was after Richard's wife's funeral. Anne.

They had all gone, to support Richard, of course, but also because it was necessary and appropriate. Peter did not know Richard's wife. They had met briefly over the years and anything he did know he gleaned from Richard who spoke of her in vague references and usually in the context of medical procedures. 'Prognosis' and 'benign' and 'remission.'

Peter was late for the funeral, parked on a verge. He rushed to the church doors carrying his jacket, stood at the back. Droning organ music, a good turnout, many of those gathered were older women and a large number of colleagues. Eventually, Richard's daughter stood up to speak, clear and articulate, not a suggestion of grief, a contained catalogue of her mother's life. And then, as she mentioned her father, her voice broke.

Peter, alone and standing at the back beneath a stained glass window casting red and blue and yellow onto the floor, broke too. He could not say why. Later he would speculate that it had been the heat, the light, the painful precision of Richard's daughter in her choice of words that had conspired to produce a near unbearable proximity to grief.

Peter remained lost for three days. He called in sick, retreated to his bedroom and took the opportunity to torture himself further by taking an eviscerating inventory of his life. From his bed he had to acknowledge that days, stretching to an entire life-time, had gone uncatalogued, unattributed, unwitnessed. And he allowed himself to admit that he was, despite his careful moor-ings, capable of unbraiding at a rate of knots.

On the fourth day he woke and found that he was well again, the books balanced, the return filed. And yet, now, here he was again, a little over a year later, drifting and searching and lost.

With regret and deep sadness we receive the news.

Peter's office was suffocating and so as a temporary remedy for this creeping malaise he decided he would get out. Perhaps a drive. Fetch a coffee. Maybe drop in on the Brandt house, go past the Residence. No one was doing any work.

———

September had his bread and milk. He stood outside the store and looked up to the sun. The sky began to crease under his gaze. He knew that under it, the city was ripening – its flesh softening and warming. Soon its pulp could be pressed with even the most unwilling thumb. And later, of course, the flies.

The king is dead. Long live the king.

———

Gin glanced at the clock on the dashboard. After ten. The sun suddenly disappeared. She switched the dial on the radio.

President Nelson Mandela has died, a spokesman for the family has now confirmed. The office of the Presidency has announced ten days of national mourning.

This day of all days. She wished Peter would stop calling. How did he even know she was back? Under the car park security boom she drove. It lifted like a guard of honour. It took two turns to get herself lined up to park. When she was done, she could feel her body seep into the driver's seat as the engine settled back into its metal, as the key shut down.

She opened the car door and stepped out. The air was heavy with car fumes and engine heat. Gin felt that one more thing, one more layer of demand would be enough to overwhelm her entirely. The heat, her mother, Mandela, even Peter, and the woman with the melting face. It was too much. Too much was needed from her. And everything was wrong. Everything was too much for just one day. She felt her mind skitter this way and that, try to fix its sights on something solid. There was nothing. She was entirely without an anchor, a star unhinged from gravity with no orbit nor constellation to call it home.

———

Neve sat with her tea and stroked Juno who curled on her lap. She only just fitted. She was not exactly a dog built for laps in her arrangement of limbs but her heart said otherwise.

It was clear Gin was having the party to make herself feel better for having flitted off, just like that. Met a man who promised her the world, or at least a New York exhibition, which to Gin was the same thing. Off she went. No priorities. She could have married Peter. He still adored her, always calling and asking after her. She had told him Gin was coming.

One time she, Neve, against her better judgement, had met Peter for lunch and he had done nothing but talk about Gin. At the end of a rather tedious few hours, Neve had eaten a large salad with cheese and pears, a dessert and two coffees. He had eaten nothing. She was rather too intimately acquainted with Peter's slightly drooping posture. Had he from a younger age assumed a more heroic stance in his posture, he would have had every hope of being attractive. Instead, he tended to fidget and slump, and, on the day of the lunch, he undermined himself further by talking too much.

So enraptured was he with his thoughts of Virginia. Memories mostly for there was so little between them these days. They had quarrelled, she suspected. She never understood over what. Some of his thoughts on Gin were quite insightful but for the most part he described a girl she, her own mother, did not recognize in the least. He called her brave and extraordinary. But as Neve recalled it she was simply stubborn, overly bossy and too clever for her own good.

———

The smell of coffee floated over like a high note of deeper promise as Gin arrived at the doors of Mother Cuppuh. Peter disparaged her coffee drinking. 'A gateway drug to sloth and poetry,' he had called it, and thought it very clever. (It was, but the fact that he knew so and therefore repeated it proudly and often, only made him sound desperate and attention seeking.) Only a man who once fancied himself a poet and had become a labour lawyer could say such a thing. She pitied his lack of sloth and poetry. Why could she not stop thinking about him now? Was he still handsome? Was she still beautiful? He had tried to call twice. She hated him again.

Over the speakers, loud and bold so that it filled the whole room, came 'Young, Gifted and Black'. Behind the bank of hyper-polished, hyper-stylized chrome-topped coffee machines stacked with cups the barista was swaying left to right, her arms outstretched, head thrown back and eyes closed, betraying just half a set of kingfisher-blue false eyelashes, alive with tears, her every cell still brimful of youth.

She could not have been older than twenty. Her weave looked as though she had lost the ends on one side. She was transcendent. Gin watched her, too scared to break the dream. From behind the machine a baritone voice interrupted Gin's reverie.

'Cup sister?'

'Large latte, full-milk, extra hot.'

'One Serious, full, *shisa*.'

The girl with the kingfisher-blue lashes had seamlessly transferred her swaying into a lunging and stacking of the mugs coming out of the dishwashing machine in the kind of weightless choreography that only oblivion can produce.

She is built for space travel.

———

Neve was dead-heading roses in the garden. One, two. Satisfying work. Poor Peter. He had always been a bit of a wet rag. Good looking though, in his way. Always had a good job. At least Gin would have food on the table. Not that she eats. God. Children, to still be worrying about them at nearly eighty. Or exactly eighty.

What a miserable day. And poor old Mandela. What is it to become irrelevant to the world of your own making? Aunt Virginia had a better idea. Walked into the sea at Plettenberg Bay in her sequinned evening dress. She was always a funny old thing – face like a bird – married though, it's not as if she was on her own. It was years ago now.

Neve often thought about Aunt Virginia and her strangeness. She wondered too if it was a mistake naming Gin after any sort of madwoman who walked into the waves. Too late to worry now. She just ignored Gin when she came home from her latest numerologist or astrologer, convinced her destiny was held in the mysterious numbers associated with her name. Thank God she seemed to be seeing fewer of those quacks or, at least, seeking out a better quality of quack.

What will become of Gin? What will become of her?

Something smashed in the kitchen. Mercy. She could not be pleased about this party. Neve dropped the flower heads she clasped in her fingers onto the grass (Talent would collect them) and went back inside with Juno.

'Mercy? Mercy where are you?'

'Ma'am, I am here.'

'What a mess. I am very sorry about this party. You have Virginia to thank for that.'

'It will be a nice party. Happy birthday, Ma'am.'

'Mercy. I am trying to forget. Thank you. Do you think Jacobeth or Nozi could help us tonight? Anna even, although she is rather old.'

'Not Nozi. Tata Mandela has passed. She will not leave.'

'I hadn't thought of that. We should put on the news.'

'Jacobeth told me. I think he died in the night.'

'Can you just imagine the goings on down there?'

————

Every day Virginia sat in her writing room that overlooked the sea. It was beautiful. The life of everything beyond that room, the water that stretched out forever, somehow reached inside and found its place in her own strange oceans, those shifting tides that washed through her all and every day. And from out at sea, the ghost ship called insinuating all the whisperings that rustled through her head from the moment she woke up.

She knew the only way to make them stop even just long enough to notice a gull or look out to the lighthouse was to write. Some days she would wake with the shape of a paragraph already finding its way through her mind to her hand, so that she would notice her fingers twitching, rehearsing for the coming morning with the pen balancing lightly, poised and inked to begin.

Once a book was finished, which was to say, those particular ocean spectres were quiet again, Virginia would go to her bed and sleep for days. Sometimes as long as a week, surfacing only to take some soup or fruit. She knew a book was done because she would wake in the morning and realize after a few moments that the whispering had gone and the only sounds she heard were those of the garden, the house, life.

Sometimes though, even before she had finished the one she could feel the next approaching. A new voice, lighter, darker. A wraith of a different rush and drag will have made its way up and through and would, even in the aftermath, be foaming towards the shore. She would know with certainty that it came from a different place. This was language that had been bellowed up, from beyond the hidden fathoms of the sea. She would have to ask the newcomer to wait its turn but, just in case, she would take down in notes what it was saying for use after a time of recovery.

She never spoke of these things. Who would hear her? Her family thought she spent hours plotting her books to specifically include insult and injury, that she actively sought controversy. Journalists, other writers came to the house and spoke about bravery and defiance. Every time they did she felt the shame of her fraudulent persona. Activist, humanitarian, she was none of these. Rather she was the coward, who knew that to resist these ocean ghosts, the work, the daily pen, would be certain death to her.

———

Gin watched the baristas, going about their work and thought about space, the place where she would finally relinquish control. She suspected that there would be no language to describe the feeling of orbit. The language born of gravity would be meaningless once she was up there. She would have to create a better language, scratch out new hieroglyphs, to send messages back to earth. Once you have described eternity as eternity and blackness as black, expansiveness, infinity, infinity, infinity, then there is nothing more to be said. Or perhaps she would just surrender to silence and send her last message saying that there was, after all, nothing to be said.

'Serious latte,' said the barista from behind the chrome machines.

'Thank you.'

Suddenly and inexplicably Gin felt she might cry, or shout. She wanted the heart on the top of her coffee foam to be a gift he'd made for her specifically. She knew, also, that it was not a declaration of love but rather Mother Cuppuh policy.

The girl with the kingfisher-blue eyelashes had interrupted her mug stacking job and was tap dancing around her mop as she cleaned a spill on the floor near the door. The unencumbered soul.

I could have been you once. I was you.

Angrier though and more serious. But there were those long nights that bled into weeks of screaming highs that left her defended by the bass of the speakers for days. Or so it had felt.

Rows of shot glasses lined up along the counter at Colour Bar, the place of her social tribe, as if the way they all dressed and spoke and danced and rolled along, allowed them all to speak with the same tongue.

———

They were rainbow nights for the new Rainbow Nation, lawless and blood-full, so that all four chambers of the heart raged in unison. After dominating her childhood, it seemed as if the police were all but gone. While violent crime played out in suburbs and townships across the city in a way that made Gin fear her own breath in the dark. And there was no one there to save her, not her parents, not her friends. Certainly not Peter. So she embraced it. The whole city was an accident of death. This one was in the wrong place, that one, his time was up. A roll of the dice. Wrong house, wrong petrol station, wrong time and your day was done. Death was everywhere and came in every form. Just to be alive was dangerous and to survive a defiance.

On one day the man who worked at the corner store was there, on the next he had 'gone home'. Which was the code for announcing that he had gone home to die. No one seemed to know what to do about the disease, only pretend it wasn't happening. Eventually civil organizations sprung into being and began to roll out anti-retrovirals paid for by the French, the Canadians, whoever.

One weekend, her childhood friend's parents were killed in their driveway for a watch and mobile phone. The next, a house-keeper down the road was shot for her keys to the house, but not before she was tied up and taunted and raped.

This was no time to stay home and wait for death. Death had to be met head on. And so she had, tearing reckless through the city on four wheels after a night of drinking. A final rebellion.

And the raging, the raging, the raging of feeling so alive as she screamed along.

And perhaps this was where she and Peter had finally started to part ways. Her launching into life so hard and so close that she knew the coin could at any time flip. She demanded that all of it, life and death, look her square in the face and he, all the while, was softening, losing his nerve, turning away.

Gin stirred in the sugar and felt the spoon briefly grind the granules against the side of the cup, reminding her of the spring of the palette knife that just registers in the forearm as she mixed pigments on her palette.

Two women walked past, or it may have been the same woman twice. In this part of the city either could be true. Gin's spoon stirred to the same tempo as their heels, punished feet, bronzed legs and thick opaque faces, motionless yet panicked. How is such a motiveless existence possible? Would she have become this had she stayed? She knew she would not because death is always preferable to that. The coffee was rich and dark. Stronger than it ever was at home. This was the coffee of bounty hunters.

———

September felt the heft of the placard he was holding weigh into his shoulder. The cardboard was not the problem. It was the tall, narrow plank that he had nailed it to that caused him pain. Its surge ran from his shoulder where the wood rested, down along his spine and into his left foot. And also ran up from his shoulder into his head so that his brain always felt like a bruised mango squashed into a tin can. Or at least that is how he described it to Dudu, when she came to see him. She would bring him water and sandwiches and fruit so that he would at least eat as he kept his vigil outside the Diamond.

He had been there every day since the widows and families of the victims had lost their application in the High Court to have their legal costs covered. So, the struggle continued, for restitution, for justice.

A full year had passed since the miners had been shot with live bullets as they came down the hill, the great rocks behind them made gold by the setting sun. By the time the first bullet was fired, the strike was already five days old. One union said it was legal. Another denounced it as a wildcat strike. But many among the strikers had felt that to fight in the dust like a wildcat was no bad thing – when the stakes are high you may need to bare your teeth. September and his comrades continued to sit out under the skies, and over the five days private security companies were replaced more and more by the state police: armoured cars, fat-bellied officers.

The strike torch-bearers felt that the arrival of the police was uncalled for. The leadership's anger, conveyed to September and his friends, began to come from a deeper place, the words became more bloody. They must resist, they must fight to the end, they must slay the oppressors.

On the fifth day, there were so many protestors that they covered the fields outside the mine that lead to the great boulders. They held their *pangas* high, their *knobkierries* announcing their battle. As each negotiation session came and went, the deadlock intensified and so did the tension that hung in the air between the men on the koppie and the men wearing riot gear.

The miners wished for more and that more seemed possible when they looked about the city where mothers took their children to school in cars the size of a shanty-town shack and fathers called to wish those children goodnight on telephones dipped and baked in platinum and gold, the same gold that September's comrades dug from the belly of the mountains until they were sick from exhaustion.

In front of the Diamond, September ran a hand across the spent agapanthus. Their flowers were gone. The loaded seed heads remained.

He turned to look back at the Diamond. A floating jewel, yet all the while made from the blackest of carbon. It never seemed to cast a shadow.

He knew that his vigil was nothing more than the hope that someone would bear witness to his body. And that the one who had seen him there would in turn bear witness to another and then another and that over time, these few would become many and would knit together in a beautiful constellation, glittering across the nation, connected by the story of the man, September, who had daily walked with his burden and borne witness for all of those who fell silent on that fifth day at Verloren.

On this day though, he felt a little too far away from himself, the faintest of cracks had begun to open between the man standing in the plaza with a board across his chest and the man he knew he was, and all the time, the heat had begun to clot his hope.

———

The security guard paced up and down, with one eye on September and the other darting to his phone.

September called to him every day, 'Falsehood is worse in beggars than in kings!'

Around him, pigeons began to land. And though they were a strange and unpromising congregation, nonetheless he did what he always did when he felt the darkness sit too close.

Fear no more!

He called out his message of love but the birds scattered and flashed their dark silhouettes across the face of the Diamond.

———

Lungisane looked up from his phone to see the man with the hump shouting at him. But he chose to say nothing in return and went back to sending messages to his new girlfriend. He had met her on the long bus journey from Ixopo back to Johannesburg. The morning they had left, the valley had been misty and green and she had slept in the seat next to his. He had never seen anyone so beautiful. A dream. Twice he had tried and failed to say something that might impress her so instead he had made her laugh. When she had sneezed twice in quick succession, he knew he was in love.

———

The night had been long for September and he knew this day in front of the Diamond would be a difficult thing. He was entirely made of pain, still and again. And today, which accounted for the difficulty he was having, it seemed to come from his heart. He had been troubled by dreams of happier times and this had left him broken not only in his physical body but the one beyond that too. The body of his soul that held the paths to all his ancestors and all his yesterdays, had now, he believed, also begun to tatter. The pain that registered there was often so much worse than any bullet or twisted spine. For there is no other line of defence for a man once his soul begins to rent and fray.

Dreams, the beautiful ones, made the moment of waking so much harder, as if the first breath of the day, the realization of where he was, delivered a blow so sudden and so violent that it took him the best part of the morning to recover. For to be alive is not always a beautiful thing.

September had dreamed he was a boy again, that he was running with his father's hunting dogs along the crest of the mountains. His spine was long and straight and he could feel it arch back, like a bow when he released a spear, outstretched fingers flinging it across the open sky. Oh, to fly, to fly would be a wonderful thing.

His father was there too, he knew that. He did not see his father's face but heard his voice and felt the heat of his horse's breath on his back. Even in sleep, the horse's breath (original, uncomplicated) felt like prayer that passed along his spine, where there was no hump yet, only the smallest sense of a bend, a break in the long straight path of vertebrae. His father called his name.

'Sechaba, Sechaba, it is time to come home.'

And when September woke he thought, why has my father called my name, why has he called me home? And just to think on that, had made him unseam a little.

September was sick. He had been to the mine doctors for years and they had done nothing to help him. They had said that his hump meant that he would be in pain. Pain was who he was now.

On days when he was very tired and angry and fallen apart, he would imagine that he could sleep on his back, feel the full stretch of the earth along his flattened spine, like a long adder that rested flush with the earth. He could feel this tender, ancient heat bring comfort to his body, as if it was his own mother's hand.

Since he had left the mine (for how could he go back there?) he had paid his money to the taxi driver and made the long, difficult ride to the clinic downtown. He explained to the doctors there that it was not his hump that was causing him pain but rather his head, which screamed and flashed with pain that was so electric it caused him to see lights, comets, flares. He explained that before he had been trampled and kicked by the policeman all about his head and his hump on the last day of the Verloren strike, he felt no such pain. And in any case how could he not feel pain when so many had fallen, when all about him they fell.

The doctors told him to leave.

————

Peter could not shake the sense that something was wrong with Richard. They had gone for coffee but in the end nothing of substance had been said, despite the dramatic opening gambit. He had expected to defend himself, felt he had perhaps misjudged Richard's views on the whole ongoing mess of the strike. As they had walked along the outside of the Diamond along the rows of agapanthus to the little cafe (which was outdoors, but sheltered by those safari umbrellas), Peter had been planning his defence and distraction even while he was asking Richard, are you off to the beach again? Will your daughter and her children be joining you? And so many other things that he eventually, after years, felt he had earned the right to ask.

They sat and ordered a coffee each and then Richard had said to the waiter, 'I'll have a croissant too. I shouldn't, only today demands one. Will you have one, Peter?'

'No thank you.'

'Discipline. I admire that.'

'Do you truly believe we …'

Richard was looking up at the trees between the umbrellas. Distracted and blinking. He brushed a fly aside without commitment.

'Fantastic birds, weavers, aren't they? Work like the devil, one nest, down it comes, try another, on and on until it's just right. They learn that skill over a lifetime, did you know? Don't think I'd have the energy for it. And they keep on making nests, hoping their lady-love will take a fancy to one and let them in. Can you imagine a fellow doing such a thing?'

'No.'

Peter had half a thought that Richard was having a stroke. He watched him, patrician and immutable, sigh, stir his coffee though he hadn't added anything and, when his pastry arrived, almost smile, as if this were the nicest thing that could happen. He had eaten half of it and they had sat in silence for long enough to make Peter feel rather uncomfortable. Eventually he ventured, 'All OK Richard?'

'Yes, yes. Pity about Mandela isn't it?'

'He hasn't been active for a while.'

'True, true. Now, tell me, what do you think of Mogomotsi?'

'He's tough. Very smart. He's handling Verloren rather deftly, I think.'

'Well, he is keeping us clean is what you mean. I find him very capable.'

'He shifted the focus. It was prudent. And necessary. He's very effective in a crisis.'

'Yes, he is. Good fellow. I'm pleased to hear that. Met his wife the other night. Did you? Might be even smarter than he is.' Richard chuckled at this.

'May I ask what you're thinking?'

Richard took a breath and looked up to the weavers again. They were chirruping noisily as they worked. In the one acacia there were as many as five or six nests. Richard never replied.

As the two walked back to the Diamond, Richard setting a languid pace, Peter thought he heard him say:

'I miss Anne. I should like to go and live by the ocean.'

*

The lights would not change. A blind man and his companion stayed there next to Gin's car. Both men lifted their faces to the sky. Gin heard it too. Voop voop voop, the blades of a helicopter, voop voop voop. Perhaps heading for the Residence, carrying family or the police or the press. The flies were descending. The traffic light changed and she was off up the hill to the mall, with the roar and muscle of the engine, the sun on the dashboard, some old-time jazz playing. Oh, this is swell, thought Gin. A fat, sumptuous, party balloon of a word. Just swell. Aunt Diana liked to say that; she'd be there tonight.

At the mall, through the boom of the parking lot and up, up, round and around until she reached 'Roof Parking' where she could leave the car to bake while she bought the food on her list. She had written the list on the plane. Eighteen whole hours to make a list that would help her get things done. In the end it had taken only twenty minutes, finished even before the flight attendant arrived with her trolley and deposited the tray of food. Gin had tried to eat, but it had been impossible.

Remembering the meal allowed Gin, out of habit, to flick back the hair that had fallen forward and then casually run her fingers along her scapula, decades of retracing the form beneath the skin, the comfort that she existed and that there was a clear and original boundary between herself and the world.

She knew the precise weight of all her bones. She had remade them all for her exhibition, Sticks and Stones. Every bone in her body, the fingerbones like chicken wings, the femur, her pelvis, remade, cast to their exact weight and size, then hung like totems from the gallery ceiling. This same set of bones repeated on and on and until they began to form a more recognizable shape and eventually a skeleton, her skeleton. Depending on which way the visitors entered the long lab-lit space, they either experienced her coming together to wholeness or shattering to the stars as they moved along. She wanted people to understand that depending on their perspective, the point of entry into her world, they would either view her, all of her, as working towards integrity and strength or, alternately, soon likely to disintegrate completely.

She waited in front of the bank of elevators that would take her from 'Roof Parking' to 'Upper Mall' and counted the lights as they ticked past, one, two, three, ping. Her hand reached to her scapula again.

I exist.

Ping went the lights and the doors opened and out came women wearing clothes so tight-fitting that Gin, just looking at them, could hardly breathe. One woman wore a leather bodice and leather trousers and a jacket to match. Platforms heels and hair that did not move and nails that did not allow her hands any kind of unfettered joy or work, which is its own joy.

Gin stepped into the elevator. The doors closed. Ping again and they fell. Too fast. Without perimeter or boundary.

We are falling too fast.

But no one else in the elevator, a man in blue overalls and a woman with a child, no one blinked or held the rail.

I should not be here.

Suddenly, again, Gin felt that everything was too dangerous, the woman's melting face, the helicopters, the beggars. Every sense assaulted. She should not have come. Everything was wrong. Here, where dangerous things happened, the metal cage continued to fall. No one else held on. She felt herself pull in towards her own body as if bracing for the fall and the impact that would surely come.

I should not have come.

She held the rail hard until the elevator stopped. And she waited for the lift to empty when the doors opened.

I am alive. I am alive.

And the moment passed. She stepped into the mall as if nothing had happened.

———

Juno walked the perimeter of the garden, soft paw pads. She did it a few times a day just to be sure nothing unexpected had happened. She would plan her journey: take a drink of water before she set out, then make her way to the side of the house under the hydrangeas before hopping over the low boxed hedges and through the ferns. Then it was a little winding path she trod all along the boundary. And every time she went there was something new to discover. Sometimes she noted a cat had strayed over the wall. Light flickered through the leaves of the trees producing little orbs and flashes that fell all around like small spirits, ghosts making their way down to earth. This sense of company, combined with evidence of cat, produced a happy frisson, a rush of information through her nose and up through her nerve endings. For the rest it was birds, humans and the rustle of rats in the far corner at the back of the house. She would sniff the drainage pipes she knew they used to enter the property. They lived over the wall, a dank and dark-smelling place where leaves were never cleared, only left to accumulate where they lay. Through those pipes, she could smell humans and food, both fresh and decaying. And rats, the most important part of it all.

―――――

Neve sat in the shade of the trees outside her bedroom, the bench reassuringly uncomfortable. Juno was rootling around the back of the hedges and flower beds.

The desire to start counting cutlery was nearly overwhelming. But she had no idea what Gin was expecting to feed her guests. Soup? Out of a can probably. Not in summer. Hopefully even Gin would know that.

It is a strange thing not to know your child. To see them begin to emerge from their bulbous infant form and begin to be, to actually be, and not understand them. And perhaps not naturally take to them. Virginia had always been so serious and withdrawn. Difficult even. That was it. She was just difficult. Neve felt both betrayed by her daughter and guilty that she had failed as a mother to produce a happy, pretty child who laughed and was sweet and grateful. And so, at a certain point, early on, she let her get on with it.

Gin would hide at her own birthday parties. Six or seven years old, saying she didn't like all the noise and why was everyone looking at her? And then, there was that Sunday afternoon when Gin claimed she was being hurt by her brother and his friends, only a couple of years older. Neve remembered what happened next because for some reason in that moment the earth stopped and she was paralysed, eyes locked with Gin's, and all she could hear was the sound of tennis balls, pop and a pause, pop, pop and another pause. Neve had told Gin to stop making a fuss and go back and play with the boys.

'They aren't hurting you. They're just teasing.'

'Mum they are, they're hurting me,' and she held out both her arms with red marks all over them, along the upper arm. (So thin and summer brown.) Despite the brown the red showed through.

'Well Virginia, get used to it. They're only playing. And they are our guests. So if you can't play without making a fuss, you need to go to your room.'

Gin let her arm fall slowly to her side. For a moment Neve thought the child might cry but no. Rather, her face seemed to change, its texture even, and she looked as if in some kind of physical pain. And instead of tears and pleading, Gin turned away, walked a few steps and turned back again.

'I will never, ever be your friend again.'

Pop, as a tennis ball sailed across the net in a high arch, lobbed so high that Gin's father (tall, blond, angry, determined to win) had to squint directly into the sun to try and return it.

The ball fell. Unplayed. Game over.

———

Dudu was drinking her tea. It was bitter. The doctor at the clinic had told her to cut down on the amount of sugar she used. On the radio there was nothing else to hear but the news of the day. No other news was possible. And all eyes were on South Africa, said the Englishman being interviewed about how foreigners saw Mandela.

And, in spite of all that, the day was already busy. Dudu felt uncomfortable in her uniform, her plimsoles, her doek. Nothing seemed to fit, nothing seemed right, and she had to wait for someone to deliver flowers.

Dudu hated cut flowers, quite apart from the extra work of having to change the water in a vase the size of a washing up bucket, they always died. There did not seem to be any point to that. She preferred the plants that were all through the house. She tended to them with such care, and a kind of observance that went beyond her duties. She liked them and she worried they would not be properly tended when she was not there. The plants and September the same. The last time she had gone away she had returned ten days later to find they were both underfed and faded. But, she carefully set to work and returned them all to their healthier ways.

Her tea was done. She had not seen September. The familiar guilt sat behind her, a woolly shadow that whispered to her even in her dreams. When they were children, September would talk in his sleep, strange half-thoughts and sentences. But even then she had understood exactly what he had meant. She could watch his dreams.

But now, he talked in riddles more and more. Sometimes he spoke as if it was before the day at Verloren, as if he was still whole.

His face had been so handsome. Even looking at him the way he was these days, she could still see the memory of that face in the one he was left with. He had always had his hump, that was true, but he had had a good face, open, and a good heart. And that could help you to do well.

When she had gone to him earlier in the week, the day it had rained and rained and would not stop, she had asked him if he felt pain.

'No sister.' He was eating the beef and yellow rice she had brought him. He had not been able to keep dry in the deluge. 'There is no longer any pain. When it comes I only feel light. I feel it, all through me. *Ezulwini.*'

'Heaven? What does that mean, that you feel a burning? Heat?'

'No, I only see light.'

'What kind of light? Why do you talk in riddles all the time?'

'Perhaps it is the sun.' He took another mouthful from the plastic plate of food she had brought him. He found it harder to eat without messing since Verloren. 'Did I tell you Tata Mandela is dead, only they will not speak it? Though they will not speak it, I know that he has already gone.' He patted his heart with the flat of his hand. 'I know it.'

'He is not dead. He is ill.'

'No. Tata has already gone to his reward. Though they dare not speak it, I know it to be true.'

When he had finished his meal he had sat so quietly on the upturned beer crate he kept on the pavement outside his garden. She sat beside him. The streets still shone. She felt such quietness between them. Some would call it love. Suddenly he had grabbed her hand. 'Duduzile, I may die. The light is getting stronger and in my dreams our father calls me home.'

'Do not speak of that.' She rubbed his hands with hers, she wanted him to know she was there, to feel her there, so she squeezed his hands, kneaded them like a rough dough, to bring him back, pull him back into his body just for a moment so that he could still see she was there. She wanted this for herself although she knew it cost him to be there. For one as soft and precious as him to be trapped between his twisted spine and the steel prison bars of his ribcage was a terrible thing.

'Tell me what the light is? Perhaps we must go back to the clinic. I will come for you on my day off.'

'Why do you love me, sister?'

He looked at her with such need. She wanted to say, because who else will love you? You have no one in all the world but me. But these were words she could never speak. So, instead she held his hands even tighter and leaned forward to let him see her better and said:

'Because I am my brother's keeper.'

Neve felt she should do something, count plates, something. The trees were restless with birds now, all jostling and fighting for the fruit Mercy had put out on the little plastic feeders. There were weavers and tiny little Cape white-eyes and grey louries with their crests erect and tails fanned out. 'Kweeeh' they said and Neve almost responded. It was a language she knew.

I was born in a tent in the middle of No-Where.

And she was. These days it was called Mpumalanga. There had been golden grass and monkeys and scorpions all about, holding their breath as Neve had found her first. Later, there was a house to live in and she was set out in her crib under the marula tree where the shadows were long and the cool was deep and satisfying. There she slept until, stealthy and wicked, baboons came and scooped her up in their bristly arms. Her mother Olive, in a cornflower blue dress and pearls, witnessed this pillage and knew she must act but knew, too, that the baboons would not respect her in her dress. The baboons knew that only those with trousers traded in bullets. They continued to play with the infant child, dangling her by a leg, sniffing her face, playing with her bonnet that had now fallen to the ground. Neve still had not uttered a cry, perhaps wisely assuming that noisy children are punished.

Olive had scrambled into her husband's trousers and tucked in her dress to assume a more manly aspect. She grabbed an old hunting hat and the gun, though she had no way of knowing how to use it, and ran out across the deep polished floors of the verandah, straight at the baboons, shouting with the deepest, darkest voice her lungs could muster.

The baby was dropped, plop, into the grass, plop, like an early fruit dislodged by a scurrilous bird, and the baboons scattered, screeching and calling, their own little ones riding on their backs.

From that day on, Olive never again wore a dress in the daytime, the only woman in her circle to wear trousers. She made her own by cutting a pattern from those in her husband's wardrobe. And while he was out on the site, she told Julius, her gardener (so good with roses, prone to drunkenness) to teach her how to shoot.

'There will be no victims in this family,' said Olive.

———

Peter's office was unusually quiet, unadorned. Quiet enough that he could hear choppers flying overhead. The end of the year. He had put the television on but was forced to mute it when Louise, one of the junior attorneys, had come to sit opposite him and talk about things. She was clever and brisk but, and it had been discussed, lacked any kind of jeopardy, the sort that could get a man's attention. He kept glancing behind her to the screen, which showed that people, citizens, were making their way to the Residence already in large numbers, carrying flowers and cards. The ANC Women's League was making a statement, the unions and every last political carcass from days gone by. Even a few old apartheid stalwarts were wheeled out for comment. Louise droned on. 'Shame,' she said. 'Shame.' Most days she bored Peter half to death and today was no different. He wanted to leave, to go out again for a bit, to not talk about Mandela.

Louise. Less a name and more an assembly of sounds. He would find a reason not to use her on the team for the big retrenchments they were planning for the new year. Thirty thousand mine workers would have to go over two years. And that was just the start.

Gin. He would let her wound him again no doubt.

She had spurned him. That was the only word he could use. Somehow – and he hated himself for it still – he could never let it go. Was that too dramatic? Probably. But he felt so changed by it, to a point that he felt he was entirely unrecoverable.

They were younger of course, nineteen, or there about. The days were uncommonly hot and little rain fell over the course of that summer. They would drift around the city between this place and that person, it never seemed to matter. Only Gin among them was never a drifter. Always working in the studio she had rented in Melville. He remembered it had a large jacaranda outside that was always full of birds. He would find Gin sitting on her folding chair underneath the tree, pulling at the threads of her trouser hems, with blue flowers falling all around, shimmering like a deep magical sea.

Come evening the city would cool, being at high altitude, and they would swim in the pool at Eden House. They would float together, the thrill of the night and the too cold water compressed between them like a shared skin.

'Do you have goosebumps?' she said.

'Yes. You?'

'Yes,' she said and kicked herself up and over in an arc and then down trailing a line of bubbles behind her and then a splash as her feet disappeared after her into the black.

He wanted to say 'I need to touch you' as she submerged, but he couldn't. How could he? Nothing had passed between them – only his every waking breath, his every fantasy.

What did it matter if she didn't know it yet or wouldn't say it back. He was going away for a few months, all across Europe. He both dreaded being away from her and craved it, the respite some sort of physical distance might offer. He knew she was everything that he needed to make himself whole. The kind of wholeness he knew from childhood, lying on the carpet under the table draped to the floor with linen, and hearing his parents laugh and chat. That was the engulfing, captured kind of shelter he sought. And he found it in the danger of night swimming, with her, in all that blackness with nothing but Venus and a sickle moon to navigate by.

She breached the surface with a gasp.

'It's cold, I'm getting out.'

'No, wait.'

'Wait? No, I'm cold, you swim.'

'Will you come with me?'

'What? Where? On your trip?'

'Yes, come with me.'

'Why? No way.'

'Why not?'

'I went last year. I am working for my show. I'm getting out.'

There was a rush as she lifted up the stairs. Her body was beautiful. He was aching.

'Come with me.' And then like a fool, the man who would pull Venus away from the moon and undo the sky forever, he said, 'I love you.'

He had said the worst.

Gin said nothing. She rubbed her legs a little with the towel. He knew she was thinking, that she was waiting to say something, and then she had almost turned to him. She could have, she might have.

72

'I'm cold. I'm going to bath.'

And she walked away. Into the golden house, leaving him with nothing but her wet footprints that lead away from the water's dark edge.

———

'It is important to mark these occasions,' said Gin to her mother the night before. 'If you cannot enjoy it for yourself then Mum please, please do it for me.'

There had been silence into which her mother had thrown, 'I might not come. I'll see how I feel.'

Gin had, of course, parked her mother's car in the wrong place to get to and from the food market with any ease, but this way she knew she would not get lost. She found malls so disorientating, and it allowed her to walk a bit, past the shops and coffee shops full of women who looked like they might have been sitting in exactly the same place since the day she had left Johannesburg nearly twenty years previously. Her skin prickled in the cool artificial air.

As she passed the boutique kitchenware shop, she saw in the window, rearranging the spatulas and whisks in their silver ice buckets, a girl she had attended school with however many years ago. She was exactly the same as she was then, mannish but neat and thinner than she had been before. Gin adjusted her hair. She had nothing in common with that girl with the spatulas who understood which tins would make which cakes and the best way to whip egg whites once they had been perfectly separated from their yolks into two matching bowls. These were girls built for marriage. These womanish things, all of them, were the same to her. She chose not to understand them so that none of it could hold her.

Gin lumbered the shopping into the back of the car. Too much perhaps, wasteful amounts even. She could not tell. But people always ate more than she felt they would or should. She judged them.

She sat for a moment in the belching heat of the car with the windows open, trying to let some air through. She took the phone from her bag. Missed calls from Peter. Already, even without speaking to him, she was being forced into the position of being contrary. He did not allow her to be kind, he gave her no agency. The way he was, his insistence, never allowed her to ease into any kind of softness. He attached to any hint of ease in her body or her voice the suggestion that she had thrown the doors wide open.

No, she would not speak to him now, and perhaps she would not have time, with the trip being so short. And she was there for Neve and her birthday party, there wouldn't be time for anyone else.

She passed through the boom, down the ramp and along the avenue, deep in shade. The jacarandas on either side of the tarmac reached across to touch one another, a permanent verdant embrace. Bliss. To be alone, the air coming through the windows setting her skin on edge, through the speakers a cassette playing, miraculously, one of her father's, Louis Armstrong, a sad, past midnight song.

Stars shining bright above you, night breezes seem to whisper I love you.

Surely this was love? This song, the avenue, the air and now the light, beginning to dapple as the trees began to space apart. A moment of transcendence, just a breath of it, but enough to justify waking the next day and the day after.

The sun was gathering flame. September was tired. He wanted relief. He placed his board in front of him so that its message obscured his face. Above him he heard the familiar voop voop voop of a helicopter. He looked up, straight into the sun. He could hear the blades cutting through the sky, just as they had at the mine on that dark day at Verloren when the police chopper had flown over again and again. It had flown lower and then lower again to scatter their number. But the strike leaders had called out, hold fast, hold fast, they will not scatter us to the wind.

The leaders were right. They could not be scattered, so angry were their hearts. They had not, he remembered, begun their five day strike with vengeful hearts. Rather, to begin, the miners had come in peace and those comrades who had shown their fury, who had threatened to become ungovernable, had been quickly disciplined by the strike leaders. Focus and discipline. That was what they had all been told; we can give the bosses no excuse to abandon negotiations, no excuse to divide us.

What was more the strikers knew they were protected. Their safety had been arranged with the *muti* man. He had leaned on his powers and spells to summon good favour with all the ancestors. He had given each of them special charms and amulets to wear. Such was their faith, that they had continued to go to this medicine man every night since the strike began, to reinforce the charm.

But, during the days, the helicopters, great and thundering, had continued to stalk them, flying lower and lower. The miners held their course. They would not disperse, they would not be cowed until negotiations meant a pay rise had been won.

Each evening the sun would dip below the mine dumps. The dust and smoke from the townships hung low over the horizon and the sky would bleed pure crimson from its heart. Then, when the sky was already red, the helicopters (still swooping, voop voop voop) were given muscle by the arrival of armoured police vans. One and another and another came, until they made a long wall. And out of them came the uniformed men in their blue shirts and their big black boots.

Before 1994, September remembered, these boots were filled by apartheid-white feet.

Even now, as he sat outside the Diamond, September curled in on himself to remember what happened next at Verloren.

He, being small, was behind a few lines of taller men. They called out their protest, carrying as their shields nothing but the *muti* man's protection. Some Basotho men had their blanket tied at their shoulder to drape across their front. That was all. The police gave instructions to disperse, 'Stand down, stand down.'

'No,' came the defiant reply, 'You once were comrades. You should stand with us, support your black brothers against the mine. You are traitors now.'

The sun dipped further. The day would soon be done.

Then, inexplicably (for these were still the rainbow days) a hurtle. A boom. A flare. Flash bombs, tear gas.

A screaming retreat, the miners caught off guard, more and more the deep thud of canisters being launched. As he ran, all September had thought was, I must not fall in this rush of men, I am too small and too bent. If I fall, I will get hurt. I must not fall.

Oh, but he could not know, never imagine what worse was to come.

For September, even remembering it all raised in him a terrible sorrow which had become so impenetrable and painful that he knew that if he was ever asked to write it down, he would lack the correct alphabet to describe all the monstrous, shameful things.

The miners, the leaders in the front, the large and the brave, began calling:

'No, we will not be cowed by their stupid bombs. They are nothing but tears and smoke. We are made from greater things.'

The miners turned back to face the police vans. September was shaking, his heart in his head, his breath short, eyes burning, full of dust and gas.

The police, the miners, edging closer, eyes locked, loaded. Both saying, 'We will not blink first.'

The chopper, voop voop voop overhead, dust and blades, the chaos of gas and grit, lower and lower.

Then, an instruction, and still, still, no one will say where from. No one will say whose voice was heard but the black boots and the blue shirts were emboldened yet more. One more surge from the miners, through the down-draft of the blades, fists raised and voices too. *Mayibuye! iAfrica!*

No more than a second, no more than a blink.

The police let loose their guns. Casings clacked and flew. Bullets. Hot. Hot and alive, rent all through flesh, alive, the walls of hearts, alive, mothers' sons.

September saw his comrades fall. Saw them try to claw through the dust. Through the dust and the gravel, crying out. And he saw them fall again.

September was crawling. (Save yourselves Comrades! Stay low, stay low!) He could not breathe. Someone cried out, 'Help me, *Nkosi*, oh God, please help me,' but he could not say who.

And then (oh my father, my mother) September fell too. A bullet shaving off the side of his face (he fell) so that he bled, in the way that skulls do, fast and crimson red. He tried to stagger up with half of his sight and all of his slaughtering pain.

He fell.

So silent the dust. So easy to fall. A moment passed, another.

So easy to fall.

He thought he might see God. But no.

'Stay down or I'll kill you, *bru*,' he heard a man's voice say.

The gravel next to September's pulsing cheek turned red then black. Standing over him, the stride of a policeman's boot.

'Traitor,' said September or perhaps he only thought it.

Here I lie. My face in the dust. A boot on my hump.

He drifted here and there, lifting out of his body (which made it all bearable) and then, terribly falling back into himself, calling, 'Help me, *Nkosi*, oh Father, oh God.'

September lay, in the middle of all of that, the Verloren hill behind him. Its single boulder mocked his own, cowering back. And with every last capillary firing and fighting and raging against the creeping dark he felt an unfamiliar cold gathering around his fingers, his feet.

Verloren. Nkosi. I am lost.

Later, and he could not say when, he woke, trying to remember his identity number for the police for he could still hear helicopters, gun fire. Later still again, when he was being carried by his comrades so that his clothing tore, he could see through different helicopters. They were white, a big red cross on the side.

All through the longest nights was the voop voop voop from the sky and sometimes the lights of the police choppers as they illuminated the mine hospital and the long flat hostels and surrounding shacks.

When he was eventually allowed to go home with Duduzile (she had wept to see him, held his hands) and his face was patched with gauze, the helicopters were still there, but now with 'press' and 'news' written on the side.

September tried not to remember that day and yet it was the remembering – the sorrow and anger that would instead rise up in him where once he fell – that fuelled his purpose and allowed him to live each day.

He had to remember Verloren if he was to walk from his garden (the vines so rich and with new leaves and just that week, flowers too) across the island. Then, further along the streets, past the Residence and the deep shaded avenues to the front of the Diamond. And he did this, daily.

When a man has no shelter, his anger must become his home.

Still, while he was forced to occupy these darker precincts, he could, at least some of the time, still imagine himself lying flat on the mountain tops, sweet grass, the air of early winter, a flock of birds, his father's horse, a dog. In his heart he carried all of this: the scars of his terrible slaughter and his longing for kindness and beauty and home.

Late morning

Home, and Gin stared at the chickens she had bought at the supermarket. Great bulbous domes of transparent flesh that Mercy always said reminded her of white babies. And that is exactly what they were. Gin marvelled that after hearing that from Mercy, she could still eat chicken but had never looked at white babies in the same way again. Though it was no loss, not liking babies in general and white ones in particular. She had no interest in them. They were tedious, noisy and as they began to walk, constantly moving, darting. They brought with them a near constant agitation that rendered her on edge, angry – a state entirely incompatible with work and contemplation and, in the end, survival.

Without her work she could not survive. When on occasion she was forced away from it, thrust back into life, she felt she had to fight with everything she had not to die. Because it was so very, very easy just to slip towards death. And her work was her best and greatest love and defence.

Gin had stood for too long at the meat fridges. Free range, grain fed, barn raised, organic; degrees of happiness for chickens. She knew she could only afford to buy unhappy chickens whose lives had been brutal and utilitarian but she felt better for at least considering the options, for at least wanting to buy chickens with happier lives. As if just wanting something altered the outcome at all. She lifted six into the shopping cart. She felt the flesh give way under the pressure of her thumb. Six little white babies. That would make Mercy laugh. Would they be enough? Her mother never ate much, perhaps her aunt would eat less too and she could do without. It was enough. She would buy trout and wine and strawberries.

Down the aisles back and forth and then back again because nothing was sequential or logical. Savoury biscuits should follow sweet biscuits and yet they were off in an aisle with other savoury snacks which was on the exact opposite side of the store. She found two items in the kosher aisle and another in the halal aisle but never found watercress. There was trout, smoked and cut and thankfully without head and tail. No one wants to know where their food comes from. A party with entire forms, heads, tails, feet all resting on a platter is not a party at all, but an autopsy.

––––––

Mercy began to sweep the verandah. Leaves and berries had blown from the trees in the storm, and frangipani flowers. She liked how they looked on the ground and decided to leave them. They made a nice mat of white blooms. She raised a hand to greet Talent who was half-heartedly cleaning the underbelly of the lawnmower with a brush and cloth. He was distracted. Mercy suspected he had more trouble with the police. Talent spent a good deal of time, and much of his money, bribing the police to let him stay in the country. A refusal to do so would see him sent to the holding camp in Limpopo, a rancid misery of a place. And then, once he was processed, he would be forced to pay for his own transport back across the border to Zimbabwe where, of course, he would simply wait a few days before walking back across through the bush, hardly bothering to hide. But it was expensive and inconvenient and the camp was something to avoid. Talent had heard some terrible things.

'Did you get rain Talent?'

'Yeah, *mamma*. My bedding got ruined. My roof leaks.'

'Still? Talent, you were meant to fix that last month already.'

Talent chuckled. 'Yeah, you know ...'

'Fix your roof. Stop spending your money on dope and girls.'

'This month. I'll do it this month.'

'*Ntsah. Wena.* This month, this month. Every month the same.'

Talent stood to stretch and tie his braided and beaded locks on top of his head. 'OK.'

'And how much does that hair cost?'

'*Mamma*, you should do your hair the same. It would look good on you.'

'Yoh. Cheeky. Does your mother know how cheeky you are?'

'Yeah.'

'She thinks you are her funny child.'

He laughed again. 'She does.'

Talent was good to his mother. Mercy liked this in him. For all the wild boy behaviour she heard him talking about with his friends on Mrs Brandt's phone (only when she was out of course), Mercy knew that every day before he arrived at work, he would stop at the house where his mother was one of two housekeepers a couple of blocks away, a huge house owned by Israelis. Talent would ring the bell, under the gaze of two guards with 'Tactical Unit' written on their shirts. His mother would come out with two mugs and they would have tea together on the pavement. Talent was not allowed in. The Israelis were not comfortable with a Rastafarian in white rimmed, mirrored sunglasses on their property. Sometimes he gave his mother money, sometimes she reciprocated. Mostly they just drank tea.

Mercy had heard nothing of the storm. She never did. One night a huge eucalyptus branch had landed on the roof above her head and all through it she had slept. Mrs Brandt would tease her about it and ask how it was that anyone could sleep through such a disaster. Mercy had no answer for how and why. She only knew that when she slept no one from the living earth could contact her, no matter how serious the storm. And who would want to be awake in a storm? Surely that was the best time to hide deep, deep under the blankets and let all the worst of it pass over. If a branch was to break, then let it break. For Mercy, to sleep was to be reawakened to her true and unencumbered soul that otherwise circled just out of sight, like a mischievous planet that because of the strength of the sun could never be seen in daylight.

Sometimes at night she would lie on her bed and listen to her own breath. She liked to keep her bed propped up on bricks, two under each corner. It was from this elevated plain that she would let the day fall away. Her radio was on, the volume was low, a gospel music station. She took in a deep breath and let the air sit in her lungs for a few seconds before letting it out again.

I am breathing in. I am breathing out. I am breathing in. I am breathing out.

It was at night, in the silence, that she felt most alone, so very far from God. She felt it in her body, a pain that seemed to sit in the marrow of her, where life was born. It was in there that she felt such distance from love. The only other feeling that came close was homesickness. And in a way it was, the yearning to be home, to be back in the fold of her Maker's arms, held, supported, protected.

————

Gin was pleased Mercy was there when she got back to the house. She had expected she might have gone down to the Residence with her friends. Mercy would know what to do with everything and say encouraging things about all the bags of food. She would be excited about the party. No one else seemed to be excited, least of all the guest of honour who had not been seen much that morning.

'Did you go to the Residence?'

'No. Not yet. I will go.'

'I think I will go too. Later. I got all the stuff.' Gin nearly mentioned white babies, but stopped herself.

'Yes.'

'Where is she Mercy?'

'Somewhere.'

'She doesn't want this goddamned party. I'm not even sure why I am doing it.'

'No, but she will like it, she will come.'

'She says she is going out and not coming.'

'No, she will.'

'I got the chicken.'

'How many?'

'Six.'

'It's enough?'

'I don't know. I don't really know how to calculate it all. There is other food though – all the fish. If you hear the gate bell will you call me? My friend is coming with tables and chairs.'

'OK.'

'The one with glasses, the pretty one.'

'Does she have a man now?'

'No.'

Was that what it came down to? Would her mother be kinder if Gin had simply complied, married some local man, set up a house, spent her days choosing soft furnishings, teaching art at the local primary school. Gin had a sense that this would have allowed her mother to settle into some sense of comfort, achievement, objective standard by which she could announce her own parenting, and her daughter's life, a success. Instead Gin had asked her mother to navigate an alien set of credentials. Difficult to quantify, impossible to justify when all around were simply toeing the line. By refusing to conform, Gin had forced her mother to do the same. She had forced her to defend something she did not believe in. It was perhaps understandable that Neve had become such a vocally reluctant renegade.

I should be kinder to her. I am her burden. I have asked too much.

———

The sun was rising higher in the sky. Late morning. September could feel the pain coming back to his temples. He thought he saw Dudu coming across the large square in front of the tower block, wearing blue. She always wore blue, it seemed to him. He tried to see through the great hairy spurts of the fountains, with his better eye, but in the end he gave up. It was not her. The hope of her, the suggestion of her approach, was usually enough to make him feel safe once more. She walked quickly and in straight lines, no wandering or dawdling; apart from her blue pinafore, this was how he could recognize her.

On clearer days, when he felt like he used to feel, he understood that sometimes he was just too much for her. He felt the burden of his hunched back had become her deformity too, that her spine might just as well have begun to snake and twist like his. His place, his position as the man without a home, made him in some ways unbearable for her. Sometimes, when she walked away and said, as she always did, 'Tomorrow, *Kusasa*, Sechaba,' he felt she might walk away forever.

She would never say 'I will not come for you again,' because she would know that in so doing she would kill him. If she left him he would go back to his garden. He would lie down on his cardboard, the barbets and the olive thrush singing above him, and finally surrender to his determined spine that had for years been trying to curl him in on himself, return him to his foetal place. In and in and in it would turn him if she didn't come, until all of his sadness suffocated him entirely.

Outside the Diamond the helicopters were still buzzing and hovering around the roof of the building. If he looked up he looked straight into the sun so that he did not know which way he was facing.

September thought he might like to rest his board but then when he was about to let it fall, he remembered why he was there and held it up straight again and walked closer to the front doors. The tower cast a shadow and for that he was grateful. The sun bleached a trail still higher.

These many months after Verloren there was still no answer. No one would say who had given the order to fire. The board, encased in the Diamond, blamed the police chief, the police chief blamed rogue officers and the officers said they were given direct instructions. From where, they could not say. The widows and the families of those slain went to court, again and again, yet still as September saw it, the truth seemed to recede with each passing day.

Traitors have troubled dreams and soon their time runs out.

September had time. He had nowhere to go and no job to get to. He could not work. The pain was too close. Any effort, physical work and he would feel himself lilt and sway. And suddenly his whole head would be full of helicopters with their blades whipping and slicing their way through his skull. He watched a newspaper delivery van pull up in front of the building. Bundles of grey wrapped in plastic and on the front cover, Mandela, in long rows, wrapped in plastic and the headline: 'A Nation Mourns.'

September sat down on the little wall that ran around the fountains. The clouds skittered across the Diamond and across the sun. Light and dark, night and day.

The city had, over time, reduced him to mere units of himself. As if he were some ramshackle apartment block at the back end of Hilbrow, a block with only a few windows lit against the evening smog, lights that would be extinguished, one by one.

He let the fountain mist him in what felt like dew or the kind of rain that leaves the grass covered in globes of light. He sat and felt all the pain in his body recede in the spray and felt too the warmth of the day on his back like God's own hand urging him to life. He closed his eyes and let the fountains baptize him in newness and as they did he felt his true name coming back to him.

Fear no more Tata, the father of our nation, our great leader and the spear of our liberation. I am Sechaba. This day, they have woken us from our dreams to tell us you have passed. I know in my heart, which is the same as the entire heart of this nation, that you died before this day. I know that you had already passed over to the place of your ancestors well before this morning. That day, I felt it as you took one mighty intake of air. The whole city was sucked in with it and then you were gone and as the air left your body the people, the streets, the trees, the buildings and even the powerful who squat like toads in the Diamond, even they, were spewed back out of your great and mighty lungs as the air rushed back out for one last time.

But they, the family, the powerful, those that were cadres and comrades and are now become kings, they held the news, held it to them, panicked and greedy and it took them all this time to summon enough courage to let us know that you had gone. As if we would all be driven to rage by our despair. No. When your name is spoken, we know only love.

I wept for you months ago Madiba. I wept for you then and wished you well and so much peace. You were an old man, and a tired one. Hamba gahle! Go well! Go well.

Dudu, while humming to the song she heard over the speakers, placed her money on the counter top and took the bread and peanut butter from the man there. 'Every time you buy the same thing,' he said to her. And she wanted to say, 'What is it to you with your over-priced goods?' and 'Do you not know, to do the same every day, that is what it is to be your brother's keeper. To keep doing the same over and over, because there is no one else to do it and he will not go home.'

And there was his hump of course. That was enough reason to go every day and buy bread and peanut butter.

She remembered the day she first noticed it. She was eight or maybe nine and they had been sitting in the big zinc bath, one in front of the other, her at the back, then September and then baby Mpho who had to be held up straight by September. Their mother, a soft, laughing woman, was singing their favourite song from church, as she often did, and pouring warm water across their backs.

'This little light of mine, I'm going to let it shine, *M'lilo vutha Mathanjeni, M'lilo ...*'

Each child was to wash the back of the one in front and they sang as they did. Dudu had her mother's hands to wash her back, something she felt to be close to a blessing. And it was, to have her mother rub her cushioned hands all along her shoulders and spine so that the soap ran in happy tributaries into the bath below.

Dudu had rolled the soap around in her own hands before passing it forward to September. Then she began to imitate her mother's movements, across his shoulders at the top, along the nape of his neck and then down. The foam ran in a perfect line down his spine, but then, just where his shoulders ended it took a quick detour on either side of a perfect round and then carried on down. Dudu released another rope of foam. It did the same, only it curled around just the one side. She ran her flat hand over the bubbles to give herself a clean slate to try again. Under her hand she found something she knew should not be there. A raising, a roundness where the small straight row of spine knuckles should be. She rubbed her hand across it again, then poked at the strange mound with her forefinger.

'Duduzile. Stop that.' Her mother's voice was sharp in a way that she had never heard. It shocked her almost as much as the mound rising from her brother's back.

'Mamma?'

'No. It is enough.'

'But ...'

'Dudu. No.'

Days later – it felt like many, many days though perhaps it was one or two (for time is like that when you are small) – Dudu and her mother joined the other women in the village and walked to fetch water. It was always a long walk, easier going there than coming back when the women would be burdened with full barrels of water, carried whichever way was possible. Dudu would carry the five litre bottle and her mother would carry the two much larger ones. The weight of the water would leave their hands burning.

Dudu liked the walk with her mother and the other women. There was laughing and talking, and sometimes she and the other smaller girls could glimpse the world of secret womanhood. To be a woman it seemed, was to understand so much more of the world through your body, your fibre, and know everything that existed both before and after you. Her hips were her mother's hips and her grandmother's and all the mothers before them too. Her hips were wide so that she could carry the full weight, the heritage of her female ancestors, the weight of their sorrow, their joy, their creation. Her hips said, I am strong, I can carry all of the wisdom of all the thousands of women who came before me and make safe the path for all my daughters still to come.

Dudu had always wanted daughters. One at least. For that was where solace lay. She knew that when she was eighty years old it would be her daughters who would carry water for her and if needs be, carry her too.

So, they walked, she and her mother, but stayed behind the others.

'Dudu. You brother's back is broken.'

'Mamma, the circle?'

'Yes. It is a circle now but later it will bend him, he will be bent over so it will be painful to stand up tall, straight like a man should.'

'Will he die?'

'No! No he will not die, but life will be hard for him. Do you understand child?'

'Yes. I do.'

'He will need you. I don't know how he will work. He is smart and strong for now. But later, it will bring him pain and then, I don't know how he will work. If you cannot work, how can you live?'

'I must help him.'

'Yes, always.'

'You help him Mamma.'

'Yes, of course, but when one day I cannot help any more, then it must be you.'

'I will Mamma. I will help September. He is my brother.'

'He is your brother.'

Dudu knew that this responsibility was important. She knew that for her mother to talk to her like this meant that much was expected from her, that September would be her charge for the rest of their lives. She knew this, even then.

Yet today, on this day when Madiba had passed (God rest him) and there was surely a storm coming (there were great clouds massing to the south), she still had not gone to September.

————

Neve was mysteriously absent. Gin sat in her mother's chair, the weave of its thick patterned linen now smooth with age. It had been Aunt Virginia's before.

It was in Neve's bedroom and looked out across the garden. She could imagine her mother sitting in it every morning to drink her tea before she dressed. To the right was her dressing table, her powder compact and lipstick, A Quarter to Red, in a bowl along with safety pins. Gin leaned back into the upholstery, uneven and faded and beautiful too. The chair was uncomfortable with age. There were no comfortable chairs in the house. These days they simply performed a function. This was not a house that encouraged lounging or laziness. As she ran her hand over the age smoothed linen, she heard Talent cursing the ibises who had been on the grass earlier and had no doubt left their large liquid droppings in his path.

In the kitchen, Mercy was cleaning the contents of the cutlery canteen. She was singing. Gin could scent the filigree of the King's Pattern spoons on the air, cold and detailed. And, with it, all those dinners when her mother would wear her only perfume, Shalimar. That and the scent of her powder rushed right back to her. She remembered that she was always terrified, as if there was, just out of the corner of her wary child's eye, some threat, as if the air itself could suddenly change its mind.

She had worked to overcome this, watched her every thought to fight against the things she feared she would inherit: mistrust, disappointment, bitterness. She had, through discipline and vigilance, planned her own survival, her escape.

Gin hated her mother's ability to find the miserable and the squalid and the failure in everything. Where Gin saw a beautiful day her mother chose to see a heatwave, where Gin heard joy her mother heard noise.

Should there be music at the party? Some jazz perhaps, some Louis Armstrong maybe, or Bird. Jazz and hot nights go so well together, like butter and toast, Granny would say. She would make this party beautiful and make this a grand and lovely piece of art that her mother could relate to – the domestic arts of food and flowers and gracious lighting.

She already knew how the tables would look and which plates would set off which types of food perfectly. She was ignoring her cousin's message asking if she could bring a dessert. The answer would have to be no. No one could be allowed to bring anything that would upset the balance. The dessert would arrive in some Pyrex dish and perhaps have a strangely placed glazed cherry on a blob of cream like some sickly nipple. She would ignore the message and if necessary send one back saying there was already more than enough.

The other thing about beauty, balance really, is that it could not be left to others to dictate; she understood that to some her militancy on this was a contradiction. But she believed, she knew, that poetry and art came only from discipline and work and hour after hour of uncompromising concentration. Only then did the momentary fracture of light break through the smog.

Again, the helicopter, voop voop voop. And there was a time at the old house when she was still knock-kneed and flat on top, perhaps she was ten or eleven, when she would lie on her back in the swimming pool and watch the dragonflies dip and hover over her and imagine they were Vietnam choppers from all the films she had seen. She would lie there with the dragonflies oscillating their metal-coloured madness over her, man down, floating in a paddy in the Mekong and knowing they were coming to get her out and she'd be singing the tune from *Apocalypse Now* in her head and thinking how wonderful life was. She would practice saying 'semper fi' in her head. She might need to use it one day. Until then she would just lean into the night and smell the jasmine and feel how it was to be held by the night air and yet wish, all the time wish, she was somewhere else.

To be somewhere else was to be someone else. To arrive at herself. The moment when what had previously been nothing but a loom of neurons is finally able to knit together into the thing that she will come to know as herself. And all the wilder firings of her mind and appetites would coalesce into something of substance and agency.

———

It would probably rain, thought Neve. It always did. At around four in the afternoon. You could set your watch by it. A sharp, hot downpour, set your nerves on end and then gone. But everything would be soaked. All those ridiculous little lanterns she saw Virginia putting around the garden and up the path to the front door. The party would be a disaster. Gin was so impractical. They should have forced her to go to a teacher training college. Art was a nonsense.

Now, this party. Neve felt her chest tighten just imagining all the people arriving. She would have to get her hair done. It was fine for Gin, she was happy to mope around with all that hair hanging around her face and down her back, at her age too. Neve had always cut it to a neat bob when Gin was at school. Practical. Long enough to be tied back. And what was going on with the colour of it? The ends looked as though they had been dunked into one of her paint pots. Ridiculous. Like a wild woman.

'Virginia.'

'Yeah?' Gin was standing in front of the cutlery canteen, counting out serving spoons. Her hair was curled in thick ropes down her back.

'Why don't you cut your hair? It looks terrible.'

Neve saw Gin jut out her chin the way she did when she was trying to say something rude, or just before she did.

'Is that all you wanted to say?'

'I'm going to the hairdresser myself. I could do without it. But there you go.'

'OK.' Gin went back to the cutlery, taking out handfuls at a time and laying them with a clatter on the dining table.

'Dear God we have so much to do.'

'You don't have to do anything. Go to the hairdresser and then get a coffee or something and I'll sort out all of this. Really.'

'You are impossible. You don't even know how to work that oven.'

'It's an oven.'

'They aren't all the same, Virginia.'

'Jesus Mother. Just go to the damn hairdresser, OK? It's all fine.'

'No need to be short. I'm leaving Juno of course. Keep an eye with all the comings and goings. Is Bea coming, she's a good friend?'

'She's helping me with tables soon and obviously coming tonight.'

'She's a sweet girl. Another one in a mess. She knows how to cook though. She can help you.'

Gin faced her mother and blinked slowly. Twice, so that it verged on brazen aggression.

'I'm off. You'd better get a move on with the cooking.'

———

Juno could feel, in her pelt, that something was going on in the street. She used her paw to scratch behind her ginger ear, the one whose colour extended all the way over her eye. There were too many people and with them came noise and scent that left her feeling both tantalized and overwhelmed. As the gates had rolled back and the car had left, holding Neve, she caught a glimpse of the streets. They did not seem as wide as usual and instead there were people, going this way and that. Not the usual traffic of feet she liked to sniff under the gate.

Early and late were the best times for seeing what was happening, and around midday on weekdays three dogs who could not be properly held on their leads would pass by on their walk with the gardener. Often they would stop near Juno and bark and spit but other than that and the bin men it tended to be quiet. Today was different though. So many feet and voices and the sense that something exciting was happening just the other side of the threshold.

———

Even from inside the house, Gin knew something was gathering pace at the Residence, choppers everywhere, louder singing, the noise that was starting to build told her that. There would be ten days of national mourning and ninety heads of state would gather. She went through to the television room. Her mother's old square set like a monolith, a coffin. She pressed the buttons, she knew it would already be on a news channel. Her mother was addicted to misery and disaster. Oh good, breaking news, she would say, as if there were no lives attached to the headline, and perhaps there weren't any more, it was just information. She flicked through the channels, CNN, BBC, Sky, Al Jazeera, all showing the house down the road. Headlines: the family have gathered, there are preparations for the funeral and memorial of Mr Mandela, no word from the family, ANC says as always Mr Mandela will never be forgotten. Thank you Tata, thank you, says the nation. The family is gathering and the sky is full of snoops and rifles.

Gin felt tears rise. She turned off the television. She wanted to say that she loved him, out loud, a stupid, single voice in a shaded room with no one to hear it, while the rest of the world walked in the street outside to show Tata their love. All she could do was speak it. But to speak it was to render it truth.

I love you, I love you, I love you.

———

The hairdresser was the same one Neve Brandt had gone to since she had moved to Johannesburg when she was twenty or maybe twenty-two. Later when the children arrived they had sat on her lap while the rollers were put in place and left to set her dark hair around her face, thick flat ribbons of liquorice to frame her white skin and her red lips, also the same colour since she could remember. A Quarter to Red.

As Neve lay back on to the basin, the porcelain lip cold in her neck despite the towels the washer had placed there, she felt that she could at least have a few moments here, away from Ginny, away from Mercy even who asked too many questions instead of just getting on with it.

The water was too cold – it made her scalp tingle.

'Is the temperature OK Ma'am?'

'Yes.' Neve closed her eyes.

She liked having her hair washed, not for the fingers on her scalp (she did not like to be touched), but for the efficiency of it, the hands that rubbed and kneaded her head, right into the neck, all across her forehead and temples and then deep into her crown. Rubbing, scrubbing, getting the grime out. The clean and the cold pleased her. Some foam slid into her ear. She indicated as much with her hand and with one hand still rinsing the shampoo, mint and sage, the washer raised a corner of towelling and dispelled the offending soap.

'Thank you, Rebecca. How is your daughter?'

'She is well thank you, Mrs Brandt. She's had her baby.'

'Oh good, but now the trouble starts, yes?'

It didn't occur to Neve to ask the name or sex of the child, they were all just work in the end. She continued, 'And what about Mandela now?'

'Oh shame, *Nkosi*, but it was time.'

'Yes, I think he'd had enough. I don't blame him. You can live too long. And some of his family are already causing trouble.'

'Ja, those young ones ...'

Neve wasn't really listening. She could understand why Mandela had had enough. He had been trapped really. You get assigned a role and there is nothing else for you. It occurred to her that once she became a mother that was her lot too. There was no other option available. Her career of course but that was just a layer that sat over the top. From the moment her children arrived screaming and shocked, there was nothing else she could do with her thoughts. And the worry, the endless worry that she was doing it all wrong, that no matter what, she would never, ever be enough. And she would be judged for it.

She tried to be strong as a mother. She had been tough, she knew that, but it was for Virginia not for herself that she did it. It was a sort of training, an education you might say, in whatever a child might need to survive. Work, discipline, manners, sobriety, all these things mattered, or should matter. And still, despite all that investment, Gin remained resolutely beyond the bounds of what was sensible.

She did call every week. That was true. On a Sunday usually, as she had done for years. They were such pedestrian conversations. Dog walks, visits to the doctor, who she had bumped into in the post office, news from the cousins and Aunt Diana. And in return Ginny would listen and ask questions and be kind. She was kind and caring, there was a terrible softness to her, like an overripe fruit. She would cry over things, strange things, humanity, people she saw on the news. And yet, and yet, a bloody-minded survivor no matter the weather. It was a stubbornness to survive, in an utterly self-obsessed sort of way. It was as if one day the child who felt everything had decided: I will survive with or without you. Gin would thrive in spite of her frailty. Neve knew this. She admired it, appreciated it and saw herself in it, having been sent away to school at five years old. And yet she still found it so strangely alienating, frightening even.

How can this girl who calls her mother all the way from New York to tell her some Irish poet has died and be in some distress over this be so incapable, so cynical, militant about men and love? Was it just arrogance, an exceptionalism that she held herself over and above them all? None was good enough. Some were good for a few weeks. Perhaps she was right though. But it would be helpful to know she was taken care of.

Neve, in the chair, looked at herself, hair wet and wiry, her eye make-up slightly smudged on one side. She righted it with her forefinger and then drank the last of her milky coffee. She always had coffee at the hairdresser. Nowhere else. Then, Neve found her lipstick and reapplied another coat. First the top lip and then the bottom. Did she look eighty? No.

Who were the twenty coming to the party? The usual suspects; family, probably some of Gin's friends. Hopefully none of the Nicholsons were coming. They were so dreary and when they weren't, they had usually drank too much and then they were far too exciting.

———

Peter didn't bother to tell anyone that he was going out. And usually it would not matter, but he felt guilty. Before he started the engine of his car, he took a deep breath and held it, letting his spine settle back on the seat so that the leather creaked a little. He had called his doctor for an appointment, frightened by his momentary stupidity on leaving his apartment that morning. But he had cancelled. There was nothing the matter. Possible blood sugar, a lack of concentration. Fucking madness getting lost twenty steps from your own front door.

And yet, to feel so brakeless.

He had thought about going to get a new identity picture taken, one was needed and there was a kiosk across the plaza. He was repeatedly being told he was not who he claimed to be on account of having aged a few decades over the past couple of years. The plump security woman at the turnstiles of the gym kept telling him that the man in the picture was blond, whereas he quite clearly was not. He explained that he used to be blond but on account of no longer going outdoors except for a run before the sun was fully up, his hair had darkened. She had begun calling him Blondie and he had begun shrinking at the sight of her.

He drove out from the basement and into the day. There were clouds though; it would probably rain around four o'clock. The morning's complaint he deduced was less getting lost than feeling lost, which are not the same at all. He had the sense of having mislaid his bearings, which is not the same as being incapable of locating oneself in a known geography. It was more a forfeit than an outright defeat. Peter was pleased to have argued the point to himself.

But now, perhaps to try to find his way again, he chose to head for the Residence (and why was he even going there?) via the Brandt house. There were endless other routes he could have taken – which made his decision to drive past the Brandts' one of pilgrimage or worse still, devotion.

What was he doing? He knew he had nothing to throw on the table, nothing that he could conjure that would devastate her, render her spellbound. And that was the truth of his pathetic mission. What a thrill to shock her with some news of his own magnificent life. See her face register surprise and then immediate regret at having not stayed with him, or yield to him and say yes.

In truth, to her his life was entirely without substance, and consequently he was nothing more than vapour in her fully parroted life.

———

Gin was alone in the house apart from Juno whose nails clipped along the floor as she rushed to meet whoever alerted her.

'Hello, it's me, it's me.' Gin bent to stroke Juno's ears; all the silk of India and beyond seemed to be held on top of that little head. 'I love you. Yes, I do.'

Mercy was in the courtyard out the back, on the phone to her friend who worked in the house opposite the Residence. She was making all the noises of a concerned mother, clucking and chittering like any number of birds. Gin glanced through the door into her mother's room and saw that a box, her leather covered box of jewellery, was set out on top of the dresser. That was at least a sign that she may deign to come to her own party. Jesus. Gin had packed the food into the fridge It didn't look like much. The cool that floated out from the shelves set her hair on edge. A moment, a prayer. She rubbed her arms to settle her skin.

Perhaps that was what did it, the cool, the shift in air, a pressure change, a rush of altitude and suddenly Gin was spinning out again.

How would any of this ever work? She had no sandbags to stay the life that seemed to be gushing out of her as she stood there. She needed Mercy. Mercy would know what to do, or at least pretend to, and that would be enough. But she would be a while on the phone.

She had no shelter when taken away from her work and her days that started the same and were punctuated by blocks of steady creation and ended with the same walk home along the Brownstones, the canopy of trees above her. Street lights, the Korean store on the corner, the same number of blocks to walk, knowing that to walk each block took a single minute. All of this – ritual, work, structure – gave her the roof over her head and the walls to keep out the gales. Without them, life, everything that was tapping at the windows of her day became impossible so that in the end she needed to work so much more than she needed to be loved.

It is getting late.

And it was. The day was becoming something other than its origin. Mandela aside, on and on the news seemed a harbinger of a greater tide that would soon rush out to sea, and take everything that she felt to be valuable with it. A great flood, that was what she felt as she let herself crumple downward and come to rest in front of the open fridge door.

Everywhere, everything was wrong and there was nothing she could do to stop it. Another war began in the deserts of Syria and Jordan and Egypt, the poets and writers had begun to die. The great towering conjurers, thought Gin, all dying from the horror of it. They must have seen the news images of the rows and rows of babies with black hair and now green faces swaddled in their bed sheets. And not a drop of blood, mused the news reporter, not a drop of blood but around their mouths, blue veins and dried foam around their nostrils which is the nature of suffocation. How strange to gas children and mothers and fathers in their beds so that they would twitch their way to death. How strange, thought Gin, thinking about the poets and writers who had died. And Mandela too. This was no world for soothsayers and seers, to be sure, another will soon die.

I cannot make this work. And I do not care, for what would it matter? A party when the world begins to crumple in on itself and babies are gassed while they sleep.

Gin felt the walls edging closer. She managed to get to her mother's room (the jewellery box now forgotten), lay on her mother's bed and felt the uneven mattress pull her into the middle. Juno hopped up and onto the bed, turned twice and settled in next to Gin. The pillows, faded blue, baby blue, smelled like her mother and all the cotton and talc of her years. Lavender. Even when she had been in hospital for that week and then through the endless treatments that followed, Neve had demanded lavender and Gin had been charged with bringing it. Gin had been charged with bringing everything because somehow, her father was incapable of lifting even one finger to go there. As if the mere fact of this terrible mutilation relating to breasts meant he could not possibly get involved, this was women's stuff, women's bodies, women's work.

All of this meant he could not drive the seven minutes from the house, the old house, to the hospital and deliver a bottle of lavender eau de toilette, some chocolate, a book.

Later, Gin had shown Neve Picasso's women, fractured, one-eyed, one breasted, powerful and immortal. She always remembered and appreciated the silence in Neve as they had sat together and flipped through the pages of the book.

'Thank you,' said Neve. They never spoke of it again.

Though for years Gin would always send a postcard of these women when she saw one in a museum or store. Other than Neve's address, Gin never wrote anything on the card.

Gin rolled onto her side. She felt the weight of the journey the day before, the hopes for the party, the songs of the mourners that even now she could hear rising and falling in song though the Residence was blocks away. She lay deep and let herself sink, she may have slept, there was no way of telling what was sleep and what was simply the terror of being awake. And the woman with the melted face, the whole screaming, sweating city seemed to sit down on the bed with her. Ghosts were rising.

———

September let his eyes close as he sat in the shade at the side of the plaza. The banks of agapanthus formed a violet haze. He could hear weavers in the nests above him. The moment was so beautiful. The cool, the light, the promise of seeing Dudu. Horizons were suddenly available. He felt as if the day had offered him a gift. A moment of clarity, a subsiding of fracturing pain, his body his own again and whole.

And yet – and it may have been the fountains, their powerful jets – without warning, September felt a sharp chill rush up his arms and up his spine, all setting his hair on edge. And he knew (because these days everything was so clear to him) that this was death, perhaps not his, not a death attached to this man or that woman, but the kind that sends great waves to rise from the belly of the ocean.

This thing that he felt, this thing of midnight and of flood, could send God's children to walk the desert looking for a home and find, everywhere, no room in the inn. This was an expression, almost unnameable, that would see poets and kings breathe their last. September felt great chasms break, deep, deep in the oceans and he knew that no matter the struggle, no mother, no child can out-swim that kind of tide.

Nkosi, Nkosi, hold us close, protect us.

———

Gin started to the sound of the gate bell. A terrible alarm. It would be the furniture, brought across the city for the party. The tables would be cleaned and rubbed to reduce the oil and studio paint that may still be clinging to them. Gin didn't lift the receiver to confirm who it was but pressed the buzzer, which immediately threw the great wooden gate back on itself as it rolled from left to right with a great clatter and roar. It was probably not prudent to open the gates like that with the streets so full of people. She heard a group of men singing as they passed.

Her mother's bed had felt deep and Gin knew she had drifted off, if only for a few minutes, her body still demanding a sleep cycle attached to other countries. Her legs, somehow exiled from the rest of her body, wouldn't respond to instruction. As she had staggered from the bedroom through the dark entrance hall to press the receiver button, she felt as if she was swimming with weights.

She ran a hand through her hair and as an afterthought had traced her mother's lipstick around her mouth. It looked ridiculously prim with her undone self, loose black top and tight jeans below. She stuffed her feet into her boots and heard herself jangling like a gypsy pony as her bracelets and necklaces swung around her. She would never be able to sneak up on anyone. This amused her even through her haze. As she stepped onto the verandah, she shook her hair to try and shake off the fog of sleep.

'Oh.'

'Ginny.'

'Peter. Hi.'

'Someone let me in. I've been trying to call you, multiple times in fact, I thought I may have had the wrong number so I took a chance. Took a chance and came to the house. I'm on my way to a meeting. Am I imposing?' He was hardly drawing breath. 'Have you been out there? Quite the mass gathering. Unions, Women's League. I might go. Pay my respects. Not that it matters. Anyway, how are you? You look great, fine.'

———

Mercy was about to go back into the house and tell Gin the news from down the road, and that buses of mourners were arriving, that the news people and even the police had arrived. There was great displeasure at the police arriving, as if they assumed grief would naturally become anger. No. Grief was grief and there was so much love there. That was what she had heard. A man had arrived, and Ginny was with him. This gave Mercy a few more moments to rest. She sat on her bed. Her back hurt and the day had only just begun.

She might have cared more readily about the fish and the chickens, she knew. She did care, but more specifically, she was thinking about going home for Christmas. From her bed she cast an eye over the bag and box she would be using to take things home. This party had been unexpected and it had rather set her back as this was the afternoon she had planned to do some shopping, food, gifts, school supplies, such things, to take home for the family. Just less than two weeks and a night in the bus and she would be there.

The bus ride itself, though tedious, was somehow part of the joy. It was hot and endless, there was always some man, large and sweaty, who sat too close and took up his portions of the seat and then hers by spreading his knees too far apart. Last time she had at least had a window towards which she could lean but then, outside Harrismith, the fat man had started peeling an orange and the smell, along with his open-mouthed enjoyment of the juice and methodical spit spit spit of the pips as he went, near drove her to speak out. Though she did not. This was a bus after all. Not hers to complain about.

Mercy, with no apology, counted the sleeps until her departure. She allowed herself to do this about a week before. She did not like to tell her children or the older women when she would be coming home. That way if something went wrong, and with this job, there was always something, they would not be disappointed and the disappointment would be only hers to hold.

Ginny had not bought the best chickens. But she was trying and needed help. Mercy knew that in the end, she would be doing the cooking and making it all sensible while Ginny made everything beautiful. She always did. Even when she had still lived at home. Her bedroom had always been beautiful. There were always flowers or branches of leaves and little bowls of things here and there. Pine cones, shells, stones. Mercy never understood why she kept them but whatever it was she did with them, they somehow seemed beautiful. It was to do with her work, her art. She collected little boxes of things and each box had labels on it saying what it was and where it was found and on what day. And always so neat.

Mercy had seen pictures of the things Ginny made. The last thing she built was a great room full of string that went from a stone to a feather to another stone and then a little piece of glass and on to a photograph and then a shell. All around this went so that in the end it looked like a great bird's nest, a spider's web, or as if telephone poles and wires had gone round and round, but neater. This was what Gin did for a job. Sticks and stones.

———

Peter. Gin felt some shock at seeing him there, just appearing like that. She wanted to say 'like a bad penny' but stopped herself. He wasn't a bad penny. But he was nervous, and that pleased her. She liked to see him plucking at sentences as they fell through the top of his head. So formal, so correct. So chaotic. But he is attractive, she thought. I am attracted to him, still.

I can see in him still what I felt from him before. He suffocates me.

'You look very corporate.' By which she meant, you are so changed. And he knew it. He walked like a man with a need to defend his suit.

'Well.'

She knew she could still needle him. Just like that, turn the screw so very much tighter, pull at his fingernails, let the wasps in.

'Come and sit down. Take the sofa.'

'Yes, thank you, briefly. I have a meeting.'

'You said.' There was nothing to say that would not wound him. 'Would you like some coffee?'

'I'd better not.'

They sat with all of it hanging between them.

He looks exactly the same. Slim and strong and too intense.

His hair was still full. Light brown. Neat features. He was what Neve, without irony or even a suggestion of shame, would describe as 'refined' as she nodded appreciatively.

'You look exactly the same,' he said. 'You look fine.'

She filled in the rest of his sentence for him without speaking it out loud: You look as though your life is unencumbered, as you wished it, unfettered by anyone or anything. You have never needed me.

'Yes, I am. I'm here for my mother's party. It's tonight. She is eighty today.'

'She said you were coming out, that's why I'm here. She didn't mention her party, not that she would have, to me.'

'Oh, she didn't know. Not about the party. I'm not sure she's pleased, you know her, how she is about parties.'

'Yes, still. I'm sure you'll make it a success. You always do.' She felt he meant something with that, there was judgement in that – you make it work, you always do, make it work for yourself.

You will never forgive me.

He looked the same but perhaps not she thought. Now she was anxious. The debt she thought she had cleared. What was he doing here, sitting so close on the sofa? She could feel the heat gathering under his shirt sleeve next to her.

'How are you Peter, same job, right?'

'Yes. It's not ideal I suppose, but, I do care about it somehow.'

'Do you? About the company?'

'Yes. No. I care about the people there. Richard, others too.'

'You've always admired him.'

'I have.'

'I'm glad you came here today, I'm glad to see you.'

'Are you?'

'Of course! What a stupid thing to say.'

'You don't contact me ever.'

'No.'

'Why don't you?' He couldn't help himself. He had to push.

'Oh. You know why. Because it becomes difficult. I have a lot on. And sometimes, I just don't.' She paused to straighten her back. 'Because you become difficult.'

Always so otherwise as her mother would say, always so tediously otherwise.

'I suppose I do. Do I? Yes, perhaps. I expect things, don't I?'

'Yeah. You do.' She smiled. She liked him for admitting it. For knowing his part in the mess that always seemed to follow him and her.

'Are you seeing anyone?' Of course, that's what he really needed to know.

'In a sense.'

'Would you marry him?'

'Ha, no, of course not, I will never marry any one, you know that. What a stupid thing to say.' She knew she was wrong to call him stupid, again, but he was, to ask that of her.

'Ah, so I still have a chance?' There it was. He had laughed while he said it but Gin felt the room close in around her so that she could have run and run and run into the heat and kept going until no one could find her ever again.

You stupid, stupid man. You had to say that didn't you? As if you only know how to be in one position with me and insist on putting me in the other. You make it impossible for me to be kind to you and you love, oh how you love to be the victim of my spite. Any attention will do.

She stood and fetched a cigarette from the table just through the French doors. 'Anyway, weren't you getting married for a few weeks there?'

'Just for the few weeks.'

'What happened?'

'I changed my mind.' He answered too quickly.

'Ah.'

There. She had slayed him. She liked how it felt. His head was low and cloaked. He was sinking fast and she could feel it. It was the way he always was, sinking, because he had been rejected and could never get over it. The familiar anger she felt towards him began to quicken.

As if you were entitled to me. Get over it all. There is no room in my lungs when you are here with me.

'You should come to Mum's party. You must come. She would love it if you were here. You know how fond she has always been of you.'

'Oh, I couldn't intrude,' he said.

'But you must. It would be lovely. And we have so much food.'

———

Eventually, the lights changed and a taxi had to hoot sharp and high to get him moving. Peter didn't care. She was still beautiful. Dark skin, dark hair. Too wiry maybe. It made her look hard. Angular. A jawline like an anvil. Un-needing, haughty. Just as she was when she refused him.

He could feel it all begin to blister again. It registered in his arms somewhere, just below the skin where the nerves were sitting. He sat halfway across the intersection, waiting for the flow of traffic to let him through.

Nothing moved. Grinding, grinding, grinding through the heat and the cars that produced their own heat to add to the day. Taxis coming down the wrong side of the road as if the lines meant nothing. Maybe they didn't. In the end they were unenforceable. You just trust that the others will stay on their side and not wander over. And why don't they? All the cars just riffing and weaving and crushing and stuck, stuck, stuck.

Fucking Gin.

He had been so impotent, so wordless. No wonder she dismissed him. She just rolled in and out of the city, breaking everything that he had set up for himself, his ploys to make himself whole again.

Even so, he had never been whole. Not since he first understood that she was different from him. Perhaps they were thirteen or even younger and she had put her arm through his as they walked down the dirt road to get tadpoles. As her arm had brushed along his, he had suddenly felt as if he would die. His every fibre reacted in a way that shocked him and shamed him too. His therapist (he had tried, he had) told him he could not separate love from shame and until he could he would be doomed to misery. He immediately stopped going to therapy.

He should not have gone to see her. Particularly on a day when he wasn't feeling as he should. When he should have been in his office dealing with the case and the directors. He shook his head slowly to the hundredth hawker or beggar, and they were sometimes the same thing, who rapped on his window saying buy this phone cover or these sunglasses.

One more tap on my window and I will do something I cannot salvage.

Heat and glare coming off the wind shield and the German engineering air-con doing nothing. The lights changed.

Along the road endless press billboards, small scrappy paper things that announced the day's tragedies. Today there was only one. Father of the Nation. We love you, Tata. A Nation Mourns.

He half expected one that read 'Virginia Brandt Returns for Mother's Birthday, Taunts the Man who Loved Her.' He still loved her though, surely, something like that, or else why was he so – he had to pause – so *lost*.

He should not have gone. But he knew that a few days would pass and he would decide that all the misery and fury he was feeling now would be worth it because of the thrill it gave him, she gave him. Just the anticipation of seeing her before the gate had opened. That thrill that comes from the skin, the anticipation of the skin of someone you know won't remember that touch in the way you will. The shameful holding it to yourself. The mere fact that she had placed herself out of bounds, was everything he needed in her.

So, Peter shut his eyes against the traffic that would not move through the early lunchtime Friday gridlock. He allowed himself to imagine. To imagine forcing himself on her, making her see him and feel that he could be powerful, primally so. And how she would have to relent, finally.

Midday

There were flowers to pick. Blue agapanthus, hydrangeas and iceberg roses, colliding across the mass of green. They were like fireworks across an evening sky moments before the rain.

Gin felt the weight of the secateurs in her hand. There is a kind love, a reverence in picking flowers for someone else. Cutting the heads, the stems resisting between the blade for less than a breath, and then relenting. Quick and clean, gone. The agapanthus dripped a thick white serum from their stems.

As Gin walked, the sap from the flowers bled a trail across the paving stones. She took the bunches of blue and pink and white into the kitchen, filling the buckets she had topped with water just before. Back out into the garden, Juno's tail brushing her leg, the lightest of memories, of other dogs and other days with bare legs and parties to come. Around the side of the house they went together, to where the hydrangeas billowed out in a deep cushioned bank along the boundary wall. They had conspired to grow their own climate, cool and dark and sanctified. This was juicy architecture; Juno disappeared into it. The bushes were taller than Gin. So full and deep so that she felt she could fall through them and find herself in another world. Cloud upon cloud of faded marshmallow and lapis lazuli spheres. The leaves were shining and lush as though they dreamed only of water.

After these too were taken back to the kitchen, arms-full, cradled like great holy bubbles, they were dropped into deep basins.

Frangipani, clusters of sugary stars, so clean and waxy it was if they had been cut from sheets of confectioners icing. Gin touched a single petal. They were real. They were high above her so that she had to stretch up through the pointed leaves and the nobbled branches to reach a stem. She had brought paper with her, knowing that as she cut the stem they would haemorrhage their milk in torrents. Blinking against the sun, trying not to lose a single flower from the spray, she cut. The milk flowed, it dripped along her hand and down her wrist and round like the cut of a blade. It burned her skin. A beautiful blood-pact with the garden.

Mother's milk.

She wrapped the whole crown tenderly, slowly in the paper and laid it down. Her wrist tingled. Another, through with the blades, cutting and bleeding and the race of poison along her skin.

She took five, it was too painful to take more, to pillage and maim this tree that should not have even survived where it grew. Not at this altitude, with its bitter frosts that would burn the tops off trees and starve your lungs of oxygen.

————

The years and years that had passed and then today, this day. Peter suddenly and again felt he couldn't breathe, was again lost and was back, painfully, terribly, to the night she broke his heart, the night he knew she would leave Johannesburg forever. She didn't even blink.

It was a hot night, a party. There were so many of those. There was music and the kind of food older people liked. They had been invited along with some others their age to fill numbers and bring some life to the night he assumed.

Gin was casual and radiant. They were twenty-two, maybe a little older. He remembered she was wearing peacock feather earrings and a deep emerald coloured silk top, paisley swirls, the type she bought from the Sunday street markets. The fabric kept falling off her shoulder. And she would raise it up. Too slowly for it to go unnoticed. He had counted the times it had happened. She was telling a New Yorker gallerist about her work, an older guy who wore his smug internationalism so well.

The longer Peter sat there, listening to her, going on and on, the heavier he felt. She was oblivious to all but what she was talking about; balance and form and how she was quantifying the human soul by weight and shape, and exploring its innate three dimensionality. Emotions too, because they aren't all the same thing. So, disappointment was heavier than hope unless it was tinged with fear and she planned to fill the gallery space with muslin sacks that she would stitch in gold thread and each would be filled with pure washed river sand to achieve exactly the desired weight.

'And ...' said Gin, quickly stooping to the ground to place her glass on the floor between herself and the man, '... each bag, for all its weight and dimensionality, precisely measured, casts on the floor ...' She pinched the air with each hand '... nothing but a shadow. Just a shadow. So it has to be properly lit. The shadows are just as important to the installation as the bags.'

'Of course, there is such poetry in that sort of use of a space, poetry and science too in its precision,' said Myberg Kamerling, leaning in so that his glass tilted dangerously close to spilling its contents all over Gin's exposed chest.

It was pathetic, Peter had thought as he watched, though he knew he too was no better than Myberg Kamerling or any of the others who could never take in all of Gin without losing so much of themselves. Kamerling was so entranced, so enraptured by Gin's disregard for him as a fawning stupid puppy and her full regard for him as someone who could help her, help her out of here and into the world, the great big and wide and shiny world out there.

'Have you ever sent a proposal to the Winnburg Gallery in Manhattan? They have a very close association with the NYU graduate programme and they might be sympathetic to your aesthetic. I happen to be very good friends with the owner and curator there. They show very important works. It is a very good incubator for someone starting a career. I would love to come to your studio and see the work. I think that would be important, you know? But you should send them a proposal and mention me, please do, and I guarantee, I do, that they will take you very seriously.'

And Gin leaned forward over her glass that was still on the floor, its golden stemmed cup, like a trophy, and touched Myberg Kamerling's forearm with just three fingers, as light as a cat testing water.

'Thank you Mr Kamerling, I would appreciate that hugely,' she said in her darker, late-night voice he had heard her use in the bars and clubs that had begun to pop up under motorway bridges and down forgotten roads.

It made Peter sick. The jolt of a voice for summer intimacies being exhaled from the deep of her throat, here, in this brightly lit room with these people, revolted him. It shamed him. Not so for Myberg Kamerling who reached into his jacket pocket and retrieved a business card.

'Please call me and let me know when I can come to your space and again before you send your brief so that I can make sure they're looking out for it. I will make sure they take you very seriously.'

And Peter knew then as her fingers touched Myberg Kamerling's arm that she would be taken seriously, that this man would see to it.

That, then, was the end of how things were. He knew it in a way you know a storm cloud when you see one. Even as Kamerling and Gin were interrupted by Nan (whom he had always fancied though she was almost old enough to be his mother) he knew that something had shifted. He had become, forever, invisible.

He had to leave. He had to escape into the garden before whatever it was that was raging away in him came out in a cry, in a shout or tears.

In the safety of night and darkness the lawn stretched out ahead of him. On either side, arches covered in wisteria, roses, jasmine. At the end a sundial and the reflection pond, planted with willows, azaleas and banks of white arum lilies to form the perfect mirror, invisible now in the dark.

He tried to breathe away the anger which he was directing at just about everyone and himself too, for being so passive and dull in the face of the gleaming snare and touch of Myberg Kamerling.

Gin wanted the world and that man could show her, open the door to Manhattan galleries and curators and peacock people who would call her brilliant and listen to her talk about her work and take her very, very seriously. And here was he, a career in law, planned out to the last. A good career he hoped, with a big firm. But how would she fit into that, who would she be to him?

He could feel his feet sink into the grass, it had the depth of damp to it, they must have irrigation. He'd have to go back in, eventually, but there was nothing he could do now except let the dark cloak his gall. He felt so sure everyone there had seen his humiliation, heard her voice, seen her touch the man's arm and known that this meant that she had, just like that announced, as if with a megaphone, I do not love you Peter Strauss.

There had been others of course. This Kamerling with his linen suit and careful, horn-rimmed spectacles and mannered laugh was not the first to be touched that way, it wasn't about that, no it was because Peter knew beyond all doubt, all conjecture, that this man would take her away. She had the funding to show her work locally already and so, if Kamerling's people took her on, it would be nothing more than administrative. He stood facing the pond, wondering if it would be cold if he walked in. And then from behind him in the humming garden he heard her say, 'Pete? What are you doing? Come, we're going through to supper.'

And he turned and saw her shaped by the light of the whole house like a halo. She was holding her hand out to him. She had come to get him. He loved her still and all over again and felt so stupid for having doubted her as she slipped her arm through his and said, 'Isn't it beautiful here? I would love a garden like this, one that is better at night. Are you having a good time? I've had too much wine.'

And he heard himself say, 'Yes, I'm having a good time. I'm glad I came.'

'Me too. Come. We'll sit together at the table. If we're quick we can move the place names if we have to, before people sit down.'

He loved her. He loved her so painfully.

––––––

Lungisane, who was employed by the Diamond to circle the square and the fountains held in its centre, was approaching down the long row of acacias that had been planted along the east and west sides. He swung left and right in his black trousers, tucked into military boots, a white shirt with epaulettes and the private company's insignia in red. Also on his sleeve, a little badge bearing his name: Lungisane Ndlovu. A little black beret sat askance on his head. It was too small. Over all of this he had on a bullet-proof and an AK-47. The great liberator of Africa, thought September. And yet on this man, in this place, he knew its bullets would not be used for freedom. The guard had slightly out-turned feet. He would be a fast runner.

The guard's form came closer and closer, down one of the two long sides of the square where under the fever trees were planted rows and rows of agapanthus (to soften the edges, dull the glare and, like the trees, to give a sense that this was a homegrown plaza, its very existence indigenous to this land).

September knew he would be moved along. He and his placard, which seemed so much heavier today, the heat more ready on his body. He lifted himself up from his seat, or he tried to, until he was standing again, albeit shakily. As he stood, he had the unsteady feeling that he had not in fact managed to shift from the seat after all. That the reason he could not find his feet was that he was still very much sitting down.

He was at once standing up and moving away but also still sitting, waiting for this man with his gun to do him some harm.

This sense that he was paralysed yet could see himself walking away left his very heart rent wide open. There was nothing he could do to protect himself.

There were flashes of light bouncing off the Diamond, birds hidden deep in acacias that the thorns conspired to hide. But, the birds spoke in strange tongues. A lizard, green and basking, told September the language of the birds was Greek.

September watched himself walk away towards another man, tall and straight like a lightning conductor, a great bullrush of a man and as the man turned September knew it was his father. He had come to call him home. 'Come Sechaba, today is the day.'

He felt such a momentous and terrible fear building in him that he thought he might cry out or beg for mercy. He felt so very painfully apart from himself watching himself beginning to tremble and weep for the fear of what must surely be coming. A bullet, a boot.

The guard passed him by. Passed both the one sitting and the one trying to walk away.

'*Kunjane*, how are you?' said the guard by way of greeting. A Zulu man, thought September.

September nodded. Or at least felt his body, his neck and its heavy, swollen head respond in a way that he understood to be nodding.

I un-seam. The green maize husks are being stripped away from the taut yellow head. I long for shelter. Why today? Why do I begin to fray on this of all days? Perhaps it is the news of the passing of

the king. Even though I know he died months ago. This nation's
great untreated grief has come to rest in me.

My spirit spills over the top of a swelling wave. The tide retreats.
And I, with it, recede. The salty rush. There in the foam and the
bitter iodine like a waxy weed my spirit is being tossed this way and
that. Further out, beyond the break, I recognize the spirit of those
who have gone before. Our king is there. The king is dead, long live
the king. I can see him, he rises above the waves, as do the thousand,
thousand before him, all the kings and queens. There too an old white
lady. She is beautiful. Long, like an egret. I do not know her. She
glistens. And, again, I see my father. He calls to me: 'Call back your
spirit Sechaba, call it home.'

But it is already too far out. And I do not know how to swim.

September's skin was still on edge. His hair raised and prickled
like a porcupine waiting for the lion's charge even though he felt
no threat from the guard. He decided to carry his placard back to
the benches in the shade. To feel himself return. The guard had
passed, the flares had settled and all around him the plaza had
once more assumed its pallor and pace.

The guard had been kind. He would call him brother, but
there was a risk in that. These days it was more complicated. The
lines between comrade and king had for many years begun
to fray.

September hoisted his placard over the top of his head, its
sides catching the sleeves of his shirt and grating against his
skin. He turned the sign around to look at it. He had spent so
long deciding what to write. Anger, sadness, fear, betrayal, all of
this, but he had to say something that said *everything*. Something
that spoke of history but laid bare the present crime. He needed

the cuts in his flesh and the pain in his feet to be acknowledged. He needed them to know that every day his sister carried his burden too, that she had to walk through rain and heat to bring him food, that at night, if he could not sleep he felt fear creeping along the walls of his garden, other men, bad men who would kill him for the few coins he had left in his pocket. He needed to proclaim that the very marrow in his bones, the straight and the crooked, yearned for home and the fresh mountain air in a way that was close to dying. It was the longing to be close to God again after a life of cruelty and sorrow. All of this he wished to say.

And yet, what could be said? So, instead, he wrote: Verloren. And under it: Here I am.

———

Neve did wonder why she never liked parties, company in general. She had decided long ago that it had to do with being sent to boarding school at five years old. Too young really, by any account. And from that moment, she missed a home she never really knew. Longed for the evenings at a dinner table, dreamed a thousand different scenarios that would play out in the house she hardly remembered. From the miserable night she was first left at school, she would be surrounded by others, hundreds of girls, no room of one's own, just long, open dormitories where nothing was ever only yours. Later when she had begun to work at the hospital, she had moved to a residential hotel just below it, and there she shared a room with another girl, a radiologist. After that, marriage. Such an upstanding man, straight and honest.

So, finally when the children had left and Gin's father was in his grave, then she had moved to a house that was hers. All of it.

She rose when she wished, ate when she felt like it, but more than that, she guarded access to her secret place as if her whole life depended on it. Which was dramatic. She knew that, but what was true, was that she had spent her whole life waiting for it. To have a place of her own.

And now Gin had turned up, swanned in with her typical disdain of everything. The way she touched a finger to Neve's collection of English porcelain dogs and scoffed, saying, 'I cannot believe you still have these things.' She arrived, as if entitled, dressed like a teenager, and had effectively thrown open the doors of Neve's house to the street, exposing her own mother to guests and violating the space that held her safe all those days and nights when she, Gin, was nowhere to be seen.

It was so much smaller than Eden House, it was true, but it was hers. Gin accused her of being dewy-eyed about the old house. She claimed it was always remembered as more beautiful, happier, wiser and somehow, self-healing, as if it never caused a day's worry or an inconvenient tradesman's account. Gin accused Neve of refusing to remember anything unpleasant.

Well, how else to survive?

———

Peter had to steady himself in the car awhile before he got out and greeted the car park guard as usual, as if he were disproportionately thrilled to see him. He ducked along the side of the building and out the front, to the public entrance that formed part of a smaller square, before the main plaza. There was a tower on each side and in the middle trees, gardens, benches, little wagons selling coffee and sandwiches. More of the same.

He bought a coffee and added one brown sugar, hating as usual the little paper sleeve that remained. Detritus that marked us as uncivilized, eating out of paper, standing up, walking. He felt embarrassed too that he was so prissy about these things.

Peter slouched towards the benches that ran along the margins of the main square. Was the Diamond the ugliest building in the city? He couldn't decide. Agapanthus leaned over from the raised concrete walls someone had seen fit to fill with gardens – clivia at the back under rounded trees and in front the blue balls of the agapanthus that formed a guard of honour as the suited men, and they were mostly men, walked along the gilded paths and into the open mouths of their buildings, banks opposite each other, separated by the great floor of fountains that roared and spurted and sent thirsty birds darting for cover. Peter found a bench that he would not have to share, the agapanthus now forming an ostentatious canopy to shield him from the sun. The hunchback with the board was still around. He knew him from the mine. He was a bit of a pest but nothing more. The sun was bleaching higher into the sky.

Fear no more the heat of the sun.

Peter closed his eyes against the few shards that still forced their way through. Jesus, Gin was still so infuriating. And she judged him, he knew that.

He had never been what she wanted, never been enough. The sparrows were dipping into the fountain where it ran over the stones into the gurgling channels that ran around the perimeter. No one was enough for her and she was too much. Too clever, too independent, too hard, too calculating – just too everything.

———

As usual, Dudu had too much to do, too much ironing, too many shelves to dust. During the brief half-hour she took for herself around midday, she retreated to her room. Dark and over-full. She had removed her doek and let her braids fall about her face, her back, their weight thick and satisfying. She began to rub some oil into her scalp, carefully and deliberately. The dark of the room, the smell of the oil, this little moment, so painfully her own, apprehended from every other second of the day, allowed her to call back her spirit and let her centre return.

No one knows where I am.

She was lost in the darkness of her room, unseen, deliciously so. The sensation of her fingertips as she tapped the oil into the skin, all along her skull, along the line of the braids, like the careful furrowing of a precious field, released all the tight and terrified coils that held her in readiness throughout the day. When she was done, she allowed herself to sit, just for a few minutes, perfectly silent. Her body swaying ever so slightly to the rhythm of her heart.

———

Peter had given Gin a huge bouquet, one afternoon when they were young and he still hoped to be loved. A bouquet, if one could call it that, agapanthus, blue and white, carefully cut to be enough of the one colour, so as not to unbalance the other. She was an artist, he had thought, she will notice things like that. Blue and white. He had brought them to the old house, Eden House, before Christmas one year, when he had had no money. He could hardly remember that feeling, but it had been there. He hadn't minded it – being educated and good looking, poverty was always only temporary, a rite of passage.

He had written a card to go with the flowers, 'Agapanthus from *agape*, for love.' So, he had carefully balanced it upon a bouquet containing nothing but the blooms of love and on seeing them she had said: 'Oh, can you leave them in the kitchen?'

'Do you want to read the card? It explains what they are.'

'I know what they are, stupid, come on, the others are at the court already.'

He had followed her across the lawn, burning, and as he did, he had grown more and more petulant, wounded. Again, as she always did, she had played him without even knowing it. She had sent another arrow into an already ruptured pelt and had not even realized. As his humiliation grew, he, as he always did, made it worse, so much worse by playing badly and hitting every shot into the net, perhaps on purpose. He couldn't even tell so that once they had finished a set, Gin had said: 'Well that was hardly a good game was it?'

She had a way of posing a question which was always and only ever an accusation. Obviously, she had learned that from her mother.

Any another man, a different more confident one, or at least, one not in love would have thought no more of it. But he retreated to the house and retrieved his bouquet, that mocked him (*agape*) and left. He had known even then that the only way to survive her was to leave, leave the country too and its stupefying smallness. Yet it was he who had gone and come back and she, later, who had gone but never come back at all, except for these brief recalls, none of them related to him, always related to her mother and later because of her father dying.

But why had he spoken as he had today? 'Are you seeing anyone?' 'So I still have a chance?'

Gin was in the city for her mother's eightieth birthday and he had to make it all about him, his need, his endless loss every time he thought he caught sight of her. He had wanted to ask her if she would come back but she had seemed so on edge, so ready to react as if he would lunge at her. And he had, 'So I still have a chance?' exposing him as the man he would always be, her old dog, in need of a kind look or a soft hand. Or a kick.

Early afternoon

Dudu had not yet gone to September, and though it was getting late she decided that she would, if only to send him back to his garden to rest. In the summer when the heat of the sun seemed to make his pain worse, this was her main task.

She crossed the road and walked as briskly as she could. She checked the time. Nearly two o'clock. She would find him at the Diamond. She worried that he might be hungry. She had visited the day before, given him *pap* and meat and bread and a big bottle of milk. Still, she needed to find him and give him money and water. She had kept aside one hundred for him and would take him oranges too.

She hated the Diamond. Why did he stay there? Every day with that sign of his. Some days he was worse than others, babbling, talking in tongues, not answering her questions: 'Brother, how are you? Are you sleeping? Are you hungry? Do you know who I am?'

Instead he would talk in rhymes, words and worlds she did not recognize. She thought it might be because he smoked *ganja* too much with that *tsotsi* that begged on the other corner. But it helped him sleep when he was cold and afraid. She knew it was bad for him, but what else did he have? And he said it took away the pain in his back and in his head where the bullet had sliced him.

But one thing she knew and held on to: no matter what was unweaving in his head, he had a forthright heart. He was straight and honest. This gave her comfort. No matter his mind, he had love in his heart. God would judge him kindly.

It was that day, at the mine, that everything changed for him. He had a job there, cooking, peeling potatoes, cleaning. It was a good job for someone with his troubles. He grew tired from the work, it hurt his back and his legs that were growing more useless. But they were kind to him there, the other ones. They would find him something to sit on so he could rest as he peeled and chopped.

But then there was the day of the shootings and that was a day like no other. He should not have been there, it was all those Xhosas marching with their *knobkierries*, fighting for something they would not win. One union said march, the other said do not march yet, first we will negotiate.

But September and his comrades went anyway. A wildcat strike that lasted for five days.

Afterwards, when September was in the hospital and could finally speak (but never again with the clear soft voice of the mountains) she had said:

'What were you doing there? You had no business there. You work in the kitchen.'

'They told me to come. So I did. They invited me.'

'But it was not legal.'

'We had protection.'

'From whom, September, who protected you?'

And all he did was look up with the one eye that was not covered in bandages and open his palm to the sky and she knew they had been to the *muti* man. That was their only protection. A medicine man, casting a wish, a dream, a spell.

'You gave up your life for two hundred rand? You paid a *muti* man? And where is he now September? Where is his medicine now?'

'He said the bullets would not find us. He made us invisible.'

'Do you feel invisible now?'

'No, sister.'

That was how it had been. And now, there was September, there on the other side of the fountains. Resting under the flowers. She would send him home. The sun was too high.

––––––––

The plaza was punctuated with groups of men in suits wandering across between buildings. A few women too. The lunchtime migration, a moment to apprehend some light.

See how they waddle in mottled flocks. Keen and grey and glossy,
like ibises scavenging after the rain. A worm, a grub, a maggot.

September felt the heat in his head return. He wanted to see Dudu. To hear her voice. He knew that she would come. And he needed to rest in his garden. The sun was too high.

The sharp hot pain reached across his crown in a band from one ear to the other. It had come after he was beaten and trodden with the big boot of power at Verloren.

He did feel, he did hope, that perhaps the pain would disappear, his body heal, his own self return, if only justice could be done. Once his vigil had been acknowledged and actions taken to remedy that terrible day, to set the universe back into its natural, easy motion, then perhaps he would wake and his body would be whole again.

It was his duty to speak for those who could not, he was called as much by his own ancestors as by those who were slain on that mound of gravel and blood. He could hear them pleading with him to speak their names.

He found, more and more, that he could hear a middle-voice, neither spoken nor thought, like dialect of language he had yet to learn though its sounds were still familiar.

As a result he had, these past weeks and years, begun to appreciate the reliability of ghosts. He learned too that he had misunderstood childhood. He had thought then that he, being small, still had all the world to understand. But in the end he had known it all since birth, heard it all, every secret whispered into his ears – only now was he beginning to remember the words that had been spoken. Now he understood.

———

It was getting late.

The afternoon malaise was deep. Peter would have to go back to his office, do something, be seen to do something, to earn his packet. He longed for sleep. He had called his mother, because Mandela had died and he knew she would like to offer her two cents on that. She had been out and his father, audibly exasperated by having to answer the telephone, had explained he could not stop to talk. He was late for tennis.

Richard had sent a message to say he was gone for the day.

He had done what was needed and signed the documents. He would come in on Monday for a few hours but after that he was leaving for the coast.

Ten days of national mourning had been announced. They would run until the national holiday on the sixteenth of December, and then half the country shut down for Christmas anyway. That was convenient. And a state funeral, heads of state would come from all over the world. Another funeral would be organized by the ANC.

There was a time when Peter would have rushed to the Residence. He would not have even gone to work which, before working for the firm, was for the unions. Labour law was the same no matter which side you worked for. He had seen his relationships on either side of the divide as an asset. It was a facilitation rather than a compromise of something fundamental. He no longer even thought about what he did. With whom his affinities lay.

He stood and watched as a small slim woman in a blue domestic worker's uniform (apron, pinafore, doek) embraced the man with the hunched back and the board. The man he knew from Verloren. Peter registered a faint shock, a discomfort. This moment of intimacy, so unexpected. And immediately he felt guilty that he should be so shocked that a homeless man, a hunchback, had someone to love him, to share a tender word.

She showed him a bag of oranges and some other things in a shopping bag. Then, together, the man with the hump and the woman in the blue pinafore began to walk towards the street side of the building. They walked with the same sway. She was the man's family. There was such tenderness between them. The woman took the hunchback's shopping bag back from him and carried it. She slipped her arm though his. They chatted. The man leaned his head towards her to hear her better as they walked. At some point they stopped and she turned her back to the hunchback man. He stretched out and lifted her long braids in his hands, unhooking something from them around the nape of the woman's neck. A necklace perhaps.

Peter turned away.

———

Gin placed the vases in a row on the table, the silver catching a reflection of the tablecloths underneath. She ran her fingers over the little bumps, the cloth was so smooth and the bumps, little knots of cotton, were so coarse that they felt like half-formed tumours on skin. Little cancerous bulbs to be rooted out of their earthing.

She had not slept in any substantial way for days, instead, moments stolen here and there. Furtive retreats to allow her fibre and nerve endings to re-knit themselves. Since her arrival she had, of course, been trapped between the time zones, bleeding from one to the other yet never settling in either.

And even when sleep seemed close, all through her head ran lists of ingredients and fantasies about table settings, her mother's linens and her grandmother's silverware. There were forty or so guests, family and close, close friends. Many, the most loved, were dead.

Gin knew that Neve saw the party as a kind of imposition, a moment for Gin to absolve herself given her absence. And Gin had had to ask herself whether that was true. But in the end (and she did believe this at any rate to be true), to lay a table, smooth the corners, calculate the length of the drop, the space between vases, all of this is a kind of reverence. For her, to make something beautiful, balanced, whole was an act of devotion. She wished to show Neve, on her birthday, this same consideration. She had put as much into the planning of her mother's birthday tables as she might into a new work. This was a site-specific installation, designed and curated for only one viewer. There would be others there, of course, but it was never them she had in mind.

And so, over and over she ran through which guests would come and which might not. If no one came it would be a disaster, too depressing to be a party, more of a wake. She had tried to talk to Neve to explain why she was doing it. But for Neve in the end it all came back to Gin's lack of skill. Her inability to fulfil the role as hostess, operating in a new medium, one she had never mastered. It was as if choosing not to marry, not to have children, somehow disqualified her in Neve's eyes from anything even vaguely domestic. The inventiveness and reach of her art had met its limit.

It was true she did not know how to cook. She was not interested in learning. Perhaps she should have paid more notice, growing up. It was the mechanics of preparation that eluded her, words that meant nothing, measure this, weigh that and all to be violently consumed in an unthinking moment. Where was the art in that? But no matter her effort to dismiss it all as worthless, she knew that on this day, it was the very thing to hold her potential failure.

If she let herself think long enough, in the car, waiting for the gate to close, letting Peter out, the misery of it all came back in. She wished Peter would stop telling her he loved her, in his dope-eyed way, in his stupid jokes. His insistence sapped the life out of her.

But, when it came to her mother, to the violence she exacted with her every word, her action and lack of action, her stupefying indifference, there was nothing more she wished for in all the world than to hear Neve say: 'I love you.' How she said it would not matter. She could say, 'It was perfect,' or, 'Thank you.' Gin would know what she meant.

The vases formed a guard of honour down the middle of the long table. Candles now. Taller candelabras, shorter ones below.

Who was she before she became a girl, a woman? Who was she before her original self was covered in its first layer of varnish and then another and another until the face and the raging, thundering heart underneath it all was barely visible? What was the texture of her unencumbered mind before she was female and Peter male?

She had known always that the entire force of her full self, as it existed before her femaleness, had become too much for Peter, or any man, to bear. And its arrival, instead of being a celebration, a moment of expansion into fullness, rather became a liability or a stain. Instead of some glorious rite of passage her transition from girl to woman had come with a sense of jeopardy she felt entirely unequipped to protect herself against.

She could trace the precise moment she became a woman.

A scorching afternoon. Swimming, sunbathing. The gravel was griddle-hot. It had forced the two of them to take short quick steps. Peter had leaned across her to guide her to the left where he had spotted small tufts of grass that they could use as islands of safety for their feet.

His hand brushed her arm. Her skin charged and surged and all along her arms, goosebumps had appeared like a thousand hot little volcanoes. She knew he felt it too because he looked at her, quickly, with shock. They rushed to the house and drank deep glasses of juice. Later when he was gone and she was alone on her room floor, sharpening pencils, preparing to draw the fat, juicy seed pods she had found that morning, she realized, horribly, that she had become a girl and he a boy.

And she hated him for it. Even as she had made a leap away from him towards the first tuft of grass which was cool and soft as pudding, everything had changed. In the end she would always be an object of affection, an object of fantasy, an object of attention. Her every easy laugh and unchecked sentence interpreted in relation to her new position.

So here she was, lining up vases, trying to correct a life's worth of deficit with her mother, apologize for not being more fully a girl, and for leaving her mother to defend her choices on her behalf in her absence.

It was as if her whole life, her art (which was her life), was a sort of sacred quest return to the wholeness of the person she was before. She weighed her emotions and rendered them sandbags, disassembled her body, reduced it to bones and put it back together again. Her whole life a series of excursions and lurches and queries trying to get back to who she was before she was marked as a girl, exiled from that genderless place where all of her, boundless, limitless, was possible.

––––––

September closed his eyes. It seemed as if the whole day was suddenly drenched in sugar. He could still taste the oranges on his lips, so juicy and optimistic. Just for that moment his entire self hummed to the harmony of the universe. His garden was damp and cool. He felt held by the afternoon, by something beyond himself, something eternal. A moment of grace.

I am made of light. I am made of light.

––––––

Gin decided on five bowls of flowers, three larger ones and two smaller ones. She had old newspapers on one of the chairs to catch all the leaves she would strip off. 'SA Democracy under threat,' it read. She felt no connection to it. She did not care. As if somehow time passes and things that before were the very parameters of your breath are suddenly so distant that you can no longer recognize their silhouette, no matter how close they get.

She had once heard an exiled musician say that his worst day in exile, New York as she remembered it, came when he woke and realized he was no longer dreaming in Zulu. Even his subconscious had been exiled to a foreign land. Fighting for freedom his exile had colonized his language; his magical fantasies and nighttime mysteries were no longer native to his tongue.

The newspaper with its anxious headlines was being covered over in waxy leaves from the hydrangeas as she pulled at the stalks. The cool green of them felt so incomparable to any other feeling, as if she could not even dredge up a simile. The paper began to drag under the pools that the damp leaves created.

The hydrangeas anchored the bowls with their capacious loveliness. They seemed to be the suggestion of shape more than shape itself. One in each of the smaller vases and two more for the larger ones. They would be beautiful. The flowers, at least, would be beautiful. Next, the clumps of iceberg roses, their fussy petals just about holding on, some more blown than others. Their beauty seemed to fill the whole afternoon. A few fell, white saucers floating on top of the foaming lace cloth. They too were scooped up to cover over the rest of the newspaper.

Gin was leaning over the vases and the piles of flowers, feet bare on the cool slabs of the verandah, aware of the dryness of her soles as she turned and bent, rocking back on her heels a bit.

This is exactly who I am. I know who I am. In this moment, I exist.

She added some lavender. Neve would like that (it was only really there for her) and lastly, because they were the show piece and the reason it would all be magical, in each bowl a whole head of frangipani, each with dozens of perfect marzipan white blooms and a scent that could catch you at the back of your brain somewhere and reel you back out through time to another place, as if through sleep.

'It is beautiful,' said Mercy.

'You think it's OK? I thought about buying some, but I think this will be nicer.'

'It's OK.'

They stood for a second looking at the bowls down the length of the table, they looked romantic, old-fashioned. They looked like the flowers her granny might have placed on her big ball and claw mahogany table in the house out past Rustenberg. The same tablecloths, the same vases, roses and frangipani.

'My granny would have liked this.'

'Oh?'

'She was tough, you know, really strong, and she loved beautiful things, always flowers. Her house was always beautiful.'

'Then she will be here. She will come tonight.'

Tears sprung to Gin's eyes, painful and shocking.

She nodded. Ashamed. 'How do those white babies look?'

Mercy chuckled. 'Healthy.'

———

Mercy felt the frustration of language. There was so much that she could not say in that moment. But there she was, again, on the wrong side of her mother-tongue. She wanted to say – your grandmother, all your grandmothers are here in this moment, and always. They are sitting at the table already and wait to sit at the tables you have not yet laid. They are waiting to eat the food you have not yet prepared and they prepare it with you, they guide your hand as it curls around the potato, peeling it, fat and solid in your hand, the wetness just seeping through. These women put their knowledge and their memories into you before you were even born.

She wanted to say all of this to the girl pretending not to cry, but there were so many things to prevent her, to frustrate the words, which were a kind of love.

———

The gates rolled back and a small white van came through. It did not smell familiar and as the doors opened, nor did the men who spilled out of it. But they were calm and easy in their way so Juno welcomed them. One leaned down and scratched her ears. It felt good, enough to reassure her. His message confirmed him as a friend. After that the two men ignored her and went about their work with tables and talking to Gin. The gate didn't seem to close. That was new. Juno walked closer to the border line between gate and street and stuck her nose through. She could hear even more clearly the sounds that had started earlier. There were people in the road all going in one direction, all moving along on foot. Juno nosed further ahead, wishing to catch a clearer read on a scent that was passing her just then, three women.

And then, with a heavy rumble, the gate began to move. She had to leap forward and to the side to avoid being rolled over by the metal wheels. The gate clanked shut against the pillar and Juno, turning slightly, realized that she was on the wrong side, outside.

*

Walter and his brother arrived with the extra tables and chairs. They worked at the gallery in Rosebank, now run by Gin's friend. They were on their way to set up at the space for some end-of-year event. Walter was worried he was late. He did not accept tardiness. Not in himself or his children. The woman who came out to meet him looked worried but did not mention the time. There was a housekeeper there too.

'*Kunjane* Mama.'

'*Kunjane*,' said Mercy.

'Thanks. Hi, are you Walter? I haven't met you before, but Bea mentions you.'

The white woman offered her hand. They shook.

'Yah. This is Simon. Where do you want them?'

'Can you put them on the verandah?'

'Yah. Simon, patio.' Walter gestured with his hand as they spoke.

They placed the tables and pulled out the legs cramped in under the metal tops.

'Can we get some water, Ma?'

'Of course. Come with me.' She led the men to the kitchen and handed them a glass each.

Walter found himself looking past Gin, once, twice, three times so that she turned too. A painting of horses in the veld, large over the dining table. It was beautiful.

'I'm seeing your horses there.'

'Oh, yes, my grandmother used to live on a big farm that had horses.'

'You ride them?'

'Yes. Well, no, I used to. As a child. But only on the farm.'

'Fast? Like racing?'

'No. Just messing around.'

'You know about Seabiscuit?'

'Yes.'

'You've seen the film?'

'Yes,' she said. He knew she was surprised he had mentioned it.

'I cry when I see it.' He took a breath and smiled. 'I love that horse.'

———

Peter had been in with Mogomotsi who had the effect of motivating him to focus more keenly, mainly out of anxiety. Mogomotsi was all outcomes and strategies and no excuses.

Peter sat back at his desk. He still felt unmoored over Gin. As if a safety rail, a boundary had suddenly been blown over in a storm. She had a way, without saying anything, of questioning his life and once he had answered the questions, it was usually guilt he was left with. He felt too that he should be feeling something or at least be expressing something about Mandela. But in the end, that might require that he begin to speculate on his proximity to imperatives like truth and honour.

He had been a union lawyer, red as the sunsets. Mostly he dealt in unlawful detentions for having the wrong permit, the wrong pass-book, the wrong anything. He knew all the Struggle songs and sang them louder, knowing any sign that he did not know the words would mark him as a traitor. Maybe he was one. Not then, of course, never then, when every waking minute was spent in prisons and detention centres trying to find out where this one was detained and that one had been sent, deported, disappeared.

He was too young to be doing it, not even fully qualified when he began. The work had to be done in halls and secret meetings in people's houses, waiting for the knock on the door. For the first time in his life, he felt as if he had something with which to announce himself, a set of borrowed credentials. His context gave him credibility. It allowed him to exist.

This had only occurred to him years later when he had been at a dinner and the dullest most predictable girl at the table (pretty but not too pretty, black dress, straight blonde hair) had announced she couldn't eat half of what was being served. So multiple were her allergies and sensitivities that she might crumple to mucus if she so much a nibbled on a tomato. As she described her symptoms in detail, he had thought she had had to invent all of this because, in the end, she had nothing else to say for herself. Without her allergies and feigning embarrassment at the fuss she makes at the table, who would remember she was even there?

Peter's mother still liked to recall, shaking her head, the time he was in hospital for two whole days after an anti-conscription demonstration had turned violent. So, other than his Struggle credentials, what could really be said about Peter?

These days, he could not imagine going to a neighbourhood even twenty minutes from his own. He lived a few blocks from the Diamond, he ate the same takeaway twice a week, had three coffees before lunch. Sometimes, another in the afternoon. He ran no less than eight kilometres each morning, except on Sundays when he rested. His pleasures were rationed. He was pleased that he had access to the company suites at the cricket oval. He occasionally bought sex from one of the girls down Central Avenue, hardly bothering to adjust his car seat, and read books on South African history. He always bought a thriller to read during his December holiday. Whichever one the bookstore told him was best.

A flaccid inventory of a life.

Mid-afternoon

No one came. The gate remained shut and though she could hear everyone, Juno began to sense that something was not quite right. A woman approached her, kind and soft and safe smelling. But then the woman moved on. Juno followed her a few paces. And then a few more. There were so many people. A whole group, many, many people, women, all passed her by and she had to cross the road to get out of their way. She followed them for a little too. She felt she had gone far enough, the group had passed, she turned back for home. A car passed, she hopped to the side and then another and then two more. She turned her back on them so that the noise and the wheels would not be near her face. She turned again, and again, back to the road and for home and set off. She kept on going and yet, she could not seem to find the gate. Not this one or that, and on and on. No gate. She would keep on. It was hot. The tarmac was hot on her paw pads and she began to pant. No gate, on and on. A road. Had she crossed a road? On and on, more and more tired and hot, so very hot as she kept on going, to get herself home. Back to the gate. They would open it for her and she could get some water.

———

September had to narrow his eyes against the sun coming through the canopy of vine leaves above him.

Fear no more the heat of the sun. Its blunt intrusions on our day. We are protected now by softer lights though they can be seen for a million, million miles.

The king is dead; long live the king.

This day, that has been declared the day of his death, should be the day that his name is sung, that his struggle is honoured. But on the day of his true passing too. I will shout out his name. I will bring him honour. I will shout out my song. It will be a song repeated across the land. The mountains, birds, all the beasts will know the words to my song.

I will bring him honour by singing freedom. I will march on the Diamond. I will sing out so that they see my face.

I will sing: Here I am. Here I am.

Flowers will be my crown. For am I not a king of all this? Of nature's realm? I will pick the flowers myself and make a crown of violet flames to circle my head. This will be my message. They will understand that though I march with the sword of justice, my intention is only love.

And it was everything that he had. After Dudu had walked with him back to his island, (and that act was love too), September had embraced her and then retreated into his garden. He had settled himself on his cardboard bed for what felt like minutes but it must have been longer. The sun told him it was later. He did feel better, in a way. The placard was such a weight, such a burden, that to have it propped up against the garden wall instead of gripping its talons into the flesh of his shoulders was, in itself, a kind of healing.

His garden was everything to him. It was his own space in the world. Its parameters, depths and shadows were his and his alone. It had become his only entitlement, his sacred, inalienable right to silence. And his moments of silence were everything so that they had become the very same as prayer.

And so September felt solid and whole. As if the weight of his bones could anchor him there, under the vines and the ancient peach trees and he would be made well again. He would be able to trace his mind from here to there by simply following the trail a thought left behind as it came forth.

Before all of this, before Verloren, his thoughts had felt like a bird walking across wet sand, one leg and then the other and behind them a clear line of jagged little stars, each leading to the next and eventually to the bird itself or at least the place where the bird had decided to take flight.

No more. Instead his mind darted left and right like a hermit crab escaping a rising tide. It made him weary. That and the pain. But here, in his garden, secret, snake-green, and filled with his own private shadows, he could find wholeness.

September curled in on himself, pushing his cardboard closer to the wall where the shade was still deep. Later it would dapple and he would watch the light trip and trill across the leaves and flowers.

It was his habit, on waking, to make an inventory of his garden and of himself. He, like Adam in his garden, called out the names of everything that appeared before him. This was a happy benediction.

The different flowers that came and went through the year, the birds, lizards, even the mice. His mother would have loved to see this house, this garden, though he would have had to lie about how he knew of it. She was a proud woman, carried the weight of a village on her shoulders. She would weep to know that he crept like a thief into this borrowed bower each night.

She was now dead ten or twenty years.

He thought about how he had come to be there and how quickly things had gone from being possible to being impossible. How even after he had come to the city on the back of a truck with thirty or so others and things had gone wrong, he still felt he could fix it, make it right somehow. He could hear his father saying, as if to spur him on, 'If you work hard and are honest and respect your parents, nothing can be impossible.' This under the old government, his father had still believed to be true. His father, a true Basotho man, always had a blanket strung around him. A sign of his tribe, his identity. The same blanket September had scorned in favour of city clothes to get on that truck, to make the journey. Then, the many, many nights he had known the fool he was for spitting on that blanket. Newspaper does nothing to keep out the high altitude frosts of Johannesburg. He knew too that to cast off that blanket was to cast off something of himself. And that was a treacherous thing.

Those thirty had worked on that building site for half of what they were promised, and September with his bent spine and his pain had worked just as hard, plastering huge walls with his trowel. He was good at it. He found that the rhythmical slop of the plaster as he scooped and slapped and spread was something he could do. The others teased him for his shape, but he would clamber up the ladders and the scaffolds as good as any and set to work. It was his work that silenced them. You cannot belittle a man when he is good at what he does. They built five houses, exactly the same. All behind high walls. Then when the houses were built, the men were all told to go with their day's wages in their pockets and nothing else.

Some of the thirty fought with the developers, but the police were called and they were *shambokked* and thrown in the back of the truck and that was that. This was 1997. These were Freedom's first days and September had no intention of going into the back of a police van to have his permit and possessions burned, so he kept quiet thinking that there would be more jobs to be had. And there were. That was how he began to cook at the mine.

September brushed off the tiny leaves that had collected in his hair while he had slept. He shook out his flattened cardboard box and propped it up on its side to keep it from getting too damp from the earth. In his bag he still had a half-loaf of white bread and the oranges Mercy had brought him. He took two pieces and tapped the mostly empty can of beans and Vienna sausages. Nothing left except a bit of sauce he had saved and now, some greedy ants. He tapped the tin a few more times to warn the ants. Those that didn't heed the warning would be scooped up with the white slice and swallowed.

Then, out of the corner of his eye, September saw something move. Something white, or partly white. A spirit, a memory? He could no longer tell. But this spirit held its shape. He placed his bread and the tin back down on the shopping bags that held his clothes and pots and the precious things. He peeped around the reach of Star Jasmine that formed the one side of his home. There the creature lay, gasping for air.

Gin had laid all the tables, chopped and cut and tucked away into the fridge, bowls of things she would need later. Mercy had reassured her that she had done all that was necessary.

Her mother was still out. She seemed to have been missing for hours. She had phoned Mercy to say she was buying some things for the party that she was sure Gin had forgotten and then having coffee with 'dear Nan'.

Dear Gin lay on the bed; oceanic waves of blue from the blanket, too warm for the time of year but such a comfort. A sea to sink under, on this day, a day for drowning.

I am without shelter.

She had wanted to go to the Residence. She would go, as soon as she had managed the food. The flowers were done. They were lovely.

She ran her hands over her stomach, concave, a little bowl that sunk between her hip bones, that sat proud, like two handles of a pot. She cupped them over with her palms. Such comfort in that, such old reassurance.

To know these hard edges was to know where her body ended and the world began, it was a mark of her being, of her existence. Anything softer would blur the edges, a charcoal smudge disappearing into paper, nothing more. These bones were their own gesture of art. The place where her composition began. A sign of her mastery over life's terrible jeopardy.

She knew why her mother would assume she could not prepare for a party, that girl who has not eaten a solid meal since she was thirteen can hardly be expected to know what one tastes like. And perhaps she didn't.

A great cheer rose up from down the road. Ululating, whistles, drums. Perhaps someone important had arrived. And just that, that thinking of it all allowed tears to rise. Again, nowhere.

The tides are too strong. They will drag me too far out, unrecoverable.

And why had Peter come and why did she care? Every time she had to cut him down, cut him back. He was too thick skinned. She might have let him love her, in another life, a life where she was softer, more easy in her own skin. But what good would it do to let someone closer now, let them come to lean on you when some days, lately most days, she felt death sit so close that she could just about smell its breath on her pillow when she woke. The closer he came, the more weight he exerted so that to be near him was a daily death by suffocation.

To let him love her, she knew that she would have to give him everything. Every last sacrifice would be hers. And after all that, when she was left with only her shell and no defence against life, then she would need to lean on him and demand his help. She knew he would never have been strong enough to keep her from herself.

One day, perhaps soon, even she would not be strong enough. Because to be as she was, so entirely alone in every moment, took its toll. There would be a night when it was no longer possible to carry each decision and navigate every last consequence without another voice in the room. She knew that some day, in this reaching and grabbing at life, she would simply fall to death. It would be she who would choose it. Seek it. None of this sitting around waiting and pondering it in some sentimental way. Her mind was too metal for that.

Death was always so close, the possibility of it, especially in this city. On the streets yes, traffic lights, the darkest hours of the night. Women who walked to and from the taxis along dark tree shaded streets, children left alone for lack of anyone else to watch them, all of this contained the kernel of the ultimate violence. The vacant threat that sat licking its teeth behind every door.

For Gin it was the place too. The denial of death by replacing it with near permanent newness. Johannesburg was a relentless rush to rebirth and rebuild so that in the end it was all built on a pit of bones. Each year another layer was added. Other people's lives, their great and pitiful histories, were piled deep beneath the incandescence of commerce.

Why was anyone surprised? The entire city was meant to be a temporary shelter for those in search of gold. Very little had changed, its streets, buildings, lives, all had the permanence of a tent settlement. Their ropes were always overstretched and fraying in the heat of the sun and softened anew by each afternoon storm. What lay beneath those tents was the promise of gold — but in truth it was mostly granite and dust.

Even tonight, the forty people who would come to her mother's party. What of them? None of them would change or move or ever dare to whisper: 'Is this it?'

She knew from early on that if she was to survive she had to leave. The suburbs that pretended to be part of the city, the lawnmowers and terminal afternoons. The housekeepers in their near identical pie-crust aprons and the endless, endless hours spent listening to stupid old bigots who still liked to believe she left 'because of the blacks'. No one wants to hear that she left because of their tubercular white intelligence, the arrogance of just about every person she was ever expected to talk to. Their entitlement, their laziness, their smug racism, their endless, endless choking jokes about blondes and birds and doll-faces.

All of this, the need to live with full, untainted woman's lungs, made her leave.

Her mother didn't understand how much she hated it, how it threatened her survival, how even another year would be the end of her, so that when the stars aligned – at the most perfect time, when she had just put together a show, just received a letter of funding for the next – she happened by chance to mention to a man – a friend of a friend of someone at the most boring party in the world – that she was an artist and he, Myberg Kamerling, had leant in and told her that he would visit her studio and see what she had on offer – so that then she knew she had to make him get her out. No matter what it cost her. No cost could be too high – she was fighting for her life. And when she was offered the show, the funding, a place to study, Neve had immediately said – no.

'You throw yourself at that man, Virginia, he is twice your age. And what does that make you? What kind of girl does that make you? Answer me?'

'Mom I have to leave. I have to get away from here.'

'Oh are we that bad? Well, I'm sorry you feel that way.'

'It's not about you. Not everything is about you.'

'Well then, what is it? What's wrong with this, everything we've given you? Not enough. Never enough.'

'No. It's not enough. This place, this city is not enough. I can't have the same conversation with the same five people for the rest of my life. Don't you understand that?'

'But what of your eating? What about that? How are you going to be at the other end of the world with all the pressures and no one there to look after you?'

'I will look after me, Mum, I'm not an idiot. I need to get away from here, please. It's this place that's keeping me sick. Mom, I can't survive it. I can't survive in this place, I just can't do it anymore.'

'God, that's ridiculous. Yet again Virginia, you are being an oversensitive drama queen.'

'Mum? I'm drowning here. Can't you see that?'

———

Eventually, Neve went home. Even Nan, light, easy, energetic, could not provide shelter beyond a certain point, and all the time Neve had been dreading what she would find on her return, nothing done, a mess or Gin in a panic pretending everything was in order. That child was in need of constant supervision. The gate rolled back. The frangipani tree looked so clean and lovely against the blue sky. Some clouds coming though. It would rain. Neve glanced to the side of her car to make sure she would not roll into the dog. Not there. Where was Juno? Probably upstairs. Or with Mercy, eating toast crusts.

———

Richard was pleased to be home. He needed the silence and the cool. There was rain coming. He could feel the pressure building. He always got a headache before the storm, an altitude headache. He never got those by the sea.

After putting his briefcase in his study, he went to sit in his chair next to the window. It looked out over the garden. The birds were all splashing in the birdbath. Doves, weavers, a gaudy barbet. It was pleasing.

Inexplicably, he felt he would like a drink. No. It was just three. That would not do. If he moved to the coast, he could drink beer in the afternoon and have Bloody Marys for breakfast. The thought of this wickedness amused him, knowing himself to be a man of such terminal moderation that he owned only one shirt that was not blue or white and he had never worn it. The one time he had put it on he had felt so shocked by his own reflection that he had removed it immediately.

He was pleased to be leaving the city. It could overwhelm a man. Pleased too that in the end the decision (which had somehow already been made) had simply drifted in that morning. He had thought about Mandela and Anne, all gone, and then there had been something about the way his own hand had looked holding the edges of the newspaper. He had looked down and seen his hands, fine wrinkles, knuckles protruding, the fingers bent, liver spots, the faintest of tremors as he turned the page. An old man's hands. And the surprise of seeing those hands, his hands combined with this day, was in the end all that it took.

The ocean, the sky and all the blissful infinity they both suggested.

Soon, I will leave. I will let myself drift on the tides.

———

'Virginia!'

Gin heard the emergency. She managed to get her head together and rush towards her mother's bark.

'What? What's wrong?'

'Juno is gone. She's missing. I told you to keep an eye.' Neve was shaking, eyes darting each way, digging in her handbag for her diary. 'I'm going to phone the vets.'

Mercy stood behind her, chewing her bottom lip and shaking her head.

'Have you looked properly?'

'Of course I have looked properly. Do you take me for a fool? Juno is missing and it is you who have lost her.'

'She won't be far, I'll go find her.'

'The street is full of people Virginia. If anything has happened to her I will never forgive you. You are so self-absorbed you can't even look after Juno for half an hour.' Neve was making her way to the phone but was turning this way and that as she went, as if she had lost everything, as if all around her holes were popping through her life raft.

'I'll find her Mum. Don't be so dramatic.' Seeing her mother unseat so quickly brought panic to Gin so suddenly that hers too was real and raw as she went to snatch a leash and a gate console. 'I've got my phone, call if you find her.'

'You had better find her. I will never forgive you.'

––––––––

It was just like Gin to lose Juno. Just like her. So busy with her party, gates opening and closing and all these people coming and going that she hadn't bothered to make sure the dog was inside the property before she had hit the button to close the gate.

And now she was gone. Neve saw Gin rush to the gate, on foot with her phone and a leash and nothing else.

Neve went to the telephone and called her vet. She had to steady her hands to dial. Old hands. They did not have Juno but would look out for her. And then she called the vet down the hill that had rude staff and the one on Eleventh Street too.

And on my birthday. Juno.

And with all the hundreds of people and cars everywhere for Mandela. Juno would get run over or stolen. She was so trusting and sweet she would hop in the first car that opened a door.

She is my only solace.

———

For Mercy, the problem with Juno going missing was that she, naturally, would be blamed. No matter what had happened or who had left the gate open without first checking where the dog was, no matter at all, she would be blamed. To be the domestic worker in a house meant that even though no decisions were yours, all responsibility was. If a spoon went missing, it was she who had lost it, though of course what was being said was that she had stolen it. If a machine broke, it was she who had done something wrong. Used it incorrectly, cleaned it badly. It was nothing at all to do with the machine itself, which may after years of service, have simply died trying. Mercy knew this and accepted it as a fact of her employment.

With the dog though, things were different. Mrs Brandt had food in the fridge that was reserved solely for the dog to eat. Good food: chicken, pieces of liver. She spoke to the dog with a kindness she never used for her or even for Ginny. That the dog was missing was not good. She felt the slight turning of her stomach that told her this day was becoming too much for her.

'I will go the other way Ma'am. We will find Juno.'

'Take a leash, Mercy.'

She rolled the nylon rope in her pocket and opened the gate. It rolled back on its girders like its own kind of beast. She stepped through. Always a little nervous somehow, as though she expected to be confronted by some or other malice. The street was busy. It surprised her. So many people walking along towards the end of the road and then down. All moving with the same intent along the same path. A pilgrimage, she thought, the path that everyone must walk until they found their place, the voice they would use for prayer. This was a place that Mercy knew. She knew too that even those who do not know God have a place that only they know about. It is their altar.

For her mother it was crocheting with her checkered rug over her knees and the grandchildren, as many as possible, gathered around her feet. Mercy needed a church. She craved it, the building, the people, the fellowship she felt after the service was done. Such singing that she felt the love rise out of her chest in a beautiful explosion of joy.

———

A small beast. A lion. White and gold all at once, a long nose, a great white tail like the sail of a boat, a body that was long and low. Who could this little spirit be? And even as September thought it, he knew. He knew that this was the small one that the old white lady drove around. She went every day at the same time and the little lion sat on the front seat of the car, like a queen. He usually saw them passing near the man who sold peanuts and *vetkoek* on the corner opposite Shadrack, the barber. This was who the small one was.

Here I find you, the small one, covered like a little lion, thick around the neck and with a strong heart. You are an African. Yes, yes and of course I can hear what you say. But you are afraid. You are not in your body, when you are tired and afraid you begin to leave your body. Am I right? It is how we all survive. And you begin to doubt your own lion heart. I know this to be true.

You are too warm, yes? You have travelled far and cannot find your way home. It is too far to go from where you are now, there are many perils. But rest here, small one. Fear no more the heat of the sun. Hide from the scream of car tyres, trucks, beasts in the sky, police with guns. Shall I sing to you?

———

Ginny was out looking for the dog and Mercy knew she should be too. Mrs Brandt had gone back into the house. Mercy hesitated. She needed to walk. And she needed to see where the people were going. What was there, who was there? She wanted to see the faces that were singing the songs she could hear, so many songs one on top of the other, cramming under the bowl of sky like an over-full bus. She wanted to see it all, on this day, an important day. She would look for Juno while she was walking.

The gate closed behind her. She was on the wrong side. She was outside. She felt she should have something in her hands to justify her proximity to freedom. She took the leash from out of her pocket. To the left, in a long row, were Mrs Brandt's white and blue agapanthus. She snapped off a blue one and then thinking she preferred a white one, took one of those too. They were slightly wet, and lovely. Mercy looked up, rain was coming, she would be quick. She turned left onto the road and began to walk towards the Residence.

———

September lifted Juno from where she lay in the damp leaves. She made no protest. He sat where his bed had been with his legs crossed, the dog panting in his lap.

I am September, small one. That there in the middle with lights on it, that is my island. What is it you say? The streets were wide? Yes and you could not see where you were for all the people and the noise and the singing. You weren't far from home. Your people come from over there, in that long line of trees. There is a raising of the nation's voice for the fallen king. That is what you heard.

*They are hymns of love calling out to his ancestors. Your person
will come to find you. Or else I will take you home to that gogo.
I know her.*

*You do not move, but I feel your heart beating still. If you should
die with me, I will bury you, do not be concerned about that. On the
day that you die, I will bury you when the sun is directly overhead
or after it has rolled off the edge of the earth for the night, so that
there should be no shadow on your grave. Do you know the Bible? It
is written there what I must do. Ruth said, where you go I will go,
your people shall be my people and where you die, there shall I die too.
So, small one, I will go with you.*

September considered what to do. The small dog lay so quietly
in his lap. She was tired and had travelled far to be there. She
seemed peaceful. And yet, he had to get back to the Diamond.
His day's work was not yet done. And on this of all days, when all
the world was watching, a tide had washed the foreigners to
African shores. September knew he could not afford to be idle
when there was still so, so much to say. September knew this, felt
the terrible ache of destiny and today of all days felt as though it
might be immense, immeasurable even, as though something
entirely beyond his belief could happen.

*You have a strong heart little lion. You are an African. As am I.
I must get to my place in front of the Diamond. The biggest you
ever saw. As tall as a hundred men and in it, the mining men sit
with their drum bellies.*

I am late. I am late for justice.

*Little Lion, come with me. I know your people, I will take you to
them. They live down the long road of trees, a big green gate, perhaps*

there is a palace behind it, it is along the road from the king. Nkosi.
May he be blessed.

———

The wet of the sweat seemed to rise from Gin's waist up while
sinking down from some awful dank place on the top of her
crown. She walked and ran at intervals, calling for Juno. She
stopped those walking on the streets, asking them all if they had
seen a white and ginger dog with a plumed tail. They had not.
The heat was so encompassing that Gin felt a kind of anger with
it even as tears began to fall. All of it made her wish she could
escape her body and swim into a cool and endless depth of cold
with just the bubbles as they passed her face on each exhalation.
Into the deep she would dive and then with a flip and an arch of
her spine, she would disappear.

Up and down the road she scanned for a tail, flash of white, a
little sail. There were too many people. They were arriving in
multiples. The ANC Women's League in a blaze of green and
gold and black all moving together through the cars, a white
couple holding flowers, Communist Party cadres all walking and
singing and dancing, everyone seemed to be shifting and moving.
Juno would never be found. Never in all of this.

———

September gathered his bag and his placard together. He decided
that he needed to wear his placard all along the road despite its
weight. It would free up his arms to carry the small one. Even as
he slid the boards onto his shoulder he could feel the heat of the
pain spike through his flesh. He remembered where Juno lived.

He knew the streets of the neighbourhood like he knew his
own heart – all the little arteries and veins pumping and pulsing,

the sidewalks, the rubble that blocked the blood's flow from one place to another. He knew he was looking for a green gate halfway down the road that intersected with the wider road of the Residence. He lifted Juno. She fumbled with her legs, then settled so softly into his arms. A soft panting prayer of a body, so very close to his own. September took a moment to stand in the shade of his garden. Birdsong. Wings. Light overhead.

And he felt suddenly that this terrible, unexpected proximity to love rent right through the walls of his heart.

————

At the intersection Gin paused. To her right was a man, ragged - her neck pricked. He was running and carrying a sack or a bag and a placard. She was shaking, upended by the streets and the dog and the day. She felt the tides begin to drift around her, the sense that she was no longer on solid ground. If a wave had suddenly come around the corner and roared up the avenue, lifted her up and tumbled her to her death there was nothing she would do to fight it because all day, she had been expecting it. She could not say that she had not been warned.

The man continued to shout. She moved more quickly.

And all along the thought of her mother. That she had lost Juno and would never be forgiven. And that was it. She would never be forgiven. Neve would forget the party no matter how beautiful it was and she would say, for years, that this was the day that the dog had been lost and it was Virginia who had lost her.

The man was far enough away now but he still seemed to be shouting at her directly. So she turned instead, walked with purpose towards the long row of hydrangeas that laced the bottom of the metres high wall. Deep and blue as if to apologize for the vulgarity of the ramparts and its electric wire noosed around the top. Along the length of the wall she stooped to look under the deep foliage, aching to see a tell-tale tuft of a tail. Calling and calling and knowing it was all hopeless.

I have lost her. I have lost myself.

She wiped her hand across her forehead and saw a man approach. He looked like a gardener perhaps, dressed in khaki trousers and shirt and fiddling with his phone so that he did not look up. She had to say twice, 'Excuse me sir, excuse me,' and then show him the picture she had of Juno on her phone and give him her phone number and make sure he knew there was a reward if he found the dog.

She would repeat this over and over to guards and security patrols and groups of nannies with children in strollers and housekeepers and other gardeners all along these streets which on another day, she might have thought beautiful or at least impressive in scale despite the wire and the gates and the guards. But that would have to have been a day on which Juno was home safely in her garden, sunning her small self and rolling over with a languid stretch in a way that humans always envied.

———

September had seen Gin, coming up the hill wiping her head. She looked as if there had been tears and he immediately knew she was looking for her small one. She was weeping for her lion and so he shouted out, 'Ma! Ma! Ma! Here I am!'

He ran towards her carrying Juno and his placard and he shouted 'Ma!' again because he knew how important it was.

She looked afraid.

He shouted, 'Don't be afraid I have news on the little lion, she is not dead, do not cry, I have her, she is out of the sun, the heat was too much so I have hidden her under this cloth. She has nothing more to fear, Ma!'

The lights changed so that a bank of cars started up the hill and September could no longer see Gin clearly. She flashed behind the windows of the cars and trucks and she walked faster too, though bent and heavy. She did not look up. He knew she could not see him. And with the great roar of the engines and the wheels round and round, and hooting taxies saying come over here, I am going to Soweto, Town, Sandton, hooting and hooting, she would not hear him either.

'Ma! I have your small one! Ma!'

A police van, two and then three. He stopped shouting. He could not afford to be seen. He knew their hearts, those devils. They would beat him all over again and burn his things, his identity papers and all his belongings so that he would again not exist. They often did this. The police could cause a man to disappear in that way.

But September's body ached each day to tell him he was still here. His hump, the line of it against the sky, told him he was alive. His hump made people look at him, stare at him even and this too made him feel alive. To be seen was the thing.

I exist no matter the papers I do or do not have. I am alive.
Here I am.

The police vans rolled towards the Residence. He was safe. *Nkosi*, thank you God.

———

Neve, having called all the vets and the neighbours and having taken the car around a few blocks, had returned home. There were too many people and she needed to wait by the phone in case someone called. Juno had a disc around her neck with her name and a number etched into the metal.

Neve felt her strength draining. Surely they could not have a party now, not with Juno gone? She went to sit under the tree again, a phone at her side.

You must find your way back to me.

Neve felt, as she sat, the unwelcome return of a feeling she had only recently begun to register. She could not name it, it drifted, unattached, a kind of untreated grief. Not so much outright fear as it was an unease, a lack of confidence perhaps, the feeling that they were all, always, so very close to death.

You are my only solace. All of the long nights, longer days, the hospital afternoons.

She felt the sun easy on her shoulders as she picked up a pine-cone. She brought a couple home from the park each day for Juno to gnaw on under the stars. She could not shake it, her sense of loss, her sense that something in her had changed.

I have lost my nerve.

Brandt women and her family of women were strong. Practical. Powerful even, if needs be. And yet there was always Aunt Virginia, the blight on this lineage of powerful women. Other women in the family had excelled in medicine, like Neve herself, others ran academic departments, schools, all while having children and keeping beautiful homes. Aunt Virginia had decided that she would write books. Not just any books either. Books that would have her in the newspapers and on watch lists, as the white

Nationalist government branded her a trouble maker. And she was of course.

Her first book chronicled, in some vivid detail, the affair of a white suburban 'madam' and her black gardener. It was of course banned immediately but Aunt Virginia had kindly offered a copy to the family so that they wouldn't miss out. Neve knew that this was simply a ploy to get them to read it so that she could shock them all anew. Attention seeking was all it was. Endlessly mortifying. 'Isn't she your aunt? Quite a gal I hear.' The less said about her the better. She did have a lovely name though, and a certain energy about her that was appealing. But possibly it was a mistake to name Gin after her. It could be construed as homage to her madness.

And she was mad. No other word could describe her. Parties in that house on the sea that went on for days. All sorts turned up, her writer friends, activists and hangers-on. Journalists, that artist and his endless women, the one who didn't seem to know how to paint but just cut out bits of paper and stuck them on newsprint. Not pretty work. The Nationalist newspapers even said she had had affairs with Indian dissidents and, oh, it was all so ridiculous. It was as if she were purposefully saying, here I am, look at me. And they did.

Aunt Virginia was feted in Europe of course and gave a lecture tour in America. As usual, that lot of lunatic liberals thinking they know better and encouraging this sort of behaviour by calling Virginia: 'brave and reactionary', 'a voice for the voiceless'. A voice that Neve would rather not have to hear. She seemed so benign when they were growing up, Aunty Virginia, a little 'sensitive' they had been told, and certainly she never liked children – whom she claimed were 'the devil's way of crushing the truth that women writers must speak'. More nonsense.

It was with some despair that Neve had noticed Gin trading on her great-aunt's notoriety. Her first show in New York, when she was still in the clutches of that awful leery Kamerling man, the pamphlet for the show, if that was what you called it, had announced that she was the great-niece of the notorious anti-apartheid writer and activist. The great-aunt of the startling new arrival on the Manhattan art scene blah blah blah. Stomach churning.

Ibises were rustling overhead. It was getting hot. Or perhaps it was the bile rising. Was Gin a startling talent? Did it matter? In the end, she had lost Juno. And she herself was lost. At least there was some hope that Juno would be found. Neve had given up on Gin years before.

———

September, as he readjusted his shoe, still holding Juno, had the feeling that the world was moving away from him. That he was moving one way, towards death, and the rest of the world, the city, was moving in another direction, chasing life. Each time he called out to someone who turned away from him, simply did not hear him, he let himself think, am I still here? That woman, that man, that family who just looked ahead behind their car windows, rolled up so high, they did not look left or right to let him know they had seen him there. He knew with certainty that every single time that happened he leaned just a little closer to death.

The day the taxi driver yelled at him as he nearly ran him over. The vehicle was so close that September felt the blast of death fan out from the side of the taxi as it shot past. There was no reason he had not been hit, skittled across the earth by the force of the impact. That day was the day it all began to change.

After it happened he had somehow managed to get off his

island. His chest, though unhurt, felt as if it was ripped wide open, exposed to the air, organs and bones all gaping into the street. When he was back in his garden (he could not say how he got there), he dug himself in under the grapevines and the weeping haze of willow leaves and stayed there until late the next day. He felt he never wanted to leave, just lie there until he fell asleep from hunger and thirst. For to be alive was, he knew, a terrible thing.

But he did wake and what he felt was not disappointment or relief but rather, unexpectedly, that he knew there was nothing more he could do to be seen, to exist. No more demands could be made. Without the pennies that were sometimes tossed to him on the corner and the bits he scavenged from the bins around the backs of the restaurants, he could do no more. He knew then that he would never plaster another wall, peel another potato, chat with comrades, easy and safe. As he lay there, the damp ground was strangely comforting. He knew, in the way that you know your own mother's voice, that the fraying had already begun. He would soon be no more solid than a head of butterflies that at any time could have their wings ripped from their bodies should the wind change direction and the storms breach the crests of the Drakensberg. And he also knew that allowing himself to say this, admit it, meant that death would, from that day, hang on his back.

———

Mercy moved with confidence. If anyone she knew asked why she was there she would say she was looking for the dog, for Juno. She was. But she was really there to see, to hear what was being said, to join in the prayers, to take her flowers to the Residence. She took them for Tata Mandela but in her heart she took them for the women too, for Ma Winnie, for Ma Graça. For

168

all the stories she heard over and over again were Mandela was this long on Robben Island and Mbeki was there too and poor old this-one was in exile for so long and poor old that-one was beaten three times.

So, that is what happened.

But what of Ma Winnie? They speak of her so poorly, saying she practises witchcraft, and she killed those boys, they said, and she causes upset and shouts at the whites when already we are meant to have forgotten all of that. Why is the woman the witch and the man the new Jesus?

Well, thought Mercy, her back stiffening, you lock me in a room no larger than a toilet cubicle, like they did to Ma Winnie, with no windows and no lights and switch the bulbs on and off so I don't know what is day and what is night, and leave me there for 491 days. You will see what I am when I come out.

You come to my home, before dawn, the birds still stretching out their wings. You arrest me in front of my children, the oldest just ten years old. Shackle me, insult me. My babies calling out to me, trying to keep me by clinging to my skirts. 'Mamma don't leave us, Mamma what will happen?' And from the moment the doors of the police van shut, I will not know who is looking after my babies. Neighbours are kind. There is family of course, but they will never know that the one likes to sleep with a light on and that drinking milk will make the younger one sick.

Mercy knew that it was only God that kept Ma Winnie alive. Taken away from her babies. No day or night. No sunlight, wind or rain to tell her she was still alive. These flowers were for Ma Winnie and the others were for Ma Graça for her care of the old man in his last days.

*

Neve tried to call Gin three times and before the fourth, she placed the telephone back in its cradle and realized that Gin was either unable to hear the ring or was choosing to ignore it. Both of these meant that Juno had not yet been found. Perhaps Mercy had found her. Juno loved Mercy.

————

Do not be afraid small one. Though you are the lion and I the lamb, I will give you shelter.

The white woman was much further away now. She must be going back to her house. September thought she looked angry. Or sad. It was hard to tell them apart sometimes. Perhaps it was because of the sun. September knew how it made him feel somedays when he turned and accidentally looked right at it. It seemed to penetrate through his skull and into the nerves.

If the woman would just stop, just rest a while in the shade, he could catch up to her and show her that her small lion was well. But she kept on. It might be the heat or she might just be too white. They are all a bit angry on account of their emptiness. His father had told him.

'You must pity the whites,' he had said, 'they have nothing but their power.' He had said this when they still had it. 'They have no culture, no identity, no ritual, when their people die they have some songs from another country to sing. When we sit under God's own sky and tell stories that our ancestors have known, stories that come out of the earth, the rocks of the Drakensberg, out of the sands of the Kalahari, stories that we have heard on the thunder, what do they do? They go to the shopping mall. These people ...' And his father would shake his head, wave a hand across himself to push away the smoke from his pipe as he spoke.

'They have nothing, you must pity them.' He always placed his hand on his heart as he said it.

September knew he would have to take the small lion to the woman's home. Every time he shouted to her on the street she ran away. He thought she might be stupid for not hearing him but then he remembered she might not speak the language. He decided to follow along behind her, a block or two to make sure he went to the correct house. Then, he would continue on to the Diamond.

Ahead of him, the woman was looking first under bushes then putting her hands on her hips and leaning backwards. Her back hurts, thought September.

Hey, sister! You looking for your culture under there? Ha!

He thought that was a good joke, and he suddenly imagined the streets full of white folk wandering all over the place looking first under bushes that their gardeners had planted along the streets and then under the motorway bridges and in rubbish bins, hoping to find their history. The history they did find would shame them so terribly. Maybe, some kindly cadres might try and teach them some Struggle songs but in the end they would not even understand the language so they would just be moving their lips.

The woman, long hair (blue at the ends, snakes), went around the corner, talking on her phone and running her other hand up the back of her neck. Her hair was tied up high on her head and was swinging left to right as she went, golden, dark like the honey he and his little brother Mpho used to steal from the bees when they were small. His little brother, long since dead from the disease, never got stung, not once. Perhaps that is why he thought the disease would never touch him. September was always getting stung, so badly that his mother would have to swathe him in cool cloths and break open an aloe leaf, thick and cold and juicy and spread the gel all over his skin and there he would lie until the burning and the swelling would stop. 'It is because you are so sweet, child, you are made of sugar.' Wouldn't be worth stinging the woman with the honey hair, too thin even for bees.

September looked up at the sky. It was less splintered than it had been earlier. The clouds were full and round. They looked like hydrangeas. White.

He felt more whole. Perhaps it was the little lion still resting in his arms. She had a strong heart and holding her allowed him to feel very much a part of the world. This was her gift to him. It was so close to love. He knew this but he could also hear her thoughts as they tumbled through her mind. She wanted to be home. He had taken his gift from her and now, to thank her, he would take her home.

The clouds. If he was too late to the Diamond he would get wet in the four o'clock storm.

———

In an hour or so, it would rain. Dudu could feel the air bristle. She was trying to tidy away the shopping the family she worked for had bought the previous weekend. A weekend never seemed to pass when they did not have something new. Toys for the children, clothes for the wife, wine for him. Always more and more and more. It added to the chaos that already seemed to rule the house. And for someone such as herself, Dudu found it unsettling. They threw away things too. Good things, hardly worn or used. Every party resulted in bags of food being thrown away as if it held no value. September always looked forward to her family's parties. It meant meat, pudding, sometimes wine.

She not only disliked the family, but judged them too. She considered them weak, incomplete. And yet, inexplicably, given their multiple shortcomings, both they and their friends felt bold enough to complain about 'the blacks' as if she were not standing there, holding the ice bucket or moving around the dinner table, clearing the plates.

———

How was it that she still looked so young? Dangerous even. All tight denim and dark skin and undone hair. American sex. Peter knew he was older than her in every possible way. He bored himself half to death. Little wonder she saw nothing in him and saw right through him all at once.

I will never be enough.

The night Gin met Myberg Kamerling, the night she touched his arm but then called Peter in from the garden so sit with her at dinner, she broke his heart again. As if one slice of the knife was not enough.

She made sure she and Peter sat side by side, moved place names on the long table, all laid out with white linen and plates and glasses that ended in gold. But also, though he only knew it once they were all sitting down, Gin had moved Myberg Kamerling to sit opposite her, directly in her eye-line and, oh the cruelty, placed Peter to her right so that she would not have to make polite conversation with someone she did not know. She had Peter. She could ignore him, make no effort at all and every time Myberg Kamerling looked up, it was Gin he would see.

Peter remembered leaving the party before it was polite to do so. He didn't care. He had drunk too much. He drove, radio on, shouting out the words to the songs, refusing to cry. No police would stop him. And if they did he had enough cash to deal with it.

In the end no one stopped him. He drove to Melville where there was another party, a student party fuelled by weed and cheap cider.

By the time the sun thought about rising, after five sometime, he left the house already knowing that he would have to deal with Deborah. (Curly haired and freckled.) He had taken her into the room at the back of the property, passed a joint back and forth and then kissed her to test her resolve. Knowing all along that she fawned after him just enough that she wouldn't mind. Even he knew it was wrong as he shifted himself onto her then into her because, as ever, it had nothing to do with Deborah and everything to do with Gin.

On the way home he bought coffee and went to sit on the bench in the park. It allowed him a view of the whole sweep of green that ended in the river. Beyond that still, a bank of trees, huge eucalyptus trees behind neat rows of shorter wilge and karee trees.

Stiffness and booze began to rest in his joints and his muscles and he saw the cars starting to arrive, park-up, three or four or five churchgoers stepped out. He had forgotten it was Sunday. They were identically dressed, head to foot in white with sashes in blue or green or yellow, women with covered heads and some of the men carried a staff. They assembled in the shade towards the river. The women and men sat separately under the trees for they would be there all day and the heat would be intense as the day got going.

Peter fell asleep, but was woken by the persistent nose of a black dog whose ball had rolled under his bench. The singing of the churchgoers filled the air all around him, as if their song was in fact rising out of the deep of him, was in him and of him, as if he too were singing. Over it all, the priest was shouting out incantations of God and hope and redemption as he held a man or woman or child in the river, baptizing them and cleansing them of their demons to appease God and the ancestors. And then, across the parkland, out of the great burning blue of the sky came a blanket of butterflies, pure white, they came in great swathes moving left to right across his frame. More and more, these banks of butterflies came. It felt like a dream, a vision. A moment of grace, in this city, in this park with its homeless camp on the far bank, its cricket players, dog walkers and drunk, lonely men.

Peter knew that if he was to survive himself, survive Gin with some kind of hope still intact, he had to let her go.

———

Gin looked at her phone. No news from her mother. Juno was not found. Only the three missed calls from Peter earlier in the day. Why had he come to the house? Probably he hadn't given it much thought, hadn't considered she might not wish to see him, might be busy. Simply arrived. Pained and pale.

He just floated, Peter, into a job, into an engagement to a girl he worked with. A relationship that lasted two years and by all accounts, confounded everyone. Some of their mutual friends hadn't even realized he was dating someone. Then, he broke it off and left the girl devastated.

He seemed incapable of seeing that his own inaction, lack of clear decision, his drift and flux was as destructive as if he had taken a hard line from the beginning. He drifted along until he found himself in a corner and only then, panicked, he reacted, when the damage was already done, the die already cast.

He lacked substance. Even his aesthetic was borrowed. His own apartment, the last she had seen it, was furnished by the developer, down to the plates he ate off.

'Would you not have preferred to choose your own stuff, or get someone to help you? I could have helped you.'

He just waved a hand across the living room and said, 'It's easier this way.'

He didn't lack an appreciation of beauty or craft or the love people put into making some things, good things, proper things, things with provenance and patina. He just seemed, over time, to have distanced himself from them. It was as if proximity to beauty might shatter him completely.

———

Peter pretended to read the changes Mogomotsi wanted made to the Verloren brief. He didn't care, the whole mess, once urgent, had become nothing more than a series of hieroglyphs scratched across a page. He could no longer engage with it with any energy. He simply let the papers wash across his desk, this way and that. And today, at least, the world was watching something else.

Gin did not seem in the least moved by it all. Had she even mentioned it? He could not recall. She was all business, organizing her party. Her party, which despite it being for her mother's birthday would, in the end, be Gin's party. Seeing her there, on the verandah, impenetrable, wearing red lipstick strangely brazen on her face, she still looked as if she was chiselling her way through her day, her life even, tap tap tap at the rock face with a kind of bloody-mindedness. He knew there was still some sort of tug, a line maybe that ran from him to her, so that he felt he might like to see how it would be to reel back towards her, closer again, just to see if he could survive it. He knew that it was an idea only a masochist would entertain.

He would go to the party.

———

Gin could feel her lungs burn from running along sidewalks, calling for Juno, the fear of what she might find. All as the day's heat began to gather towards the storm that would surely come. The air was thick, conjuring its moisture to the sky. Every last drop that had fallen the night before would be percolated and lifted just high enough to be returned to the earth again.

Her jeans stuck to her skin and her hair was heavy with damp. Everything felt so painfully wrong. As if one of the poles had suddenly lost its gravitational pull.

She tried to breathe more slowly, take in more air. Johannesburg sits at six thousand feet above sea level. Breathing in, breathing out took some focus, forcing her attention to what should be the unconscious mechanisms of living. Even while she fought for breath, she could hear the helicopters still, the constant clattering of blades and air colliding so that she could feel it in her chest cavity where the air was trying to fight through.

I cannot breathe.

Juno. The consequence of this small creature not being where she should be began to feel so monstrous, so overwhelming.

Gin needed some shade and walked to the end of the wall, close to four metres tall and devoid of any shrubs or trees that thieves might use to scale it. This was the architecture of paranoia. But then, beyond that wall, an oddly ramshackle, half collapsed wall offered shady recess.

Shade, rest, breathe.

Gin wiped her forehead and chin and tried to roll her head against her neck. What was this place? In all the perfectly built fortressing suddenly this anomaly, this carbuncle. Where once there were neat wooden fence panels mounted onto a small red brick wall, including a couple of wooden slabs for the gates, now there was a weave of planks; any old pieces of timber cobbled across one another to keep prying eyes out. They offered no real protection from intruders and the gate was slumped open, slouching into its own hinges. It was unsettling to see a house in Johannesburg so blatantly unguarded.

In this neighbourhood, no one had any idea what anyone else's house looked like from the street. The most you got was a greedy glance, grabbed as a gate rolled back on its girders. Then you would see a row of topiaries or silver birches up a long sweep or a flowering tree overhanging expensive panelled garage doors, also on girders and ready to swing up like a mouth for a car and its occupants, then slap its jaws shut and swallow before any intruders rushed in after, triggers cocked, heads raging. In for a penny in for a pound.

———

Heavenly Father, Blessed Mother, bless our father, bless Tata and
Ma Winnie and Ma Graça, bless the children and grandchildren.
Let them know love, let them find peace, let them be free from fear.

Mercy crossed herself. She would have to go back to work. There was the party to attend to after all. She had left the chickens marinating. The vegetables were cut, great platters of trout and potatoes all covered and cooling in the fridge. She knew Ginny had already forgotten the food.

The dog had not been found.

She stood back from the wide circle of candles and flowers and notes that formed an altar on the pavement outside the Residence. There were many white people there too. Behind her the church group sang, the women all together, strong and powerful and true and beyond them the Cadres: 'My mother was a house-girl, my father was a garden boy, that's why I'm a Communist, that's why I'm a Communist.' And there was toyi-toying, lines of cadres, (AZAPO, Azania, NUMSA, ANC, PAC, SACP), all the names and t-shirts with the faces of heroes across the front (Biko, Hani, too many to name), fallen and gone, toyi-toyi, one leg up and then the other, hop-hop, and flags and banners raised. Drums, deep and thunderous. Song, beauty, light, clouds whipping past so that the sun flashed. The noise echoed in Mercy's stomach.

You will hear us inside the Residence. The walls will shake with our song, the drums will wake the roots of the trees, stir the earth beneath that house, the windows will rattle with our love. And this is right. This is how it must be.

The crowd was gathering pulse, a great single heart singing and moving.

Amandla! came the call and all around Mercy, voices and fists lifted and called their response, *Ngawethu!*

And Mercy knew the next call would come and it came, *Mayibuye!*

For the first time in her life, *Mayibuye!* She felt her arm raise up in a fist, round and hard, a rock, above her head and a great roll of thunder, a flash of light through the fast chasing clouds. And her voice came out of her with the strength of all her mothers and grandmothers before her.

———

A great cry was raised from the Residence so that it seemed to carry the whole city along. Gin stood immobile in front of the open gates with the crumbling pillars and billowing, weed-choked verges.

The smell was of decaying leaves, musty and damp. The hair on her neck told her she was afraid. She stepped forward up the two concrete strips meant for car tyres, now cracked and overrun with grass, and walked into the garden. A shift, as if a ghost had materialized, expectant and waiting. More than anything she could hear birds, agitated in joyful clamour.

In front of her a house. It was sunk in on itself, deflated in the middle. The long roof drooped over the verandah, which had also begun to sag with sorrow. It was still held up on either side by identical Cape Dutch facades facing into the garden. Each facade held expansive bay windows. Much of the glass was gone and what panes remained were covered over by varying degrees of dirt and lichen. Moss gripped the outer reaches.

She walked up the five stairs onto the verandah. Its floors, she could see, had once been red polished concrete but were now faded and pocked. There was a mouldy sofa at the back and three white plastic garden chairs, an old unconnected television. Everywhere bottles and cartons of all kinds, beer, soda and milk.

'Hello? Hello?'

There was no sound from the house though the birds continued to sing, which gave Gin some comfort. Some of the bottles were clean and new.

'Hello? Anyone there? I'm looking for my dog.'

A child's cry for a lost puppy, mocked by the density of the tangle all about her. The verandah led around to the left, she followed it, noticing cigarette stumps, a hoola-hoop and more rubbish. Leaves too, all left to decay along with these shards of human detritus.

Just as she rounded the corner trying to avoid yet more broken glass she found a child, no more than ten or eleven, peeping around the corner, eyes wide against her small face. She was pretty and shy.

'Hello, don't be afraid, please don't, is your mother here? I'm looking for a dog, a little dog.' Gin tried to indicate Juno's size with her hands. 'May I look around your garden?'

The child stepped forward to reveal she was wearing a school uniform, bottle-green and khaki, from the local state school, an old and venerable institution. The girl held a baby on her left hip like a doll.

'Oh, you're just home from school. I'm sorry, I'm just looking for the dog. Do you think your mother will mind? Are there any grown ups here I can ask?'

'No. You can look.'

And with that the girl went back inside with her charge and Gin heard a screen door tap back against a frame. There were clearly adults living there, probably off at work.

Gin passed under a washing line on which hung a few terry nappies, another skirt to match the rest of the school uniform, an adult woman's shirt and dress, some men's jeans and a few socks and pieces of underwear. She looked back at the house.

There couldn't be any running water or electricity in there and what there was would have to be jimmy-rigged off the mains. Were they squatting illegally or allowed to stay there? The owners were likely the children of a deceased couple. They probably didn't even live in the country, but were holding onto the property anyway, waiting until the same business rights that had been granted to all the surrounding plots, had been extended to theirs. Then they could put the house up for sale, ask the moon for it. In the meantime they let it suffer the indignity of pillage and ruin.

The garden was artless and dense. A mangle of limbs and leaves.

'Juno? Jube-Jube?'

She knew there was no point calling to her, she would be in some sort of frozen fear, rolled up under a piece of card or in a drain just like her mother's beagle had been that time it ran up the dirt road in a thunderstorm. Lost.

———

The king is dead. I will be getting along to the other side too, soon. Soon. I can hear them calling me, my own people, my own father, calling me home to the place where the king has gone. But I have heard them for years, calling me to act, to stand up. 'Rise up!' they say because soon enough your time will come and you will lie down forever without having ever stood your ground.

And though my spine is bent I stand straight. I stand.

As did you, little lion, you stood up and walked instead of sitting and waiting. You heard the call. Smelled it on the wind. But there are those who prefer that you wait. It is the same for me. My sitting and my waiting keeps food in their bellies. And big bellies they are too, like drums, the hide stretched tight across the barrel.

So, I walk and I walk alone. I have been walking my whole life. But at Verloren I did not walk alone. I stood with armies. For the first time, I was one of many, all the fighters and comrades and cadres of the nation, the sons and daughters of Shaka, Hintsa, Sekhukhune.

I am the warrior child of Moshoeshoe, Cetshwayo. I stood tall and straight for Mphephu and for Ngungunyane, all these warriors who have come before. I stood not for my tribe, but for my nation and I am one of many in a nation who stand up.

We are the spear of the nation who will never dishonour the cause of freedom. For it has been spoken. We have heard it from the mouths of princes.

I will walk, holding my fists round and hard as ancient roots. And know this, those roots will grow until we cover the land with our beautiful vines, thick and full of fruit.

But, small one, I will dress my justice in agapanthus and willow. Acacia thorns. Butterflies, moths and crickets will all be fraying from my crown so that though they will see I call for justice, I have clothed myself in love. Here I am.

September, with Juno in his arms and his placard biting into his flesh, continued on his course for the house where he knew Gin and Juno lived, along with her mother and Mercy. It was number eight. He moved slowly. He knew he had far to go and crossed back and forth as he went to keep himself and his companion in the shade.

He liked to assign a sin to houses. The house of sloth, of avarice. He counted them as he went and assigned to each block a sin as he went. He knew he would not do it to the home of the small one (tall and deep green) when he eventually found it. To do this to a home whose people you knew was wrong. Particularly so as he held the little lion so close that he could feel her heart beating next to his. How soft, how loving, her chin resting now on his forearm. The smallest drop of saliva escaping her mouth and rolling down his arm.

*

Gin knew she was being watched by the bright-eyed girl inside the house. She wanted to ask to look inside, part of her wondering if the child had Juno in a room in the house of mystery. Had Juno arrived, the fluffy little dog she had always wanted, the dog that looked like it had flopped down off the screen of a children's film? But of course the more likely reality was that Juno was down a storm drain, drowned and washing miles underneath the city. Her body would turn up in a nest of branches and rags under a bridge, like that woman, years back. She had washed up on the river banks after the floods. No one claimed the body and eventually the papers stopped asking for information.

Gin turned back to the garden. She didn't know where to start, everywhere in the malachite gloom there were old plastic beer crates, an upturned bath, filled to the top with water over which bottles, leaves and plastic seemed to grow like a rancid fungus.

She felt so uninvited in this miserable, wounded dream. The Cape Dutch gables accused her of imposition. She went towards the banks of hydrangeas and the junk that lay underneath them.

'Juno?'

The smell of faeces was so intense that she had to hold her hand over her nose and mouth. A bed of flattened cardboard and newspapers, a rolled up jumper, some bottles, an empty can of beans. Jesus someone was sleeping here too, in addition to those squatting in the house. Juno would never be here. She would be too afraid.

The hydrangeas ran along the side of the house and wedged in the branches were babies' nappies, the modern kind, all just rolled up, covered in whatever they held and hidden in the foliage. Why live like this? You have this house, why not live here like kings, in cleanliness and beauty.

My skin is spooling out into the world. I am vanishing.

Gin felt tears rise again. The heat meant her shirt was beginning to stick to her back. Clouds were gathering, the humidity rising. She moved to the shadier side of the garden, all the time ducking down low to try and look under all the bushes and benches, there were three, in case a small, white muzzle protruded. She moved as quickly as she could so that she could get to where the smell of waste was less overwhelming.

———

September found himself on the corner of Eleventh Avenue before it ran down to the Residence. He was not far from getting the small bundle home. But the sound, the beautiful singing and hoes, hoes-hoes as the cadres danced and toyi-toyied. The drums, the women ululating, all the beautiful sounds of mourning made him stop. He squeezed his arms closer around the small one he carried, held her as close as he dared. Suddenly, as he did, and in a way he had long since forgotten, he could feel great waves of love rolling through the cloud-thickening air towards him as the people sang.

The shock of love, the immensity of it, its vast outer shores, its unfathomable reach, drenched him all through and left him feeling that he, crippled, bent and rent, had ceased to exist.

I am clothed in love.

Here came a white family, small children with flags and paper with things written on it, flowers. September let himself look at the child. The parents would not see. The child, a girl, no more than five thought September, looked up at him, wide eyes, serious, her lips pursed in concentration. September could not help himself. He smiled at her, despite knowing better. People did not like him talking to the children. In case they caught his spine disease, whatever that was. He felt this as another great sorrow in his catalogue of prohibitions, for he liked children. He felt his face pull hard against the smile, his scarred and broken face, but he did it anyway. The girl by then had to look over her should to see him, which she did, searching and squinting, and just before she carried on to the Residence, she smiled back. More or less. It was enough.

These streets are great rivers of love, and the fish that leap and swim through them are all the words we speak and all the songs we sing.

———

Sticking out of the trees like bones were white pillars, what remained of a pergola. And like a shock, Gin saw among the paint-flaked femurs, perfect bunches of new grapes. Like jewels hung from the ear of a sun-bleached skeleton. They were nowhere near ripe, still hard little beads.

The garden was freeing its ghosts one after the other and as it did Gin felt herself divide over and over again, rendering her inarticulate to herself. In among the plastic and leaves and shit, she began to notice roses too, pinks and the palest butter yellow. And lilies, poking through the grass that grew to over knee-height around them. The garden somehow continued to forge through, to show its seasons, push a bud, find the light, despite the wild that enclosed it, the vines and the decay and the stench.

Directly below her, at the base of the steps that lead to what could have once been a tennis court was a sundial, or at least a plinth where one used to stand. Through the grass and rubble the faint memory of a formal garden, quadrants, neat and square with a path that crossed through the middle and then again in the opposite direction, and where they met, the column, its concrete spine, straight and defiant, unmoved by time. Whatever sat on top, brass perhaps, was long gone, just three of four holes, one on each corner where the instrument had been held. Into the sun, squinting at the shout of it. Even with the trees so swollen, the beams would still know how far the day had progressed. Three o'clock, four o'clock.

The shadow falls.

———

Neve opened her writing desk. It had been Aunt Virginia's. The glossy rosewood swung so easily back and behind it sat all the little compartments. Stamps in this one, envelopes in that, a key here and in the little drawer that the key locked, a little pouch of photographs. She retrieved it. She knew there was a good one of Juno in there. She would take it to the park and show it around.

I cannot lose her. I am too weary for all of this. I am too old.

She found the picture of Juno easily, it was on top. She lifted it off the pile and there below was a picture of Gin. A portion of her anyway. A basket of puppies, Gin behind them, some of her head was cut off by the edge of the picture. The next was a black and white picture of herself, her sister Diana and Aunt Virginia. She didn't even remember it being taken. It was before she or Diana were married. Virginia was striking looking. You could say that much. Like an egret they always said.

When she had done it, drowned herself, there was such consternation, such outrage. To do such a thing, and on her eightieth birthday too. Virginia always had to be difficult. Just walked into the sea, they said. Who would do such a thing?

Neve placed her thumb over her own face on the photograph.

Who indeed?

———

All night Virginia's beach house had throbbed and boomed with guests, the music, mostly Count Basie, Bird, came with a belly-deep roll that seemed to merge with the thunder of the sea that boomed and drummed along the shore, boom-bissh-boom-bam-bish. It was like the old times, guests drunk and rabbling, oblivious to what they were saying and not caring. Politics, music, protest, art; all these ideas, still roughly formed and soft, not yet muscular enough to find their way into the world. Instead they bounded out across the drawing room floor like untrammeled puppies on a green lawn.

The room's French windows were open on all three sides so that you felt you might be on a ship, on the waves. Air and sea and house all became one. At night the waves felt so much closer and darker than during daylight. It was as if they might suddenly take the whole house in their mouth and let their jaws fall shut. Some nights Virginia would lie in her bed, Leo asleep next to her, and feel the sea right inside her, feel that she too was water and that the thunder she could hardly bear in her own head was the same as that of the sea, all scale and fish and empty shells and terrible, bewildering depths.

But that night she was throwing herself a party. She was turning eighty, or was due to turn eighty in the coming week. Leo, whom she had known for nearly sixty years (as friend, lover, husband, ex-husband and now friend and life companion again) had been so enthused by the idea. Unlike him, usually so quiet and ponderous.

Eighty hot summers of Virginia. Her dress was such a pale, icy blue as to seem white on top. But, as the folds thickened in the fullness of the skirt as it fell towards the floor, it took on the deeper hue of the ocean, squid ink and iodine, as if she had already dipped her feet in the foam along the shore. Heavier too, the beading around the hem and skirt, swirls and arabesques that meant the skirt dragged its weight around her feet, a jewelled anchor.

She is gracious, an egret, her silver hair swept up to reveal her neck, her beautiful nape, thinks Leo, as he passes her and smiles to acknowledge her. This beautiful night, all orchestrated to express his adoration of this woman and the admiration of the others who were still to come.

Virginia welcomed them all as they came in through the garden, up from the gravel drive to the door, bookended with lanterns and great pots of hydrangeas. The house that books built had a wide hall that opened out into the rest of the house. Though the guests cannot see the ocean in the dark, they know it is there and just that, its proximity, its jeopardy, makes the night quicken to life.

She told Leo to invite everyone, friend or enemy, the only proviso being that they were somehow important to her, even if that position came as a result of bitter dispute. Some would not come, but she noted there were a few here who drank her wine and ate her food and yet, still, would wish her ill. It pleased her.

A few of the younger ones, couples (always so tedious), had expressed disdain and declined the invitation when she made it clear that no children were invited. They were at the ocean, it was holiday-time, could not their well-behaved and lovely sons attend?

No.

The men look so handsome, thought Virginia, and so upright in themselves. So smartly tucked and tied. Though time had passed and they were no longer young and dangerous, swimming naked, stealing caresses beneath the waves, driving too fast along the dusty roads to the beach, booze in the picnic basket, all reckless skin and sun and long loving nights. Tonight though, all were correct in their jackets and their advancing years, despite the dangerous sea. And all eyes on Virginia. This was the exact result the evening had been designed to produce. Even her own vanity raised a pleasure in her, knowing that all of her, her failings and her victories, was present on this night.

Flowers billowed out of great urns on every table, roses. At the coast. Some of the women were heard to say, 'Where did she get them?' Platters filled to tipping point with Knysna oysters, crab and Mozambique prawns. A band played music that reminded them all of other times, the best times, the War years, the years that followed, the halcyon days. A dream, a happy mythology and a good one. For it allowed them to turn their heads from the tatty and the poor and the dispossessed and turn instead to the sun.

Leo would make a speech, a short one. Not sentimental but just right. They both knew too much to be sentimental.

Then, much later, as the guests continued with the night that would be forever memorable, Virginia would slip away, quietly now, quietly, down the wooden stairs from the front of the house to the beach.

Oh, this night, this magical night.

Her feet were delicious. The sand found its way between her toes and swept up behind her as her dress dragged across the little tufts of dune-grass and shells. There was enough light from the half-moon to just catch the edge of the beading as it tinkled along the wide arc of the beach. Such a night!

It is getting late.

And there she stepped, those eighty hot summers of Virginia. Her one foot falls through the surface of the cold sea, the next and the next. Her dress fulfils its form and bleeds ink blue from the ankle, up and up. Such beauty in this moment, such surrender. Weighty, cool and stealthy, her legs begin to drag. On she steps, forward again, further and deeper, with every twist of wrist and bend of knee. Drifting now, sinking and no effort to move against it.

I am made of light.

Eyes become fish, and lips molluscs as she returns to her start of the world place, the womb of all origin, and falls through the cascading rush of synapses as they roar and race and then suddenly begin to recede on themselves. And all of the time that belongs to the ocean alone, begins to close over. And through this time, liquid time, she falls away further and deeper and thinks ever so briefly about breathing, but only ever so briefly.

And later when the man Isaac, who had lived his whole life near that beach, walked the eight kilometres from one end to the other of the golden arc of sand, as he has done every morning for as long as he can remember with his fishing rod and bag and bait, he finds her there. He isn't surprised, not really, because sometimes that's just how it is with the sea, sometimes you just have to return to it because being away from it is a kind of death. He knew that. He had tried to leave it once and it had not done him any good. He thinks how beautiful this thin white lady looks with her strong, long nose, like a bird he thinks, her white hair sprayed out so that it has become one with the seaweed and shells. He feels as if he can see right though her skin, so thin is its veil between her body and the rest of the world.

———

Gin stretched forward to try and ease the stiffness gathering in the base of her spine. Would she ever be found?

It is getting late.

A cheer rose up from outside the Residence. Gin turned back towards the house.

———

Neve opened the car door and got in. Juno might have gone to the park. It was close enough and she knew the way. She liked it there.

Why had Gin been so stupid, so incredibly stupid? If Juno has been hit by a car then perhaps someone would take her to a vet. Mercy had reappeared from God knows where, also without the dog, and was instructed to wait next to the phone.

And what if Juno was dead? What then? The hair stood up on Neve's arms even to think it. She would tell Virginia to cancel the party and that would be the end. She would rather have Juno than all these hangers-on coming to the party. Neve's ire spiked as she pulled the car door shut. She felt provoked.

She knew unequivocally that she would not take part in the farce unfolding around her. A contrivance which would allow all those who attended to feel they had done the right thing. It had nothing to do with her. If it were only her she would have a nice walk with Juno and avoid the phone for a few days. Or get away, into the bush for a week. She had taken out a dress, though, just in case. Midnight blue, high collar, sprays of white orchids. With her hair cut sharp across her jaw and her red lips, she knew it suited her.

Into the street.

Parties. A waste of money too and all the dishes and plates to be washed and glasses to be cleaned and all the silver. Gin would want to use the good silver. (Was that Juno? Was that her? No, a supermarket carrier blowing along the pavements.) And what did Gin know about cooking? Nothing at all. You simply cannot feed guests cheap chicken.

Neve knew she should be kinder. But she did not know how when she was feeling so thoroughly vexed by it all. She should be more forgiving of Gin. She looked weary, a kind of life-tired that people who live on their own sometimes get.

I cannot protect her much longer.

She was still pretty though, and she walked well, it was her height that gave her that ease with her legs. A pity she could not have gone to the hairdressers before the party.

Where was that little dog?

———

Juno was hot. Uncomfortably so. And she began to worry about the man who was carrying her here and there, for they never seemed to arrive anywhere. But he spoke so nicely to her that she felt he must be kind. There was no scent of anger on him, only love and, in the end, she was more interested in getting a drink of water.

They seemed to be moving a lot and from time to time the man would have to readjust his arms around her. She tried to be helpful by lifting her weight a little before she settled back in. She thought for a moment (though there was such noise in the streets) that she heard the car, her car, Neve's car, which had that low engine noise, and she thought too she heard the sound of the dog that lived near home. But she could not be sure. And she was still so very thirsty.

———

Neve decided to walk up and down the length of trees that ran like a twisted spine through the middle of the park. The sun and massing clouds continued to create a humid shell over the city. She found the shade. From there she could look left and right as she walked and called out for Juno.

Eighty years old and never before given her age a moment's thought. Not really, despite the years and the cancer. And possibly becoming a mother so late had simply forced her to keep moving, offered her no time to think. What good would thinking about things do? Motherhood had been a complicated business. The tedium had surpassed her, so too had the overwhelming sense that she would never, ever be enough, or would fail to be there when it truly mattered, so that somehow her entire experience of being a mother was one of chasing villains and fighting disasters that had yet to materialize: an impossible task.

Eighty years old felt different. Knowing that her own mother had died at eighty-two gave her an idea that somehow this was it now, this was the hour when the coach drew up and one by one the horses went back to their stalls.

What a ridiculous notion. She didn't even like horses.

These park walks had saved her, taken every day for as long as she could remember. The dogs, too, yes, when Gin's father was so bad, at the end, it was her dogs that had saved her then. Not all these people set to arrive at the house tonight. She could simply not go, simply choose not to join in. But then where else would she go? People did have birthdays it was true. But she had never been that person and what would it do to start now?

A funny looking bird flapped its wings over there in the Karee trees. They formed such a lovely bank along the river, part of the original estate. The old orchards were still growing, lovely pears and quinces from before it was all carved up and made into a park. They could use a proper prune and some nourishment, not that they'd get any from the parks department; still, they had an instinct for endurance.

There weren't many walkers, a few in the distance. Not the safest time to be alone in the trees. And no Juno.

———

Gin was lying on her mother's bed. It always smelled the same, powdery somehow. Mercy was crashing around, talking on the phone or over the fence. She had done all sorts of beautiful things to the food. Gin had hugged Mercy, and had felt Mercy's small hands pat her back in unison, pat-pat-pat as she said, 'Pleasure, pleasure Ginny, pleasure. You mother has gone to the park.'

Gin's phone rang, first her friend Jackie and then Alison. She didn't answer. She had nothing to say to them and she would see them all later.

Two of her friends were freezing their eggs. One was sleeping with men she met in clubs and then making these men sign legal waivers so there would be no complications should a child be produced. Another, with no money to speak of and a man who was, at best, half-committed, committed herself, wilfully, to pregnancy. There was panic in the one-bedroom condominium market, reducing every first date or failed return of call to an emergency.

Where was Juno? She would be so afraid.

Gin closed her eyes.

Thank God I don't live here. Thank God.

Gin thought about eating but changed her mind. She could wait. For so long, she considered everything she chose to swallow as a specific, orchestrated decision to live. No undisciplined, unconscious stuffing of a gaping spittle hole. Rather to eat this and that and how much of each was a specific instruction to her body, an affirmation that she had chosen to continue with the business of living for another demarcated amount of time. Every day she ate, sometimes more, sometimes less. And, for the present, she had decided she would continue.

It was the same process she had applied to marriage. She had once considered it, though a brief examination had been enough to expose it as impossible. She could see no benefit beyond financial security and as such this too was redundant. She would make her own. And she had. She had made enough.

She owned her own apartment, more than enough space for one particularly since she had a studio for work, subsidized and spacious. The artist's necessity. A studio of her own was what she had always yearned for, not a husband. She did not respond well to shared spaces. To have her space, tall walls and full of light, was all she needed to produce her work and, more than that, to survive. From the very outset it was its very parameters, the square meterage stated in bold in the advertisement, that gave her a kind of limitless, boundless space to breathe. That the doors locked, that the walls admitted no eyes to see her work, that there was no number or name over the gate buzzer, all of these strictures made it possible for her to do anything at all. It was entirely down to the demarcation, discipline, stricture that she imposed on the outside world that the most radical kind of freedom was possible.

Here though, back in this city, nothing, not even life was possible and, instead, so many different ways to die.

This was a city where the blonde woman and her athletically built man led lives they believed to be extraordinary. Accountants who made jokes about 'boring accountants' and did not for a second include themselves in these ranks. Women who started nearly every sentence with, 'My husband says,' as they drove to another lunch in their four-by-four. The four-by-four bought on the advice of friends all of whom drove the same car, always silver. They continued in this unconscious parody of a life that existed decades previously yet seemed to persist and pervade.

Marriage and children was a hobby, as much as the evolution of a relationship. It was what people did over their weekends, it was how they filled silences; weddings, baby showers, bachelorette parties, pram shopping and on and on as if there were nothing else in the world of any value, nothing else to catch their eye or give them pause.

This, this endless nothingness, was what was meant to offer Gin some sort of solace. She was expected to find this sustaining, nurturing. She was meant to attach her own life to this vapour and find deep and abiding satisfaction from it.

I would rather die.

These were the women who would say to her, in the frozen meat isle, you don't know how happy a child will make you until you have one, I just didn't know who I was until I had a child and now it all makes sense and I have never been happier. And Gin would look into the pram at the bag of squirming flesh and say, I already know who I am.

For so long she had wondered why did she not feel as they did. She thought she must be missing the critical hormone that would make her want a child or make her yearn beyond all else to produce offspring. Whatever it was, she did not have it. She didn't like them, children noisy, inconvenient, slow, all of the things that make life intolerable, made her work impossible. To live without her work was never an option, because to do so would be the same as dying.

She had sat at enough lunch tables, at every return to the city, where the purpose of the lunch was not to speak and discuss and, as an aside, also meet the children of her friends, but rather for the entire adult table to point themselves in the direction of the children and marvel at their every breath. Her friends spoke in voices that Gin did not recognize, monosyllabic and infantile. She had made an effort, once or twice but soon realized that her friends would not be making the same effort to meet her and speak to her on her terms, to return the favour of feigned interest. So she no longer went to meet the children of her friends.

The friends themselves no longer cared for her single life. It was possible they found her reactionary, strange, otherwise. They could not identify her. Soon they parted. A great relief.

Juno had a tag with a phone number and name etched into the metal. Surely she would be found and taken to a vet or a kindly person would call.

I should be looking for her. Why do I just lie here?

And tonight, the party, would bring its own questions – agonized, usually well-meaning exhalations of, 'Not married? Oh I can't imagine why not, if I was a younger man I would have snapped you up.' The 'never mind' variety were worse. The offers of advice about not being so picky, the perfect man just doesn't exist. And through it all she held her tongue, never saying, 'I don't want to marry, I don't care about finding someone, I'm not too picky, I have never felt so whole. My work is powerful and I am powerful in it.'

None of this could be said because it sounded shrill and defensive. Maybe it was. She no longer cared to analyse it, all she knew was that whatever it was that they all had, was not of her, not in her, and never would be.

———

September stood at the gate. To his right was the small, plastered pillar that held the intercom system. He hoped the black woman would answer, it would make it all easier. He pressed the button that said: 'Staff', once, twice. He waited. No response. He could feel the pain beginning in his head, behind his right ear. He pressed 'House' and took a step back as if he expected a great beast to suddenly roar through the gates.

'*Yebo?*'

It was the black woman.

'*Ma! Kunjane*? I have the small lion. The small one is here.'

'What?'

'My name is September. I have the small one. The small one who was lost in the street. I have her.'

———

Gin realized it was getting late. Too late to be lying here rehearsing angry speeches. Soon enough the meat would need to be cooked. Change into her dress. To be happy and beautiful was the best defence, the only defence, against pity.

Juno, come home.

She looked at her phone, messages, aunts that couldn't remember what time to come, cousins trying to be helpful, a friend saying she was going to wear such a hot dress the older men would need an ambulance.

Mercy was calling her.

'Come! There is a man here.'

'What?'

'Juno. A man has her.'

'I'm coming. Oh God.' Gin hardly had a sense of her feet as she ran down the stairs two at a time. Mercy had opened the gate and there was the man. The same man she had seen earlier, the hunchback, ragged, wild. And in his arms was Juno.

'Juno!'

The dog leapt from the man's arms and ran towards Gin. Gin rubbed her hands all along her fur and along her tail so that she could feel her shape and make sure she was well. She looked up at the man.

'Sir, where did you find her?'

The man spoke back but she could not understand him, or perhaps hear him through his missing teeth and slurred speech. His head seemed one-sided, paralysed down the one side. She asked him again and still she could not understand. He had a large fresh agapanthus strung around his neck and a placard.

Inexplicably, shamefully, Gin felt afraid. Brutally so. She felt the man's insanity too keenly. It sat proud on the surface of his skin, a devastating kind of presentation. The surface of her arms was bristling and cold. A terrible, urgent chill, as if death were in the room. And yet she tried to keep looking at him, tried to show she was grateful.

'Wait there. I'll get you something.' She indicated that he should stay. 'For bringing the dog. Where did you find her? Mercy ask him.'

Gin turned for the house remembering that her money was in the bedroom, that she had cash there and thinking, how much is enough? One hundred? Two? Five? How does one value these things, put value on the act and the man. She took out three hundred, then hastily added another fifty. Why was it he who brought Juno home? Why him? His face so smashed. And the hump.

I cannot even look at him.

———

September began to feel as though this woman was not who he wanted her to be. He had thought she would be pleased to have her small one home. She should have said thank you, perhaps offer him some food or money for his efforts because he was clearly a man in need of such things. Instead, she had about her the look of a woman who would never trust the world. He felt that it was not so much him that she was repelled by, or his hump (though she had looked and looked away, quickly), but, rather that she expected him to be a *tsosti* or a scrounger. He knew he was neither.

He stood there as himself.

Other than the dog, it was all he had to offer. On another day it would have been himself alone, standing on his island, nothing more than a naked wound. But today, on this day, he came with an offering, a precious one. He had come to the gate with everything he knew she wanted. And still, somehow, it was not enough. It could not purchase him an unflinching eye or an open hand.

September no longer wanted to be standing there in the driveway of this woman feeling, as he often did, too dirty, too ugly, too everything. And still not enough.

That was the thing about his hump. It made him visible when he did not wish to be visible. In that way he understood that the broken, the deformed had much in common with the truly beautiful. They made people stop and turn and stare. Unlike the beautiful though, it also made him invisible when he hoped to be seen. Perhaps the *muti* man's spells at Verloren had worked after all. Just not on that day, when it had mattered.

He could hear her telling someone to hold the dog. She sounded as if she was coming back out to him. He felt himself begin to lift a little, to peel away from his body at the prospect of the encounter.

September, still waiting just inside the open gate, did not want to be visible to this woman though he held no ill will towards her. And he felt he would always have affection for the small lion who had strayed into his garden. Suddenly and unexpectedly, though, he felt his throat begin to ache and his eyes burn, wet. In other words, he felt the darkest sweep of shame. The thing he had thought he was done with. More than anything he knew he should turn and leave. But to do so would be to let her watch him walk away, his hump like a great and monstrous eye looming out of his shoulders.

He could not turn.

Turn. You must turn. Leave this place. There is no love for you here. You are nothing but a stranger, a ragged hermit at the gate. You are no messiah, no king, no prophet. September, Sechaba, you must turn. Walk towards safety.

She will see your hump as you swing your back towards her. As you walk away she will stare. Because she must.

Dare to turn, September, dare to turn. Call back your spirit. Summon your blood to rise in you. You are the son of warriors. You can turn. You must turn. Call back your spirit.

September turned.

He turned, with or without his spirit. And the shame that he knew from childhood weighed on him so that he felt his spine contract yet more.

———

Mercy let her eyes follow the length of the road to where the man with the board and the strange body shuffled down the line in the centre of the road. He ignored a taxi and another car carrying white people and their flowers to the Residence. She might have run after him, told him there was money for him, but she knew this one and preferred to keep her distance. He had never tried it with her but he smoked a lot, she could always smell the sweet heat around him, his eyes wide and red. He would call out to her, make comments about her womanliness so that if ever she saw him at the intersection she would cross the road. It only made him shout louder but at least she knew he could not grab her. Sometimes she had seen him, ragged and wrung out, bashing his flat hand on the doors and bonnets of cars, shouting, 'Fear no more! Even in the darkness we sing, we sing all that we know about darkness!'

A riddle, a nonsense and always on his head a wreath, a crown made from marijuana leaves or willow branches or agapanthus. He was the wild one, from the deepest acres of the fields and the forests. Mercy felt sure that if he ever died, his blood would drain from him the colour of crushed berries.

———

My hump holds the precise weight of the earth that will fill my grave. It casts its shape in a perfect shadow. And so I carry up this bundle of earth behind me. I will not waste a single grain of it. Now I will walk the blocks to the Diamond. I carry this earth, I carry my grave.

———

He had called himself September.

'Mercy where is he? Where did he go?'

'He was there. Up the street.'

'He's gone, then.'

Gin crossed the threshold into the street, tried to see through the dappling of the trees up the length of avenue. There were so many groups of mourners that she could not make out one shape from another. But there, so much further than she would have expected, she saw the man, bent over but shuffling away. He seemed in a hurry.

'Come back! I have something for you, come back.'

He didn't react. He could not hear her. Not at that distance and with all the noise in the street.

Gin never thought about chasing after him, leaving the gates and taking herself out into the heat and the bleaching sun. She did not have the energy for all that, for yet another scramble through the streets. And there was the party, the food, ice, flowers, all these things she still had to do. And Juno was home.

'Did you find him?' said Mercy

'He's too far away. I know where he begs, it's there on the island? I can go there tomorrow. I'll take him some money tomorrow.'

Even as she said it she knew she would dread the meeting. She could drive, and then simply hand him an envelope through the window and hopefully the lights would change and she could leave him.

She felt so threatened by him. She had been accosted by beggars all across New York: subways, street corners, under bridges and in the park. All day, all night it was a city that demanded attention, dollars, anything and everything, another dollar. It didn't touch her. And yet this man, this castaway, washed up on the streets like the city's last orphan, had left her sliced right open so that suddenly she felt uncovered, skinless, with no border-post between herself and life.

He erodes me.

The monstrous hump and a placard strapped to his side, the straps of it cutting raw into his shoulder. Gin shut her eyes against the image of him but she saw him there too: his eyes twitching, teeth missing, hair full of leaves, an agapanthus trussed up on string around his neck, wildness in him, something of the waves, talons, fur. As he had walked away she saw not only the impossible cone that forced through the fabric of his shirt but on the side of his head, a scar – deep straight furrow along the side of his skull. It looked as if a great anvil had scooped a trench of flesh from his head and dumped it on the ground.

To be next to him renders me beside myself.

———

September kept walking. And as he did he felt he might cry out, or worse, that he might not and then all the shame and the smallness of his place in the world might be stuck in him forever. In that single moment when the thin, white woman questioned his care for the small one, suddenly all the daily slights and insults, the stares and windows that rolled up when he approached a car at the traffic lights, all of this, suddenly, became impossible to bear.

He had not felt this for so many years. He had, by choice and out of necessity, begun to step back from himself, away from himself. To be absolutely present for every moment is the highest privilege. It means that your life is bearable, that you may face it square on and not flinch, and it means that others do not flinch at the sight of you. September knew that he would not only flinch but find himself flayed right through his flesh.

In his clearer moments he knew what he saw in Dudu's face. She could see the end in him. She saw his splintering as an approaching death. She was wrong. To take separate occupation of these multiple units of himself was to survive. And for her and so many other reasons he still so desperately craved life.

That very day, the softness of the small one's hair under his hand, the small beating heart, the breathing body that had come to him for help, was the closest he had felt to love from another being in so, so many years. As he had carried her home along the avenue, a small drop of saliva had dropped from her mouth onto his forearm and it had seemed to him a moment of grace. He had felt it burn his flesh as it ran along and dripped to the tarmac; a moment of beauty, a sense of love, the promise of survival.

But perhaps it was the love he had felt for the little lion and the tenderness he felt in return that had left him vulnerable to the gaze of the woman. He had let down his guard, allowed himself to expect some kindness from the world after the small lion had come to him, chosen him, sat so soft in his arms.

———

Gin took Juno inside for water and gave her some meat from the fridge. Where was her mother? Why was she never around? She felt the whole day had passed and she had hardly seen her. Mercy said she would call her but knew too that Mrs Brandt did not understand her phone and rarely had it with her.

Gin was cold. She could feel herself sink in, just a little, enough so that her feet were getting wet.

I am beside myself.

She lay on the sofa and pulled Juno up next to her. She felt the deep begin to lap at her ankles. This was a dark ocean.

She could not understand, could not reshape the man's specific contours in her eye. She felt she needed to straighten him out, lift him up so that his spine was righted. She lay there, deep in the waves of linen, and rocked this way and that as she thought about the man with the hump, the desperation of the day.

It was as if she had always known the city would kill her, the house, the people. It would pull the skin from her bones, un-seam her so that she would be left as carrion for gulls.

I am fraying. How can I do what needs doing. How can I survive?

And she knew that each moment she lay there letting the tears rise and fall on the tides, that each moment was a moment closer to the time when the first guests would arrive and expect some kind of radiance, some kind of light. They expected life.

It is getting late.

Out across the city, from the belly of the mines and out of the voices of the mourners, came thunder, deep and rolling. The clouds began to mass with growing focus. Four o'clock. The afternoon storm was finding its feet. When it came, it would be quick and violent.

Late afternoon

Thunder.

Neve could not find Juno. She felt light-headed (it was hot) and disconsolate. She would go home. But first she needed to sit down. Which way were the benches?

The wooden slats on the bench, those that had not been stolen for firewood by the squatters over the river, were dusty. But, if navigated well, one could find a place to sit between the worst of it and the bird droppings. Neve had a sense of her body exhaling into the wood beneath her. She ached. Her knees one day, her back the next, her knee again. Ridiculous. Always too hot, too cold, uncomfortable, miserable in her own body as if she no longer understood it nor recognized its contours. There is a day when you cross some threshold of age, when you are no longer middle-aged but, somehow, old. When you stop simply falling and instead it is said that you have had 'a fall'. It has become an event.

There were some dogs off on the far side of the park, stalking moles, slow and pointed, each with one leg raised so as not to disturb the earth and alert the moles to their hunt. The backs were straight, tails too and noses pointing at the ground. From Neve's distance, nothing appeared to move. But she knew the ears would be twitching, one, then the other, as they marked the movement of the creatures beneath the earth. The hunt. The stalk. The pounce.

Neve couldn't breathe.

I cannot breathe.

'Give me money.'

I cannot breathe.

'I will cut you, Granny.'
She tried to shake her head. Pinned. Throttled. Someone. An arm around her neck. A knife. Cold on her cheek. The blade pressed. Keen.

'Give it to me.'
She tried to shake, no. 'I don't have any.' Strangled words.

'Your phone, I'm going to cut you, old lady.'
Old lady. Easy target. No. There are no victims in this family. No.

How dare he? Here in the park, her park, on her birthday. Somehow (how?) Neve turned her head to the side. Just a little. Easier to breathe.

'I am too old for a phone.'

'I want it.'

'I don't have one. Take my watch.'

'Give it to me.'

'I bought it at the chemist. Two hundred rand. Take it.'

Filthy, filthy fingers, dirty nails, grappled with her watch. She could feel his filth on her wrist. She couldn't see him but suddenly she was overwhelmed with the smell of the man. She could smell the stench of sweat and filth coming off him.

'I'm going to cut you Granny.'

'You will be a murderer.'

'You think I care?'

'You have the watch. Now go. Go.'

And then she was coughing and retching.

He was gone.

I am alive.

She gripped her wrist where the watch had been. Her favourite watch, from the chemist. His hands had touched her wrist.

She checked her arms and body for cuts or blood. She ran her fingers across her cheek where the knife had been. So close. Her throat was raw, dry and rasping. Again her fingers across her cheeks and then down her neck.

I am alive. I am alive.

Already her body registered the space where her watch had been. As if the air sat more keenly and cooler in that small round of flesh. She needed to find another one. It was years ago she had bought it. She wouldn't get a nice strap like that again. Dark green. Moc-croc. She rubbed the flat of her hand across the place where his fingers had fiddled and groped, she rubbed the skin, hard, as she looked around, this way and that.

Did anyone see it all?

No. That was good. She did not want anyone to have seen. There would be a fuss. And it was just a watch, a cheap one. She would go to the chemist and get another.

That man. The stench of him. He had touched her arm. His arm around her neck.

Neve stood.

I am alive.

Dear God, she needed Juno, more than anything. No matter the man and her watch, none of it would matter, if only Juno was found.

Neve decided that, in future, she would not choose to sit on a bench that had its back to the river. All sorts living along there in their little plastic huts. The police should clean them away. Filthy. Could Juno be there? She should go and call out for her. But the man might be there. She should not have come alone. Idiot. She could send Talent. He would talk to the men, explain that a dog was missing. Take some money as an exchange.

Everything is wrong. Everything I have known. I am losing everything.

Neve felt something run down her cheek. A burn, a cut. She touched her face then looked at her fingers for blood. There was none. Only tears.

———

More thunder.

It is late.

September was nearly a full block from the green gates of Gin's house when he felt his centre begin to come back to him. Only then did he sense her shouting after him, 'Come back, come back.' He would not. He would not go back.

He had thought he might visit the Residence on his way to the Diamond, to see the flowers that had been laid out for Tata, but he decided that he had paid his respects months before, on the true day of the king's passing.

On the day that the whole world would be watching, he was late for the Diamond. As he walked along the avenue, groups of cadres, families, older women, walked towards him, all had flags, flowers, for the king. He wanted to keep on his path, heavy though it was, but the sight made him stop again.

Their hearts are broken.

The women are taking agapanthus to the fallen king, to show him their love. I have seen them from my island. The taxi stops, pulls back its metal curtain for a door and out come three or four old gogos, all neat and clean with handbags and heads covered, and in their hands, the agapanthus they have taken from their white madam's gardens. These beautiful gogos, our mothers, and grandmothers, who carry whole cities, the whole nation, in enamel troughs that sit proud on top of their heads. They walk for hours each day, carrying us all. This city's secret is that it is the women who carry the burden of all our tears. This golden place, our walls and streets were built using the sweet grains of sugar left in the bottom of their tin mugs. One on top of the other, they built us all, in their kitchens and on their stove tops.

There go some more.

'Power! Power to the mothers of the nation who have built us all! You have given us gold! Ma Winnie, Ma Graça, the nation salutes you!'

Look, all these people are going to the house of the king to show him their love and for his wives too, two of them left now. There were three, the first one has been called home to her reward. We know these people, his family, his people. We can call them by their names. They are our home.

And what of my name? Who will remember that?

I am September.

Mercy had a lot to do and yet despite the cutting and slicing and grilling, she was thinking about the journey home and what to pack. For that was what she had planned to do that night, before she had heard about the party.

She decided she would need to buy another holdall. Her room was always brimful of clothes and cups and saucers, wrapped in newspaper in boxes, blankets, shoes for the children and on and on. And she felt it was not really her room. It was Mrs Brandt's room. For until you own the land it sits on how can it ever be yours? It was her room for as long as she worked there and if Mrs Brandt demanded to see what was in there or see how it was kept, then what could Mercy do? Mrs Brandt did not do that. But there were others in domestic employment who had their rooms checked every week. Like children.

Always she had thought, that if she could just have her own apartment, or a room with a small kitchen and a chair outside under a big old tree (a fruit bearing tree would be best) then she might feel different about living in the city. More whole perhaps, more true. And often when she felt trapped, saw her life the same every day until she retired, arthritic and spent, she imagined all the things she could cook in that little kitchen. A stove that she could buy second-hand, and a small table were all she needed. It would be her stove, her table (she would paint it red) and in there she would sing out her hymns as loud as she cared while she fried *vetkoek* to sell to builders and gardeners all over the city, *mielie* fritters, beautiful cakes for white ladies' book clubs, peanut butter biscuits too. Even stew and *pap*.

But she had no such room, no such kitchen to call her own and it was this lack that she felt most keenly.

———

September sat on the fountain outside the Diamond. He watched as the light hit off the water and the reflective puddles that had collected around its base. There were fractured feet and knees and faces flashing past as the people came and went across the plaza. Came and went as if he were not there at all despite the size of his disappointment and his placard. Clouds were moving at some speed, flashing light across the city. Thunder too, somewhere further south.

He closed his eyes and let the cool drench him. On his one side, he felt his shirt begin to attach to his skin as if it were one and the same, all part of him and his tired body. It stuck to his back, wet and warmed, like the blood that had stuck, wet and warmed by his own heart.

To be shot from the front, to walk into the bullets was one thing but to be shot as you ran away was something else. And no one said any different. The reports in the newspapers and on the radio and then later, in the courts said no, no sir, the workers were wielding knives and *knobkierries* (those Xhosas, so militant) and they would not yield, they would not yield. But September knew. He knew that he had been shot from behind, just off to the side, his face and head grazed by the wild hot bullet.

Thunder. Closer. More ready. The rain was on its way.

There is that man again, that white one. I knew him back then, before. He pretends he doesn't know me. He looks heavy. Son of Europe the sun will burn you.

I hold nothing against him on account of his whiteness but I do judge him on his forgetfulness. He has holes for eyes. He has forgotten how to look at a man, he cannot meet my gaze. This will be his downfall.

He pretends he does not see my protest. I know this man. I have seen him at the mines. He is young. He should know better. He sat there and pretended to listen to us and hear our grievances but in the end he was there to bury the sins of the men who hide in the Diamond. Puh! I will have to bring my protest to his door, to his face, so that those holes he has for eyes will suddenly be filled with tears.

And he will see Duduzile too, for all the women that she is. She is all of them. When he looks at her he will see that she has been made from power lines. Long cables, whipping and flashing, pulled from the pylons. High voltage. And with a few knots, she was born. A sinew, a bolt. A woman.

Still, Dudu has to work. She lives in a room, a cell, offered by her madam in exchange for some labour, scrubbing floors on hands and knees like a dog, scrubbing, scrubbing all day.

I cannot stay there with her. I will frighten her madam and the children. Probably the dog too (I did not frighten the small lion), but perhaps I make too much noise to be allowed to stay. The truth can be heard from far hills, and I will speak truth. Speaking truth is more difficult when you have a hump and half a face. Only the beautiful are believed without hesitation.

So, I stay here on the street. And I see Dudu. She comes to me and brings me money and food and blankets. She does not understand why I make my home in the garden, why I do not stay inside the old house with the others. But they are from Mozambique and the other two from Zimbabwe. I do not know their language. So, I stay outside, under the stars, where I can still imagine beauty.

Home, thought Neve, it was the only place to go. But perhaps a stop at the chemist. Juno. Where was Juno? Into the car, window down, a cigarette. Her hands shook as she found the lighter.

I am alive.

Heavy skies, thunder. The storms came so quickly. Every day with the regularity of great, chiming bell towers. It meant it was nearly four. Neve looked down at her wrist to confirm the hour. She had run out of time.

I am alive.

————

Gin was lining up wine glasses, tumblers, a storm was coming. It was already after four. A few drops were beginning to fall. The afternoon tempest. She had given up waiting for Neve, and the longer she sat immobile the closer the terror came. She assumed her mother would come home soon. Juno was home. Mercy had done the food. The natural order was restored.

Juno sat close to her feet as she moved back and forth in front of the large yellow-wood table. She began to line up candles in glass jars all down the centre of the table. A long, straight, illuminated spine. It would be beautiful.

I know what I am doing. This is who I am.

Gin liked to think about her work as much as execute it. Hours and hours writing and reading and looking at her archive of slides, Caravaggio, Brancusi, Bourgeois, it made no difference. She would let them run as she sat in her armchair, the images flashing across her studio wall, one and then another and then another. And after a while they began to form their own narrative, they began to fall into place, the line of Christ's halo began to bleed into a dome and the dome became a void and the void the colour of ink so that she never knew where one image ended and the other began.

Eventually she would begin her own contribution to the line, the golden line that ran from one to the next. Her true inheritance. She would begin and weeks or months later, she could start to refine her gestures again and again, until they were simply the essence, a moment of pure beauty. She wanted, more than anything, to let life find its perfect expression.

She worked with line after line after line. The golden touch lay not only in the line as it lay on the paper but in the moment of its rendering too. It was how she felt it unfurl its length across the perfect paper-scape, the near airless float, the liquid roll of ink as she let gesture find its form. Later they might be reformed in a three-dimensional installation but always her work's first perfect breath in the world was this.

Gin pulled at her shirt, which suddenly seemed to be a bad choice with a storm coming, the air so crisp.

She wanted her work to pursue beauty. She knew too that growing up in this city there were things that demanded energy. There are always more urgent needs than beauty.

In Johannesburg, she felt so very far away from grace. The gap was so wide between what she sought and where she found herself, floundering and terrified that she would never, ever be enough to survive it all.

———

Neve sat in her car in the parking lot in front of the chemist. Next to it was the little coffee shop. She could get Gin a proper coffee. No, she probably had one already, she didn't need her old mother to do that for her. What went on in that child's head? It could have been today, that knife could have just begun to pierce the skin and then, in. The jugular. Sometimes she just wished she would fall asleep and her heart give out. It had happened to her mother and her younger sister too. Just like that, a little nap.

Gin was still so insubstantial, rake-thin, living on her own in the worst kind of city. She seemed to have few friends over there and they seemed to be more like hangers-on than friends. Not that she ever needed many.

Her work was doing well. That was something. How the young made a living these days was beyond comprehension. But people bought her art, museums even, a museum in Boston had bought one of her sculptures. Was it a sculpture?

I am tired. Painfully so. Do I keep myself alive for Gin? She has to let me go. I cannot stay alive for her.

———

September stood up from the fountain and arranged himself, making sure his placard was well-placed. The pain in his head was tremendous. It swelled through his eyes so that it made his stomach heave in on itself. He wished Duduzile was there. Instead he kept remembering how the woman in the house had looked at him. She had decided that he had stolen the small one. The small one who had snuffled her way into his garden like a ghost or a friend.

He walked up the side of the fountains and towards the front of the Diamond. It seemed so far away, all the gleaming water and the sun and gathering cloud hitting off it like a great, beautiful lake. He could almost imagine fields, rolling and green, falling downhill into the lake, and on it, cows and goats, all his. This was a beautiful dream and it helped him make his way. Because in truth, each step was an agony, pain reaching up his legs and the placard cutting his flesh. The woman at the house was not who he had hoped. He looked up and took a breath to give him relief. Fields, sky, a lake. A day for love. A day for beauty.

I will take this pain to the door of the Diamond. They will see me and I will not turn like I turned from the woman, I will not turn.

———

Dudu heard the first drop on the tin roof of the laundry, and then another, another and then so many she could not hear a space between the drops as they fell. She turned to watch the windows blotch and then run. Then she remembered herself and the washing too, and dashed out with the plastic washing basket and began grabbing the clothes from the line. The damp would make them easier to iron. These were fat, overfed drops. As she reached for a shirt she asked God to keep September safe and dry.

———

Peter began to feel that the afternoon might improve. Through his windows he could see the whole sky and the coming storm. A few drops had begun to fall. He always enjoyed the afternoon rain. The pressure change made his ears pop. Just gone four o'clock. There. Thunder. One, two, and the great flash of lightning. The rain was beginning to rattle and spit. He could see it moving left to right across his vista. Peter did not move from his desk, only watched it all gather its force outside his window. And then, the sky broke. A torrent. A drench. Screens of it. The worst of it wouldn't last longer than twenty minutes or so.

When the rain stopped Peter turned away from the window.

He turned on the news to see the mourners at the Residence. The reporter, wet haired, American, told the camera that as the first sound of thunder rolled out, the mourners replied with a great cry and even as the torrent fell, arms and spirits were raised higher and the singing grew all the louder. Behind the woman, Peter could make out a few people clearly drenched, but holding their umbrellas to protect the candles that formed a bank of light along the sidewalk.

Suddenly it was all too beautiful to bear. The bank of light, the flowers, the hundreds with arms open to the skies calling out their love as the clouds let loose their torrent. He wanted it to end, the love that was everywhere. He felt so beyond the bounds of all it. Such a rush, such an ache of longing that could hardly survive or be named.

I am not entitled.

Onto the screen came a video montage, splicing together Mandela coming out of prison, the roar, the love, the noise. Mandela, hand aloft, fist clenched *Mayibuye!* and the nation the entire nation calling back to welcome him *iAfrica!* and on and on, images, music, 'Never, and never again, shall this nation ...' Peter changed channel. But there was more and more and more so that he could not find a way to escape it.

He turned it off. All the people and all the things his life could have become instead of what it was. There was the Union leader he used to know and drink with, there was the Communist Party stalwart who had ordered him to leave a meeting, all of these people and places that should have been who he was and yet were not.

Fucking failed, liberal sell-out.

'You need to come quickly.'

Peter turned to see a junior, wide eyed and urgent. People were moving quickly into offices, three, four, five at a time, doors were closing, locking.

'What's going on?'

'There's a nutter out the front.'

———

'Mum? Mum? We have Juno.'

Gin rushed to the door to greet Neve with Juno in her arms. Juno wagged and wiggled and kissed Neve's face over and over.

'Oh dear God. I've been looking for her at the park. Look at you, you dear, dear thing. I've had a terrible afternoon.'

'But she's here. A man brought her. A homeless guy. He had a hunchback.'

She looks so old, as if she were sinking away from her self, from life.

'Heavens. Where did he find her?'

'I don't know. I couldn't work him out. But she's back.'

'I need to lie down Virginia. Before your party. I'll have Juno with me. She must be tired.'

'Are you ok?' She saw that Neve's make-up was smudged.

Gin felt a chill run along her arms and legs, as if yet another layer of skin had suddenly been stripped off.

I ask too much of her. I ask things of her she has no energy to give.

'I'm fine. Just hot. And driving back in the rain. And I've been so worried about Juno.'

'OK. I gave her some meat. I'll bring you some tea.'

They reached the entrance to the covered verandah. Gin knew her mother would see all the tables, all laid with Granny's cutlery, her vases and linen. The flowers were perfect, leaning and billowing as if they had grown right out of the wood of the tables. All the candles and the lines of little lights she had been hanging in the frangipani tree. She felt Neve pause next to her as she took it all in. She had seen the beauty in it, the love.

'You've been busy Virginia.'

'Yes.'

'I hope there's enough food.'

She had not seen it.

Gin's chest tightened as she stood and she had to breathe in a lung-full to stop the tears she felt beginning to burn.

'There will be.'

'I hope so.' Neve dug into her handbag. 'Here.'

'What is it?'

'You're giving me a watch for my birthday.'

'Sure. Did yours stop?' Her eyes still burned.

I will not let her see me break.

'I lost it at the park.'

'Now? Did you look for it?'

'It's gone. I got that one on the way home.'

'I can go to the park with Mercy and look for you?'

'No. It is getting late.'

———

'What are you saying? What kind of nutter?'

'That hunchback guy. Verloren dude. Going bat-shit crazy out the front at the entrance.'

'What? I'll go. I know him.'

'What?'

'I'll go down.'

His name is September.

Peter took the stairs in twos and threes, the great metal and wooden fish spine that dropped through the floors of the Diamond and into its cathedral foyer.

I will tell him to be reasonable, that we will find a better way. I will appeal to our relationship, offer to help him. Why are people locking themselves in?

Peter remembered seeing him earlier with Richard, and then again as he sat under the fountain after seeing Gin. He went down the stairs in gulps. Two, two, three, he kept his hand on the rail.

The woman, a bag of oranges. A moment.

Down, down, nearly there he could see out the front, the sun was already trying to break through the cloud. The plaza was a mirror.

Across the marble entrance. Past the reception desks.

'Sir you must come this way.' Security, flack-jacket, helmet on, AK across his front.

'I need to go outside.'

'No, sir, there is a guy.'

'I know that. I know the guy, I want to speak to him.'

'No, sir.'

———

Here I am. I sing my song at your door.

Fear no more the heat of the sun, and fear nothing for me. I am alive with light. The Diamond is alight, the sun burns right through it so that it shines from every side, and I am alight. I am on fire.

I will not turn! I have called my spirit home, I will not turn.

Fear no more. See how the water has spilled from out the Diamond's fountains and has spilled all across this plain. All the trees, the fields and the mountains are reflected in it. As am I.

Even as the water has escaped, so have I escaped my sorrow. Now, you will see me. This time, you will hear me. I have brought my pain to your door. I clench my fists against my pain.

The grass is shifting in the wind and with it, the clouds. Here the lake is, so cold and deep and beautiful. I see my father's cattle in these fields. He is close. I hear him call me. He stands like a lightning rod. See how tall he stands? His spine is straight and long. I am home.

———

Peter tried to keep the security guard at arm's length, to look over his head at what was going on. Through the oceanic sheets of reflective glass he saw, what? Was this the stand-off? Is this what was meant?

With their back to him and the building were seven guards in black helmets, backs right up close to the glass sheet he was looking though. Goggles, bullet-proof jackets, boots, the god-damned mother-load. Seven in a row, automatic weapons raised and pointing. The radios were going mad.

'South Point units, South Point units, Diamond, red, red, red.'

And there, beyond this line, ragged and torn, wheeling about, arms out and shouting, his head wreathed in agapanthus, a crown for a king, was September.

'What is he saying?' Peter pushed at the guard. 'I need to hear him. They mustn't shoot do you hear? Where's the radio? Do they know that? Tell them now. Tell them. They must not shoot.'

This was a mess already. In all those offices up to the 15th floor, interns and associates were messaging their friends saying a mad man, a Verloren protestor, was storming the Diamond, a line of security thugs taking aim. There was no way to control it. In the middle of the trial, this was the worst kind of disaster. He could hear a chopper. Police? Private tactical? Where the fuck were the board members? Where the fuck was Mogomotsi? Peter tried dialling. He tried De Wet. All the lines were just ringing.

'You have to tell these people that no matter what happens they must not shoot this man. Whose chopper is that? Is it ours? Do you hear me? Who is in charge here?'

The guard shrugged.

'The guys at headquarters.'

'Jesus. Offsite?'

'It's OK, they have video.'

'Tell them now, tell them no one must shoot.'

———

Look at them. All lined up with their guns, the white man's army. You take on a glorious son. I am chosen. You cannot touch

*me. I am proud and straight. See how my spine unfurls like a great
spear.*

I will not turn!

*I can feel the sun reach through me. Look! See how it shifts its course
to collide with this building. The great Diamond, now illuminated
with the light. That is the power of my voice. I speak truth. I call out
the names of those who fell at Verloren. Listen to them.*

*The Diamond is blinding. But I must walk towards it. I must
walk through this golden light towards the Diamond, closer and
closer. I bring my pain to their door.*

I am light now, beauty and light, I can no longer see their armies.

*Where were they? This way? That? I am blinded. I walk across
my father's fields.*

Show me your faces you cowards!

*I cannot see the enemy nor they I. I am invisible. Beauty's own
son. And my father calls my name. Sechaba, he says, come home. It
is time.*

*I am all the light of the sun and the moon in one. The stars fill my
eyes. I hold in my heart all the voltage and power that gave form to
Duduzile herself. For we are one. We are bound by birth and love.*

*I march to the Diamond's door. Stand down for Beauty's son!
Stand down! Mayibuye! Hear the names of the fallen! I call their
names. And my father calls mine.*

Voop, voop, voop. Despite all the radios Peter could hear the
chopper. It must be the mine's. The police would never get there
so quickly. Thank God. And the press were at the Residence.

Peter could see September turning left then right and looking
up, wildly, disorientated. He seemed to be looking for the
chopper.

The square was empty but for the guards and September, still looking to the top of the building or the sky. Some of the light from the sun hitting the building bounced back off the water fountains and onto his ragged shape, making mercury of his form. His head was orbited by the amethyst stars of the agapanthus.

For love.

A moment utterly still, a vacuum, muffled by the silence of the Diamond's glass. Through this, Peter saw the guard in the centre position twitch his head, a breath of a nod towards his ear piece. Then the man dropped his head away to the other side by no more than a vertebra, then back. And even from behind him, through the glass wall, Peter could feel the tension build in the guard's trigger finger. He could feel as the line that runs from the shoulder down and around the elbow and connects along the forearm and into the finger began its contraction. And he felt it too, in his own fibre, the snap of the mechanized hammering as the guns released their blood.

———

Lungisane had hardly felt the weapon in his hands. Nor heard the sound of the bullets as they sprayed out in front of him towards the man. All he had seen was the man with his arms in the air, his crown of agapanthus and the sense that this man no longer had any interest in life.

There had been a noise in his ear-piece, a voice: shoot, don't shoot. He would never know. And it did not matter. In the end the wild man whom he had seen every day since he had begun working at the Diamond was dead. He had killed him. And he could feel no terrible remorse over that.

———

Peter had finally managed to fight his way out the front of the building and into the square towards September.

There was not even a hint of breath left in him, he was on his side, near foetal and the strangest look on his face, his eyes reddish and rolled up a little, skywards and though his face was misshapen, a kind of smile. His wreath, his agapanthus crown, was somehow still safe around his head like a strange halo. Behind him, a few metres behind, was his placard, boldly in blue saying, 'Here I am. Verloren.'

What was he thinking?

Clearly he wasn't thinking. He looked so strange. A man from another place. A forest maybe, or a magical world. He was so ragged, his hump like a brazen declaration of a name or a place, a landmark that demanded to be seen.

Here I am. Verloren. Lost.

Peter felt tears rise. He felt heat rise on his face. Shame. Was it his shame? And then, because the man, September, was dead and because Peter did not know what to do about that, he took off his jacket and laid it over the man. He crouched next to the body and laid the cloth over September's face, his halo of violet flames could just be seen under the grey.

Nkosi. Take him home.

————

The guards were nervous, chattering, standing too close. Lungisane felt a terrible cool on his neck as a breeze racked through the sweat.

'Get away, get back.'

The head of security was running, with some effort, across the plaza. A nice man but all of them knew he would need to exonerate the company and himself of wrong doing even before the barrel of the gun had cooled.

'What happened here?' said Goodwill, still panting. 'Who is this?'

The white man who had taken off his jacket stood. Lungisane was surprised to see he was crying. He could not stop. 'Your guy fucking shot him. Look at him? He's completely unarmed.'

'We can't be sure.'

'Who fired, which one of you fired?'

The guards all took a step back.

'Lungi fired,' said one of them.

'Was it you?'

'Yes,' said Lungisane. He felt his hands begin to shake. The white man was still crying. He had his face in his hands and he shook and shook. It was nothing Lungisane wanted to see. The others turned away too. No one wants to see something like that.

Lungi already knew his day was done. As much as the man who lay on the ground before him.

He had twitched. He had twitched and felt the trigger push back against his forefinger, just a little push, back, a little nib of hardness and he had heard the voice in his ear saying, 'Hold, hold. Shoot', or maybe, 'Don't shoot.' How could he tell? And he had then heard something else in the ear-piece, a whistle, a scratch, and the man with the flowers in his hair had lunged further towards the line of them. The man had thrown his hand up from his sides. 'Fear no more!' he had shouted. His hands like the fury of a great and angry prophet had shot into the air.

The gesture was too wide, too wild, too high to contain. And so he, Lungisane, had pushed his finger into the metal.

And now it was done. *Nkosi.* It was his time.

———

Peter sat on the edge of the fountains.

Here I am.

His phone was still ringing. A constant alarm. De Wet, Mlauzi, Mogomotsi. They all would want to know what happened. What's our exposure, find it, fix it, make it go away. Peter's head was raging. All his fibre felt burnt and jumbled.

What just happened? He's a hunchback wearing a goddamned crown made from flowers.

Peter waited for the ambulance, or at least pretended to. It gave him some time to think it all through. He was saturated with dread. He was hot, drained. The man with the halo lay under his jacket, now surrounded by parking cones and red and white tape, the type they used on building sites.

Even as he sat there though, Peter kept a wary eye on the placard that was still a way off from where the breathless body lay. He considered moving it, hiding it, the evidence that would mark this as the shooting of a protestor versus the shooting of a homeless man which, though tricky, would have less fall out, politically. Especially now, this week as wage negotiations were still underway. They couldn't afford another strike. He, Peter, was paid to prevent this kind of thing. His eyes fell back to the placard.

He looked too at the heap under his jacket.

Here I am.

If it got out, everyone would immediately claim him as their own. The unions. He was a peaceful protestor, a placard, flowers. The mine foreman, speaking after a day underground, we used to know this man, he worked here but he went mad, as you can tell, a placard, flowers. The media, an assailant, a victim, a man believed to go by the name September, aged thirty-eight. And in the boardrooms and offices, once the doors had all opened again and the fish spine inside the Diamond was again populated with the normal pulse of feet, it was decided to put it down to a trigger-happy guard. He was mistaken. No order was given. The guard would be disciplined and relieved of his duties.

———

Dudu had been allowed to leave work early to go to the Residence. This pleased her. It was something she wanted to do, needed to do. And she would see people she knew there. She was distracted by the helicopters that thudded overhead all the time, this way and then that and never really settling, like a dog looking for a bone. Voop voop voop. Dudu felt herself relax a little in the way you do towards the end of the day, when the promise of rest and time to oneself and a meal suddenly feel close and possible. She was distracted too by the choppers and was looking up and thinking, what are they looking for?

She stepped off the kerb without thinking, without looking and as she did she heard a noise and a scream and a blast that blew her right back onto the pavement like a fist in her belly.

She clutched herself.

I am alive, I am breathing, I am alive.

'*Sisi* are you right? Are you safe?'
'Yes. I am right.'

'You must look where you are going.'

She nodded and let her hand rest on the man's arm. She leant on him, to stop the terrible spinning she felt. She recognized him as the sweet seller who sat on an upturned beer crate under a red and white umbrella.

'I was looking at the helicopters.'

'Ja. There is some big noise at the Diamond. Just now there was an ambulance too.'

Dudu kept her hand on the man's arm.

'And what big noise is it?'

'Ah some *tsotsi* was shot there. Now there is a big noise.'

Duduzile felt all the deep cold from the rivers of her childhood rush over her. She felt the peaks of the mountains rise up around her. So too the great and terrifying storms that came from the valleys below and then up over the pass to the Highlands, suddenly came to sit over her head. She felt the pebbles, jagged and keen, that littered the long road to fetch water, begin to cut through the soles of her feet. And every bee that had ever stung her begin to push its sharp and hot poison through her skin.

'*Sisi*?'

She let go of the man's arm and turned to walk towards the Diamond.

I am breathing in, I am breathing out, I am breathing in, I am breathing out.

———

Gin had felt the atmosphere of the city drop, air pressure, altitude. A shift of a plate. She could not name it. Her skin still pimpled from the storm, she went to find Neve in her bedroom.

She was in front of her cupboard, her hand running over the sleeves of dresses and blouses that hung in neat rows and arranged by colour.

'Mum?'

'What do I need to wear?' She turned.

'Your blue one is nice. Whatever you like.'

'What I would like is not to come.'

Gin could feel her skeleton collapse, the full weight of exhaustion and the whole long day finally and completely stamp its foot across her chest.

She did not move. She could not move. Only the tears came, and came again, and would not stop. Another day she would have hid them, turned away, but not on this day. On this day, she let them fall until they ran along her chin and along her cheek bones and she did nothing to hide them. Her breath would not come and she fought to find it without shame.

She felt, in that moment, as if something, possibly everything, had been lost. She had lost something fundamentally of herself too, a constituent part. Perhaps something small and unspoken but that in the end was the one thing that allowed her to appear entirely whole to the world. All of this and all of the things she could not even name, overwhelmed her to a point of devastation. She found herself in a grief so overwhelming and dense that she was, in that moment, so far beyond the bounds of recovery that to surrender entirely was the only way to survive.

All the slights, the oversights, the refusals to see her, to see what she tried to do to make things right and make things work, to live, just to live every day without any hope or prospect of shelter – all of this was finally, too much.

Neve turned. 'Virginia, honestly. I didn't mean it.'

'Yes. You did.'

———

Peter waited for the ambulance. He could hear it. Not that it mattered. The man was dead.

'Pete, we need to do something. Get the ball rolling.' Jacob Thlabi was shifting around next to him. The only one of his team who had bothered to come out of hiding and see what needed doing.

'Give me a minute. Go up and start. Can you make sure the area is shut off? I don't want people here.'

'How did this happen?'

'I don't know.'

Peter's eyes kept returning to the crown of agapanthus that now lay near the body. Strangely intact.

Agape, for love.

He looked beyond it and there stood a woman, small, pretty. She held her hand across her mouth and swayed, just a little. Back and forth. It was the woman he had seen earlier. She had given September oranges next to the fountains and held his hand as they had walked.

———

Dudu had seen all she needed to see. She lifted her phone from her pocket and sent a message.

'Uncle, Sechaba is dead. *Nkosi*, God bless him and you too.'

She sent the message to her cousin who would then relay the message to their uncle. He was blind now and near deaf too. But he should know that the child had passed. For he was always like a father too.

Then, Dudu walked to the security guards, to the one woman she saw among them and said: 'That man is my brother. I would

235

like to know where they are taking him now so that we can bury him.'

'Sorry Mama. I don't know. You must wait for the police also. Do you need to know what happened?'

'I know and I do not know.'

The woman guard lowered her eyes.

'Who must I ask about where he will be taken?' said Dudu.

'Ask that white man.'

Dudu looked across to the white man sitting on the fountain. She noticed that it was his jacket that covered September's face.

She approached him and saw him lift his head as she did.

'I am Duduzile.' She looked straight at his face. His eyes were red with tears.

'*Kunjane Sisi*. This man is known to you ...' The white man spoke fluent Zulu. It surprised her.

'Yes. That is my brother. Sechaba. You will call him September.'

'I am sorry for your loss.'

Dudu did not know what to say to that. Why was he sorry?

'I want to know where he will go. I need to bury him.'

She could see the man was watching her carefully. He wants to know if I blame him, blame the Diamond. He wonders why I don't bother to ask what happened.

'If you give me your telephone number I can let you know. I will give it to the police, the liaison officer. They look after families.'

'I will have your number. I will call you.'

The man opened his phone and out of a pocket in the cover he took a card with his name and number on it. He was a lawyer.

'I will make sure you are contacted,' he repeated.

This man is afraid of me.

236

Dudu wanted to say nothing, wanted to take the card and walk away and just sit on the ground next to September while she waited. Keep him safe. And she would.

But first she said to the white man, 'I will call you. You must know, I am my brother's keeper.'

————

Peter felt a drop and then another and realized the sky had grown dark. The afternoon storm was returning for another crack at the summer heat. The ambulance had arrived.

He scrolled through his phone numbers. He stood and walked towards the man's body. Other than September's sister, who had walked towards the ambulance and was talking to the driver, Peter was the only one who was anywhere near the body, any onlookers were held behind a hastily erected barrier. But for the most part, no one looked, no one stopped. The city had not stopped for Madiba's passing, it would certainly not stop for a crazy, homeless hunchback.

As Peter walked closer to the body, he picked up the placard that was now a few metres away. No one stopped him, no one noticed. He walked towards the rumpled limbs and placed the placard next to it, facing up. Then, he walked back a pace or two and took exactly eight pictures, making sure he captured the man, his placard and the front of the Diamond in the frame of the image.

Then, he made his way back in.

Mlauzi, no doubt sent out by Mogomotsi to see what had transpired, was striding across the foyer towards him. 'Mess, total mess,' said Mlauzi.

'Well, people are saying he couldn't see, the sun was coming off the corner of the building.'

'I don't care. He knew what he was doing. There were seven guards with loaded weapons there. He knew,' Mlauzi persisted. Peter was surprised by the force of his defence.

'But if he couldn't see? There are witnesses. He was unarmed.'

'For fuck's sake Strauss, we don't pay you to defend a vagrant.' He was casting around. 'We shouldn't talk here. Come to my office rather.'

'You pay me to prepare for every eventuality and reality, legally.'

'I suppose I do.'

'Well then you might also need to consider not only what he could and could not see but also whether he was indeed a mad bloody vagrant or a legitimate protester over Verloren. That is already the claim.'

'What? Since when has he been upgraded to a protestor, the fool was out of his mind, had a huge cone coming out his back.'

'He cannot be deemed mad by virtue of having a physical impediment. And you should be aware that he has been protesting Verloren for months, no matter his state of mind. He has been outside with a placard every day. You must have seen him, he was at court too a few times, early on.'

'Yes. I've seen him. But do other people know this? It's a media nightmare if it's true.'

'I've controlled it. So far. But he worked in the kitchens on the mine. He took part in the strike and was injured there.'

'Meaning?'

'We have tried to kill him once before.'

'Watch your mouth.' Mlauzi dropped his voice. 'We have tried to kill no one. Keep your voice down for God's sake.'

'We killed him.'

'Listen here, we do not pay you the sums we do, to hear your white socialist views, you hear?' He smiled a little as he said it. 'We did not kill him, he was mad, it was a suicide, so to speak, you'll know the correct term, do you understand me?'

'I do.'

'If it comes down to it, get one of the guards nailed for it. Trigger-happy. There are already rumours on that score. Make sure you back it up. Trigger-happy, you hear? Which they are. Half-trained bloody idiots they send us.'

Peter had nothing to say. The decision had been made.

As he walked back through the great glass walls and up the spine back towards his office, he began to send the clearest of the pictures he had taken to Jackson Maphalala, investigative reporter, Independent News Associates.

The storm came back over the city with reliable violence. It began to rumble in from the south once more and in less than ten minutes began to pelt its torrent on the streets as it did every afternoon. As the cadres sang and danced and the Women's League raised their voices, the rain washed over the flowers that covered the fences and the placements around the Residence. The thunder called out across the mourners, here I am, and they replied with ululation and raised their song yet higher. Rain and wind and thunder all joined in the tumult of mourning and celebration.

The king is dead. Long live the king.

Evening

Richard had been called back to the office. An incident. A man shot. He did not go. Instead he called Mogomotsi and asked him to handle the situation and in so doing had effectively stepped away from it all, forever. It required no more than that. The board would meet when the year began and it would all be formalized.

Mlauzi, Mogomotsi, even Peter could and would do a better job than Richard. They were younger and stronger and Mogomotsi was possessed, Richard had always thought, of a focus, a useful expedience, that marked him out from his peers.

Richard on the other hand knew he was tired and all he could think about was moving to the ocean. Mogomotsi would be a fine replacement.

Once Richard had let the thought in, so deliciously, he could not get it out. The scent of the sea. It had happened that morning, sitting in his office reading his papers and his horoscope, thinking about Mandela. Once it had formed itself as a distinct thought, a full sentence with a full stop at the end of it, it suddenly felt as if it was done. It held a form and it was as if there were simply no other option available. This pleased him. He felt he could breathe and as he pulled a tie from the neat little rows inside his wardrobe he even allowed himself to hope that he might be happy again.

———

Dudu stood on the kerb, waiting for a taxi to take her to the hospital morgue. She had given the police officer her details and had been told where to go. The first two taxis that had passed were too full to take her. Rush hour. Rain.

She felt so horribly aware of the pavement, its hardness. The terrible smell of petrol and fumes that seemed worse after the rain, the density of the air trapping all the filth under the clouds. All of this made her feel as though it were near impossible to draw breath, as though life itself was being denied her.

She had called the house where she worked, where they would be expecting her to help with the children's dinner. And she had said, my brother is dead, he has been shot. The woman had said, will you leave in the morning then? Dudu had begun to explain that he had been shot here, in Johannesburg, and that she was standing over his body waiting for the police. And instead of saying, I am sorry for your loss, how may I help you? the woman had simply said, so you won't be home tonight?

Dudu had decided then and there that she would work until a week before Christmas when she was due to go home. She would take her salary and her end of year bonus. While the family was at the sea, Dudu would pack up her things, phone her cousin who had a truck and she would go home, to the mountains and the rivers and she would not come back to Johannesburg unless she was needed for a trial or an inquest. Someone else could find the money for the aunties and the children, someone else could clean bathrooms until the bleach cracked their skin, because she had done it for years and years, carried them all, and what did she have to show for it? She had kept her voice quiet and her head down and her back bent. She had leant over so many baths and floors and washing baskets that she might as well have had a hunched back too. And for all his pain September was never a servant. He knew the stars and heard their voices too and though they had shot him and kicked him she shouted out his freedom until the last. Dudu knew she would pack her things and fold away her uniform with the pie crust apron and she would take her freedom too.

But first she had to stand on the side of the road. The car tyres spraying the filth of the streets onto her shoes. She would soon be free. But she knew too even as she stood under her umbrella, that already her heart was breaking, so hard and so deep that it would never, ever be whole again.

———

Eventually, some of the guests began to arrive, some on tip-toe through the carpet of frangipani flowers that the storm had laid out across the drive. And as they did the night let loose a sticky perfume, the crushed petals giving up their last sweet breath before beginning to brown in the water. Once as a child Gin had tried to press one of the flowers into her book, to take it home, waxy and pristine, its own kind of white, frangipani white. She had hoped that she could open her book once back in her room and again have that scent around her. Instead, she had found nothing but a rotten, sweaty mess between the pages.

But not these. They were perfect. As if she had laid them out herself to lift each guest's step from off the hard wet floor of reality and drift each of them in on perfume. Most would not notice. They were too vulgar for these charms. But Gin did, she noticed everything and it all meant something.

Gin looked good, she knew it. She knew too that she gave the impression that she did not belong here, in this particular city, but rather read from a broader map. Her loose burgundy dress stopped at her knees where it tapered slightly and its neck plunged as deep as was possible without causing concern. It gave the impression of a woman who did not care what you thought, be-jangled with her usual gold pendants and stones. The layer of silk was her last and only defence. Her mother would disapprove, which was part of the joy. Earlier in the day, before it all, she might have worn a different dress, but now, this was the only option possible if she was to hold her centre.

Older guests arrived and took a drink from the waiting trays, wine for the women, spirits for the men. Her friends were there too, Bea, her sister Fran, others too. One had married, one had divorced, one didn't care, one thought of nothing but weddings and babies and the fact that she might finally feel as if she was home. Gin knew she loved them in that distant, interested way.

But she had a whole evening to orchestrate, curate. There was Mercy with another tray of food. Gin's friends greeted Mercy, asked after her daughters. She saw Bea bite into a piece she had been offered and tell Mercy, dear God, it's absolutely delicious. Generosity. Mercy smiled.

Her cousins were standing together. Just looking at them left her feeling disappointed. Why did they not move, speak to others? They were under-dressed. She had said 'elegant'. A matter of interpretation perhaps. She knew she was being snide. She did not care.

The gate opened again. Who now? Talent, for a tidy fee, had been convinced by Mercy that he would like to be stationed outside with a console, pretending to be a guard. Gin hoped her paternal aunt was not coming. She had been invited out of courtesy but the reply had been that it was too far and too dangerous at night. Gin hoped this was enough of a deterrent. She had not spoken to her of course, this was only relayed information. They did not speak and had not for years. Gin insisted on it.

Nothing could go wrong. This would be the most perfect of nights, even her mother would have to admit it. Where was she? There was Richard. Gin kissed him and told him she was pleased to see him. He squeezed her hand and told her she was looking wonderful. And what a wonderful night. Gin remembered her mother saying he used to be such a handsome man.

Neve sat in her usual chair on the verandah. She looked so elegant. Her dark, gunmetal hair, red lips, pearls announced her as herself and had done so for years. She would be overwhelmed, to begin with anyway, while people were arriving and embracing her and chatting all at once. Gin knew that. But she knew, she hoped that she would in the end, have a good night – better than that, a wonderful night. A night to remember.

The noise level seemed to rise and fall and then rise even higher. People were laughing, one of her friends was demonstrating her yogic balance, standing on one very high black heel, her arms outstretched.

'You see? I've found my centre, I've found my centre. That's all it takes for perfect stillness.'

Older men in tennis club ties were gathered around, rapt.

*

Peter was late. It had taken longer than he had expected to get himself together. To get his shields into place. He had sat on the edge of his bed for nearly an hour before he had even remembered where he was meant to be. He could not say what he had been thinking. Only time had passed in a terrible dream.

Any number of times he had tried to stand up, to move, but he could not. It was as if there were no longer any borderline between himself and the world. Every noise, or flash of light from the street below set him on edge.

Eventually he had forced himself into the shower and with it had come some clarity. Enough to get him out the door and back into his car to head back towards the Brandts' house.

He parked in the road and stood outside the gate facing the direction of the Residence. Still he had not gone, not properly. The singing and drumming and ululating he had heard earlier continued as if it might never end. He almost turned, almost walked towards it but remembered instead the man September and his violet crown.

I am not entitled.

So he turned towards the party carrying the rain-flecked bouquet he had bought through his car window from a man on the side of the road.

Decades of habit, of cellular memory, meant that even before he had greeted a single person he was only looking for Gin, even though he knew she had invited him as a courtesy. She was walking past a group of women, she stopped to fill their glasses. She laughed at something one of them said.

She looked astonishing, so easy, almost in flight.

He wanted to be closer to her. He knew he would only look

anxious, drawn, a high school prom date holding an ostentatious bouquet as a shield. He needed rescuing.

'Hi, wow, what a bunch.'

'Gin, hello, yes, I hope she likes it.'

'God, she'll adore it, who wouldn't?'

You wouldn't.

The paper around the flowers crinkled a little as she leaned across it to kiss his cheek. What was it she always smelled of? He remembered: Opium.

'I'm sorry I'm late though, a man died, well he was shot really, outside the office, there's been a bit of a mess. So I'm late, I'm sorry.'

Why had he told her? To make himself sound important perhaps or even an excuse in case he needed an emotional alibi, because it was still early and already he felt himself so visibly unmoored.

'What? No. I haven't heard. Like a colleague?'

'Oh no, no a homeless guy. But I knew him, from before, he used to cook at Verloren.'

'What was he doing at the office then? Jesus, why was he shot?'

'He, well, I'd rather not say too much, I see Richard is here.'

'Right.'

Gin straightened. He felt her accusations multiply until they formed a tall stack of little dockets behind her.

'My mother is over there. She'll love the flowers.'

———

Gin moved away and towards the tables and then to the kitchen on the pretence of taking some empty wine bottles through. Respite. Peter looked terrible. A man had been shot. Drawn and grey. As if he were a breath away from falling, unseaming. Not just that day, but in general. She should be kinder to him.

He has lost his nerve.

'Mercy what do I need to do?'

'It's all OK.'

'We've done everything, so I guess once the chicken is done you can call me and we can put it out.'

'You aren't going to cut it before?'

'God. I don't know. Is that better? OK, we'll do that. Thanks for being here.'

Gin put her arm over Mercy's shoulder and squeezed her closer. Mercy smiled.

'It is a very good party Ginny. Do you want to serve now?'

'Give me ten minutes.'

Gin went through to her mother's bathroom and closed the door, locked it and sat on the edge of the bath, her knees cupped in her hands and allowed herself to take deeper breaths as she rocked back and forth.

I have lost my nerve.

The shower head was dripping.

———

Neve felt her energy fail. Just seeing Peter Strauss and his ridiculous bouquet filled her with dread. She smiled and thanked him and made sure to send him in the direction of Gin's friends.

She should have tried to eat a little more than she had but hadn't liked the taste of all the little bits and pieces. She had seen some of the men, Richard and some others, go back for second helpings so at least someone was enjoying Gin's offering. She couldn't stomach it. It was too rich, too much. All of it, all of this in front of her was too much. The flowers were pretty, though Gin should perhaps have bought some with a bit more colour, some pink roses would have been nice. Some of the hydrangeas looked faded.

Neve looked at Richard with his plate piled high with food, ponderous as ever. A clever man. They had all known each other for so long. For so many years, met at tennis parties, at university, at balls at the Country Club. That was how they used to live. Everything had been softer and more beautiful. It angered her that it had all changed, that life was so fast and crass and frightening. Nothing beautiful seemed to last.

She shut her eyes against the noise of the party. There was such comfort in the dark that fell. It seemed that as she closed her eyes, all the voices dropped, a lull, and through it came the sound of singing; men rolling out notes in unison. The mourners. She let all of this come over her in less than a second and then through it, through the singing and the happy voices came the other voice from a few hours earlier. The voice that said: 'I'm going to kill you. Give me your watch.'

Nothing lasted. It was folly to hope for it.

———

Gin could tell that her mother was awkward and anxious. She kept asking where Juno was. Perhaps to make a point but more likely because she was overwhelmed and needed a diversion. She was behaving exactly as she always did. And yet, there was always the hope that it would go better this time, easier, because it was a special night, a different night.

Gin felt the exhaustion of it all, the chaos of the day, Peter, Juno, the broken man who had brought her back and all the endless wakefulness in which she seemed to be eternally trapped. Standing in from of the stove, Gin smoothed her dress. Burgundy paint, dense giant brush strokes printed in large format on cream silk. She felt, now, that it was too short. She had wanted to look beautiful. Instead she looked like something her mother did not like. She should have worn flat shoes, loose trousers, put her hair up, tucked away the coloured ends. It would have pleased Neve and allowed her to feel proud.

Why do things (clothes, words, people) that make sense in one place and not in another, never quite make the translation? Here at home, Gin never felt she was enough and that this place was never enough for her. That she was at the same time diminished by it and too good for it. How these two states of being ran alongside each other, two rails raced off into forever, never meeting. She felt tears rise.

She found her mother sitting at the head of the long, candlelit table where Gin had told her she would sit for the night. The light was golden and perfect. To her mother's left was her friend Bea.

Gin sat to join them.

'Are you OK Mum? The dinner is coming out in about five minutes. You look beautiful in that dress, you always do.'

'It suits me, I think. Must I help you?'

'No. It's all fine. Bea can help me. Are you OK?'

'Yes. I suppose so. I'll go and sit with Diana.'

As Neve stood, Bea stood to help Gin.

'Ginny, imagine the fabulous party we're going to have when we're eighty?'

Bea followed Gin through the huddles and groups and into the kitchen and squeezed her hand as she did. 'By the way, your mum is so cranky. I think she's got worse. But I guess it's her birthday.'

'Thanks for being here.'

'Are you OK?'

'No.'

'OK. I know. Come on, let me help you with your birds. They look amazing, amazing.'

'They're pumped with hormones, that's why.'

'Then that's what we'll get before we turn eighty. Some bird hormones.'

Gin needed it all to work. The wine seemed to be disappearing faster than she had thought it would. She didn't like how the trays of canapés looked, three, half empty. That wasn't right. She would need to move what was left onto one platter and hide the rest. It needed to look more beautiful, better. The balance was off. And dinner was coming soon. People had to sit at the table.

I am sinking in so fast I feel I may break from the speed of the fall. I need someone to stop me. I don't know if I'm going to be OK. Not tonight, not forever.

I need someone to tell me I am enough, that I will still be enough when I am eighty and there is no one I know who will throw me a party with flowers and food and candles everywhere.

Peter wasn't sure where to put himself. The verandah seemed too chaotic and he kept finding himself on the wrong side of the dinner table that had been laid out. He could see Gin's hand everywhere. The flowers were perfect. Nothing like his awkward offering. He lifted a hand in greeting to Mercy, she smiled then began quickly, neatly, laying another place along the already crowded table. And in seeing her do it he felt immediately that it was he who had not been expected, that his presence had already become an inconvenience.

I should not have come.

Speeches. Strange and emotional in ways Neve had not expected. Even Richard stood up, thanked her for her consistent friendship during the difficult months after Anne's death. He was forever grateful. He raised a glass to Neve and she saw his eyes well and then subside again as he blinked the moment away.

Gin stood. She thanked everyone for coming, those from far away, wished Neve a happy day and sat down again. She was clipped and unemotional, vividly so after Richard's unexpected flush. The dinner began. Chatter and the sound of cutlery. Gin sat next to Bea who Neve saw mouth the words, Are you OK? She saw too as Gin filled her lungs and shook her head as she exhaled.

Gin was not OK.

Almost in the same moment Gin seemed to register something in the direction of Aunt Diana and quickly left the table, returning moments later with a knife and fork, smaller than the ones on the table.

'There Aunty Di, you might find those easier.'

Night

The dinner over, Peter felt less confined, and Bea's sister, Vanessa, was good enough company. They had been closer before, all of them. Now he felt he was no longer a part of them. His relationship to the other girls had been through Gin and when she left he had seen them here and there, but over time it became obvious that without her they had nothing in common. He became what he had to, in order to do well in the firm; and they held him, or so it felt, in mild disdain for not being more whimsical, more relevant, free, more like them.

All through the meal and the speeches, he knew he had reverted to his old self as if the years had not passed at all. He found himself at another party, another summer night watching Gin as if his very survival depended on it. He disliked being back in it all and yet he felt he never wanted to leave, the discomfort itself was at least something, a sense that he could still, still what? Love?

So, he stood, excused himself, vaguely greeted some of Gin's cousins who only ever spoke to each other. He knew Gin would have something to say about what they were wearing.

'It's a beautiful night, Gin.'

'Thanks. Do you think so?'

'Of course. It's perfect.'

She nodded without smiling. He knew she did not think it anywhere near perfect, that over and over in her head she was running an inventory of all its flaws and inconsistencies.

'Gin, I'm sorry about earlier.'

'What do you mean?'

'Just …'

'It's OK. I move quickly. I'm over it.' She put her fingers on his forearm. 'Old habits die hard.'

'I guess they do.'

There seemed a great silence between them, fat, full of forgiveness, even as a glass shattered and a roar of laughter rose up from behind them.

'Do you need to get that?'

'No. I'm past caring.'

'I'm getting to that myself. Some days, you know?'

He watched as she eased into the thought. He felt the air between them moisten and fill.

'Tell me what happened with the man. You looked upset. I don't understand who got shot.'

'His sister came, that was the worst. The plaza was shut down. It was … I can't explain it … I feel I could have stopped it. I feel I should have but it all happened outside, and I was inside and I couldn't get outside. That doesn't make sense I know, but I just couldn't get to him.'

'But who was he? Did he work for you?'

'He used to, but not for a couple of years. He's been homeless I suppose, looked it, rags, always wearing plants, agapanthus, willow wreathes, kind of a wild man, had a hunched back too which added to it. You OK?'

'And a placard. "Here I am. Verloren."'

'Ja, a protest placard. You've obviously seen him around. But that's not necessarily why he was there you understand. He was out of his mind. He just walked towards the guards and they were telling him to stop, their guns were pointed at him and he just kept coming. I don't understand why. Gin?'

'He came here. He found Juno. She was lost.'

'What? When?'

'Before the storm.'

'Today?'

'Today. Can you excuse me please?' Gin turned away from him and as she did he felt the great gulf return. One of grief and sadness and all the things she always held in her that he could never understand.

The chasm opened. Endless and ancient and black. What had happened? Why was everything so misshapen? The agapanthus around his neck, his shattered face, his terrible swollen hump. He had gone to the Diamond and Peter has seen him shot dead. He had brought Juno home, cradled her, and then walked to the Diamond. She had let him go.

Was that what happened?

Gin felt the verandah was closing around her so near that the candles might singe her, the vases break.

Had he stolen Juno? Did it matter? She only knew Juno was

home safely and she was too, but the man from the street was dead. And Mandela too.

The room, the garden, the whole house was rolling and swaying with people and music and light that seemed to attach itself too briefly to the people she knew and loved. And suddenly it was all too beautiful, too perfect and right.

How can just one day be so strange? As if it had slowed down to a whisper then suddenly all these worlds and lives collide here, in her mother's garden and the street outside. As if they had been waiting somewhere out of sight for years, for decades so that on this day, at this hour, they could all fulfil some cosmic function, a contract even and all of it find its way to her door. And with it a great unrolling of the earth and its place in the planets. Juno posting her nose into the street had somehow set into motion all of this chaos, as if breaching the threshold between the house and the street had opened yet another threshold and another world that suddenly could not be separated back out. She, Gin, must do something to make it right and set the day back on its hinges. Or else nothing would ever be safe again.

Neve was sitting deep on a sofa, Aunt Diana next to her, both listening to Richard, making long, dipping motions with his arm, like a dolphin or whale.

The man had walked towards the guns. He should have known they would kill him. But did he even know the guns were there? Sometimes we choose to ignore the things we know, the things that might kill us, or we would never be able to live.

How does life, its impulse, move in a space, a city? How does it navigate its way through the woman whose face fell from her skull, the man who was now dead, through Peter, through her, the miners underground, chipping and drilling through the core of the earth so that the very plates the city rested on had begun to fracture in strange and unnatural ways. The day she had landed there had been earth tremors.

If I am to survive, I must leave.

She watched the guests laugh and lean in. Older women who had not forgotten their alluring ways as their hands brushed the shoulder of the man they might once have loved lifetimes ago, picked from their sleeve a piece of lint, this act a subtle residue of intimacy. The men who leaned forward in conspiracy, one which produced a laugh, a smile, lightness.

No one would notice if she disappeared.

————

Dudu sat on the end of her bed, her legs crossed at her ankles, her hands upturned, one on top of the other, her head bowed. She did not weep. There is some grief that goes deeper than that. Tears float along the surface and give voice to something or someone that already has a name. By the time a woman can weep for her loss, she can already bear to speak the name of the dead, mention them in prayer, demand her God that he return the beloved. But she had not yet reached that time. It was too far off. She was still in a silent place.

Later she would blame herself, for not keeping a closer eye, for not taking him to the clinic more often, for not visiting him again after she had taken him to his garden to sleep.

And later still she would place her blame where it would rightly rest. In the cocked finger of the guard, the men who sat on the roof tops of the Diamond and finally, in the place where it all began, in Verloren. The day the workers, miners but others too, began their protest with a wildcat strike. Songs and calls and lines of men with *knobkierries* all marching towards the offices of those who would be kings.

And five days later, fifty-one were dead, shot with live rounds. And the others were injured, hundreds, and September too, shot while running away he said, running away.

'I will not run away again sister. Rather I will be shot walking into their bullets. Rather that than running away. For they will shoot you anyway.'

This he had vowed in his hospital bed where she had gone every day to see him. His head bleeding through bandages no matter how often they were changed for the bullet had gone deep and it was a miracle he was still alive, they said. A miracle.

———

Gin took the key she knew hung in the kitchen. Mercy was long asleep, they had embraced. Gin had thanked Mercy for her help and Mercy had said goodnight before taking her plate of dinner and pudding and closing the door behind her.

The key. Gin walked straight through the verandah, past the guests, glasses full, bellies replete, and away towards the gate. As if by instinct, she reached into the green canoe-shaped leaves of the frangipani and plucked a garland. It was perfect and let loose its mother's milk. Gin wiped it away on her dress.

Click and out, as she stepped her shoe through the metal frame and felt it fall, a little unevenly, onto the pavement outside.

She did not remember having ever walked these streets at night. Too afraid or at least thinking she should be. These were not streets for night time, dark as they were and overhung with jacarandas, wide and deep. But, there were others in the streets despite the time. A group of four, who looked like students, were just ahead of her, couples, holding hands, holding flowers, treading the dark. Is this who I am meant to be afraid of? And not knowing where else to go but knowing she could not be in her mother's house, she followed them.

The air was cool after the rain.

At the main intersection before the Residence she was handed a small national flag by a group of older women dressed in the green and gold and black of the Party. Canary yellow shirts with Mandela's face like a giant, golden medal. The Women's League.

'*Sisi.*' The woman smiled, as she handed her the flag.

Gin wanted to say something. She didn't know what.

Her eyes retched their tears. Violent, burned and tired. She shook her head, held it low. 'That way?' She knew the way, why did she ask? For permission to prolong the contact. Even as she said it, she felt a fool.

She crossed the road, tilting onto the balls of her feet to save her heels, a habit she seemed to have developed in New York. Her shoes suddenly felt so frivolous, exposing, so indulgent, black booties, open at the front, studded with brass and out the back, sitting proud, leather wings, Hermes in flight. She had loved them so much, still loved them so much, prized them as a trophy. Her wild feet always in full flight, ready to lift ever so slightly off the ground to freedom. 'The fly-away bird', a stupid, stunted aunt had called her.

The noise coming from the end of the street was thunderous and muffled all at once. The night was so dark, so electric and alive. She could feel the singing already beginning to register in her chest, as if the space between her ribs had been scooped out to accommodate the roar. What was the feeling? Sorrow, grief, elation, all of it filling her. All of it seemed to rush right into her as if her skin was as thin as highveld air, porous and brittle.

She stood awhile, disorientated by the push and jostle, the dancing, a song here, ululating there, all directed at the house, windows lit behind thick curtains and guarded. She pushed towards the house.

Across its access was a barricade, metal lattice-work that had been erected to keep the growing crowds from the front gates. Every last metal diamond on the fence had been plugged with flowers; sunflowers, roses, agapanthus, lilies of every colour, pinks and white and orange, yellow too, plumbago, star jasmine and proteas from the Cape, pinwheels, bottle brushes and wild orchids, all stuck between the bars. Some with notes, we love you, we will miss you, and over and over again, thank you Tata, thank you, you have given so much, rest now, rest well. And out over these flowers came song layered upon song. Songs of struggle and revolution over songs of love and longing for home and yet more hymns of love and longing, but this time, for God.

On the verge there were more flowers, mounds of them. Yet more in jam jars and in others still, candles. Other mourners had brought plants still with their feet in soil and teddy bears, and each of these had notes, some in children's writing that had run out of paper as they reached the end of the card.

Gin waited for a space to clear next to the candles, then knelt to place her garland. A new song rose, Tata we love you, Tata we love you.

Yet more songs rolled over her in languages she could not understand and songs that all the assembled knew, all those who had been there all day and those who were still arriving. Old songs, songs from their mothers, songs from the Struggle, all the sad lullabies of that other time.

Gin felt choked by it, strangled by the beauty of it, candles, song, the trees over-head releasing the remnants of rain whenever the wind stirred. The news anchors, baffled and earnest, were lit up like planets under lamps, their truck generators humming in the background beneath the music.

This is how it feels to be home.

Gin knew that she had for years been the astronaut, sent out into space to travel across the infinite blackness, guided by nothing but stars, always and forever just trying to get home. As if by travelling so, so far away through such endless nothingness she could suddenly break through some barrier, some shield of light and know she was home.

For all of it, the fracturing, the pain, the proximity to death, she knew what she had always known: beauty matters. These moments, this man, this place. All of it.

These women who have come on busses from the Eastern Cape, seventeen hours to be here to sing and lend their praise to the throng. This white family, children wide-eyed and tired in their pyjamas, these cadres singing, 'That's why I'm a Communist.' All of this in its light and weight and strange molecular movements that connected them all, mattered.

The smallness too, the daily and the dull, Gin needed it all. Despite the cruelties, the awfulness, the knowledge that in this city, something terrible, catastrophic was always about to happen, made it matter more. Every flash of beauty however glancing had to hold its own weight in gold. In this dry continent where one bad season meant a lifetime of hardship, here, love, beauty, memory had to work harder, had to hold more earth. When death was always sitting just out of earshot waiting to speak your name.

The raindrops as they landed on her hair, as the trees released them, this light. The way her nerve endings had sat up when the cold of the fridge set her skin on edge, tightening each pore as she opened the door. The way Peter looked at her for a moment before he turned away, perhaps forever, as he left the party. The mere memory of a dog's tail along her shin under the table as it rearranged its legs and stretched into its dreams, all of this mattered and made life possible.

Gin's breath rose and fell and rose and fell again.

I am breathing in, I am breathing out, I am breathing in.

And it felt like a miracle to be breathing like this, all of her body and its million, million component parts all humming and singing and drinking in the oxygen. Poets died, leaders fell, seers and men who came from a wilder place of earth, forests, plains, were killed for nothing but the truth they spoke. But through it all she was still breathing, infinity, negative infinity, and the true fabric of her and of everyone in the street that night was still reaching across a chasm towards something great and unnamed and beautiful.

Acknowledgements

There are never sufficient words to thank my agent Jo Unwin who, despite her magnificent appetite for humour and positivity, continues to support my unflinchingly miserable novels.

To most respected and adored editor Sarah Castleton at Corsair, thank you for knowing what is needed in both novels and life. The greatest creative support a writer could hope to have and always a friend.

Everyone at Corsair/Little, Brown, Helen Upton's wonderful focussed energy, Olivia Hutchings' patient support and Kate Doran's marshalling of troops for this book. Thank you. A joy to be reunited with copy editor and good-egg, Caroline Knight.

Thank you Neil Gower for the sensitive and pulsing cover design. It is perfect.

Thanks are due to Shelley Harris for an early-days pep talk and to Gillian Stern for ongoing encouragement and support.

My brother, Adrian, and mother Ruth Melrose, thank you for

being such a support. Also nieces Clara and Imogen, who are wonderful readers and storytellers. Maggie and Phoebe, always.

Even misanthropic hermits need friends and so many thanks go to: Taryn Millar, Emma Jesse, Craig Bregman, Beate Schulte-Brader, Karin Salvalaggio, Karen Heese, Thomasine Magaldi-Kamerling, Allison Nicholson and Angela Sacco.

Finally, an enduring thanks will always go to my constant companion, Ms V Woolf, for all the work that she continues to do and all the questions she continues of ask of me. Thank you Ms Woolf.